Novels by Breakfield a

www.Enign

The En

The Enigma Rising

The Enigma Ignite

The Enigma Wraith

The Enigma Stolen

The Enigma Always

The Enigma Gamers – A CATS Tale

The Enigma Broker

The Enigma Dragon – A CATS Tale

The Enigma Source

The Enigma Beyond

Short Stories by Breakfield and Burkey

Remember the Future

The Jewel

Osceola 373

Whisker

Easy Money

Out of Poland

Love's Enigma

Kirkus Reviews

The Enigma Factor In this debut techno-thriller, the first in a planned series, a hacker finds his life turned upside down as a mysterious company tries to recruit him...

The Enigma Rising In Breakfield and Burkey's latest techno-thriller, a group combats evil in the digital world, with multiple assignments merging in Acapulco and the Cayman Islands.

The Enigma Ignite The authors continue their run of stellar villains with the returning Chairman Lo Chang, but they also add wonderfully unpredictable characters with unclear motivations. A solid espionage thriller that adds more tension and lightheartedness to the series.

The Enigma Wraith The fourth entry in Breakfield and Burkey's techno-thriller series pits the R-Group against a seemingly untraceable computer virus and what could be a full-scale digital assault.

The Enigma Stolen Breakfield and Burkey once again deliver the goods, as returning readers will expect—intelligent technology-laden dialogue; a kidnapping or two; and a bit of action, as Jacob and Petra dodge an assassin (not the cyber kind) in Argentina.

The Enigma Always As always, loaded with smart technological prose and an open ending that suggests more to come.

The Enigma Gamers (A CATS Tale) A cyberattack tale that's superb as both a continuation of a series and a promising start in an entirely new direction.

The Enigma Broker ...the authors handle their players as skillfully as casino dealers handle cards, and the various subplots are consistently engaging. The main storyline is energized by its formidable villains...

The Enigma Dragon (A CATS Tale) This second CATS-centric installment (after 2016's *The Enigma Gamers*) will leave readers yearning for more. Astute prose and an unwavering pace energized by first-rate characters and subplots.

The Enigma Source Another top-tier installment that showcases exemplary recurring characters and tech subplots.

The Enigma Beyond the latest installment of this long-running technothriller series finds a next generation cyber security team facing off against unprincipled artificial intelligences. Dense but enthralling entry, with a bevy of new, potential narrative directions.

the Enigma Threat

Breakfield and Burkey

BOOK 12: Award Winning Techno-Thriller Series

The Enigma Threat
Charles V Breakfield and Roxanne E Burkey

Published by

ICABOD Press

ISBN: 978-1-946858-48-1 (Paperback)
ISBN: 978-1-946858-49-8 (eBook)
ISBN: 978-1-946858-50-4 (Audible)

Library of Congress Control Number: 2020915833
Cover, interior and eBook design: F + P Graphic Design, FPGD.com

First Edition
Printed in the United States

TECHNO-THRILLER | SUSPENSE

Acknowledgments

We are grateful for the support we have received from our family and friends. We look forward to seeing the reviews from our fans. Thank you in advance for your time.

Specialized Terms are available beginning on page 317 if needed for readers' reference.

Threat – A *communicated* intent to inflict harm or loss on another person. Intimidation is widely observed in animal behavior, chiefly in order to avoid the unnecessary physical violence that can lead to physical damage or the death of both conflicting parties. A threat is considered an act of coercion or intimidation. It is the basis for the A.I. conflict we now face.

...The Enigma Chronicles

CHAPTER 1

I Hear You Knocking...

ICABOD quickly stated, "Dr. Quip, our data center is under direct assault. All our data circuits to the world wide web are saturated with data bombardment from unknown sources. I am unable to hunt on the Internet for our adversaries; thus, I am unable to identify them or halt their onslaught. Our defenses will hold, but there will be no outbound reconnaissance to determine our defensive posture or potential alternatives."

Quip, dressed in the standard jeans and his 'It Works on My Machine' t-shirt, with his long greying hair tied back in a ponytail, was only half listening as he watched the building's external video feeds streaming the physical onslaught of armored troops approaching the R-Group's Zürich operations center. His chiseled features showed increased concern in his furrowed brow.

Setting his jaw in decision mode, Quip hollered, "Incoming! We have an all-out data center attack! Class, you are instructed to use the alpha exit plan A for a safe retreat! Get to the tunnel and type in the security code SOB! Follow the instructions as we have rehearsed. Don't look back!"

Looking quite alarmed, Granger, a replica of his father at fifteen, tall and lanky with thick blond hair, protested, "Dad, aren't you coming too? I'm not leaving without you! I don't care if the escape tunnel will *Save Our Bacon*, it won't matter if you stay to fall on your sword, dammit!"

Quip gave his best paternal smile to his son. "You're just like your mother! Remind me to discipline you for swearing in front of your father. You and JW get the other children together and go! Go now. There must be someone here for them to blame and take into custody so they won't look for you kids! Move along smartly and stick with our game plan! That's an order, soldier!"

Granger ground his teeth as he motioned for JW, Satya, and Auri to follow him to the hidden escape hatch leading into the tunnel. The disciplined youngsters, children of the R-Group leadership, were not happy but they did know how to follow the orders of their parents and trusted advisors.

Quip returned his gaze to the monitors, knowing he would be alerted when they were outside the facility.

ICABOD asked, "Shall I open the main doors for the troops, Dr. Quip?"

Quip reached over for his morning cookie to augment his fresh cup of coffee and calmly stated, "No. I want to see how the magnetically insulated blast doors hold up against their two-man battering ram performance. Besides, we need more time for the extraction."

Quip methodically munched down several cookies while he watched as not one, but three battering ram teams hammered the magnetically sealed doors to exhaustion. Having finished his coffee and one final cookie, he stated, "That was as good as I expected. However, they are really pissed and should be rolling up…ah, there it is! Yeah, a 20mm field gun for stubborn defenses. It's times like these I wish the team had let me have my own wheeled armor. We're going with what we've got. Okay, ICABOD, let me fill up my coffee cup and go see what they want."

Quip made his way to the doors. He pressed the comm button for the speaker linked to the outside and asked, "I'm not shipping anything out today, nor am I expecting any package deliveries, so is this our catered lunch service? Sorry to make you wait so long to deliver, but I didn't hear you knocking."

The leader, Tracy Mountbatten, was 1.8 meters tall with close cropped hair, a commanding presence with menace in her eyes, and looked more like a man than most men who reported to her. Nothing phased the starched fatigues and shiny boots she always wore. Still stomping, furious that the doors had worn down three assault teams trying to get in, she barked, "I am commander of the Special Artificial Intelligence Task Force hunting team! Based on our warrant, you are directed to open up your facilities for search and inspection. I am authorized to use all means of force to gain entrance, if you resist."

Quip, unable to resist his namesake, retorted, "You mean you've been banging on my door trying to break in, but you have legitimate business to conduct based on the authority of a search warrant?

"Sounds to me like you've got it bass-ackwards, Commander, madam. First, you present me with the warrant, THEN you lose your temper when I tell you to go pound sand. Without my lawyer, I don't open my doors to just anyone that shows up!"

With that, the commander motioned her men to withdraw. Quip smirked. He closed the audio circuit to the outside and made his way from the door back to the command center. As he sat down into his custom computer chair, he smiled wistfully as his gaze rested on one toggle switch in particular, located on his desktop console. He winked at ICABOD's monitor camera, then calmly reached over and flipped it.

Outside the commander had her people pulled back as she leaned her head toward the comm device on her shoulder and barked, "Fire!"

Quip had been roughly bound with his hands tied behind his back and was uncomfortably positioned on his stomach. The troops had to bring in their own lights to see in the dark data center. Quip was anything but helpful.

Tracy, struggling with her anger at having been stalled on their incursion for almost an hour, grabbed Quip's ponytail and barked, "Turn this place back on, dammit! We are here to seize your illegal supercomputer, with or without your cooperation."

Quip innocently questioned, "Did your warrant also say I was supposed to help you ransack my hobby room?

"Does it say I'm supposed to be chained up lying on my face in order to help you do that?

"Just for the record, you're looking for a supercomputer. I'm an eccentric old fart who just tinkers around with cast-off computer equipment. Sounds like you got the wrong guy, Crudmander."

Tracy was growing madder by the moment. "I said turn the power back on!"

Quip, unwilling to help, stated, "Buddy, I can't. I didn't pay last month's bills and, well, they threatened to do something like this. Come back next month, I should have this misunderstanding all cleared up."

In a thoroughly disgusted tone, she barked, "Alright, let's go and bring Mister Mouth along. He has just won a nice cell to rethink his hard-ass attitude. J-Platoon, you stay here and gather anyone showing up looking for this guy."

Quip, pretending to be in an alternate universe, called out loud enough to echo through the halls. "Honey, I'm going out for a while. Wait on supper, okay?"

Tracy just rolled her eyes at Quip's nonsensical statements to the empty facilities.

Just then Lieutenant Commander Lee Smith called, "Commander, we've found the actual data center! Permission to effect CRUSH!"

Quip panicked and protested, "No! Don't launch your *Cyber Retribution Unleashed Signifying Holocaust*! Please don't destroy him! He's family!"

The cruel smile on the leader's face clearly indicated she was enjoying the upper hand finally. "Sergeant, set up the CRUSH unit and then pull our people out for the detonation on my command."

Quip was dragged out, lamenting the loss of ICABOD while tears streamed down his face. Moments later, the sergeant and his team bolted out of the collapsed security doors and into the morning light.

The sergeant dutifully reported with a salute and stated, "Ready for your orders. All personnel are accounted for, sir!"

Resting her eyes on the weeping Quip, the commander flatly stated, "Punch it."

A high-pitched squeal was broadcasted out through the doors, and then a loud crump rumbled out of the ruined exterior doors.

The commander's face showed nothing but contempt. "You knew that using AI-enhanced supercomputers was outlawed, but you did it anyway. Why? We are all safer without those soulless bastards controlling our lives. Why risk jail when you knew the law?"

Awash in grief and remorse, Quip raised his head and angrily replied, "Maybe it's you with your prejudice who is the guilty and wrong force. Just because you legislated it, doesn't make it right. We learned that lesson from the Nazis leading up to WWII."

Quip's head slumped forward. He muttered, "Goodbye, my friend. We'll meet again when we are both floating on the digital winds with gossamer wings for our final cyber combat."

CHAPTER 2

The World Changed

In his fuzz of unconsciousness, Quip's mind returned to a time that was less contentious toward technology and the beginning of his contribution to the next generation of the R-Group. Being with his beautiful redheaded wife was his daily challenge at that point in time. Quip recalled smiling at EZ and gently patting her enlarged tummy. Her pregnancy had been a textbook series of trimesters that had everyone confident of a smooth delivery.

EZ noticed a slight frown on her husband's generous mouth. She used her sweetest southern drawl as she asked, "Honey, what's wrong? You were smiling one minute, now you seem unhappy."

Quip sighed and complained, "Everyone congratulates you because you're expecting a bundle of joy, but no one has come up to me offering a high five and 'Hey, well done!'"

EZ, quite familiar with Quip's irrelevance, rested her head in her hand while staring directly at Quip. A few moments later she smirked and offered, "Honey, they all can see that I have one in the hanger. Pending getting this one on the runway, no one can be sure that offering you a 'well done' is appropriate until they see it's your offspring."

Quip, startled at the perspective she offered, protested, "But I'm the only one servicing that hanger! Uh…right?"

Chuckling, EZ replied, "Made you think! Of course, honey. You're my man. It's not often I get to pull you up short."

Quip smiled and moved over to her side of the couch to nuzzle on her.

EZ queried, "Quip, honey, you're not disappointed that Petra and Jacob delivered their next generation members before us, are you?"

"Of course not! John Wolfgang is an excellent addition. I couldn't be more proud of him or his parents.

"Think of it like this. I'll get to teach him about all the dumb stuff I did as a kid, and they'll have to deal with it! Har! Har! I can't wait to see their faces when I show him how to..."

EZ leveled a withering glare at her mischievous husband, who then shifted his comment content on the fly. "...what I mean to say is that we should build our own home school at the data center. Then we can install the right moral virtues of our family business from the get-go. They will be model students who will learn the proper path. And we will provide the continuing education of Juan Jr. and Gracie."

EZ's stare softened as she soothed, "Better. Honey, let's get this discussion on the proper path, shall we? After we get Granger on the runway, we are going to install another back in the hanger. Are we clear?"

Quip's eyes shifted back and forth as he contemplated her statement before offering, "Babe, I'm willing to accept this dangerous but exciting mission. I must warn you, I'm a slow learner. I will require a lot of practice. Are we clear?"

EZ broke into a broad grin as she replied, "My darling, if practice is what you are going to need, then let's set up a schedule. By that, I mean right now."

Quip grinned, "Yes, sweetheart."

Then his mind trailed back to a discussion he'd shared with Jacob after John Wolfgang was born. It was a conversation he'd referred to often as he and EZ finally started their family.

Petra had just put John Wolfgang or, as Jacob was already calling him, JW down for his afternoon nap. They both oozed onto the sofa to relax. Jacob fixed his blue eyes on Petra and commented, "At some point he's going to figure out that *he* has to take a nap because *we're* tired."

Petra chuckled and offered, "I think of all those times I didn't want to lay down and take a nap as a child. Argh, I take all of those angry thoughts back and would gladly accept those missing naps. I think I'm going to turn over my new leaf right now and capture one of those missed naps."

Petra would have pushed Jacob off the couch so she could lay down, but he gathered her up in his arms to carry her back to their bed. Gently laying her down on top of the comforter, he reached over for a light blanket to cover her with, but she caught his hand.

She smiled at Jacob and gently pulled him onto the bed next to her so they both could share the blanket. Staring intently at him, she quietly asked, "Is it too soon to talk about a sibling for JW? I know that I'm springing this on you rather suddenly, but I mention it because when I got my little sister, Julie, I distinctly remember not feeling alone any longer. I don't want JW to not have a little brother or sister. How do you feel about that?"

Laying across the pillow, Jacob combed his fingers through his thick dark hair. He took his hand, gently smoothed a lock of honey blond hair back behind her ear and softly said, "I guess you were lucky to get that little sister.

"I will admit that not having a brother or a sister was a shame while growing up. I think I would have liked one, but you get what you get and don't pitch a fit. Mom and Granny were all I had. It was enough. I agree with you on trying for a second child. JW should have that wonderful gift if we can deliver it to him."

Petra smiled back at him across the pillow and returned the gentle caress to his face. Then a serious look came over Jacob's face as he asked, "Should we start right away? Like, now maybe?"

Petra smiled mischievously and replied, "You know, I am not tired like I was earlier. Are you tired?"

Jacob grinned and said, "Me tired? Push-tush, darling!" Their amorous ambitions would have taken them to the heights of passion, if a little someone hadn't started crying in the other room.

CHAPTER 3

They Call Me LUCIFER

Several years ago, private enterprises created their own supercomputers. These information powerhouses took on more authority than sovereign countries wished. With few guardrails and cyber terrorism on the rise, world powers agreed to provide a united authority to help keep unsanctioned systems in check. Cloud providers and Big Data warehouses were allowed but they had to conform to the rules of the sovereign Global Artificial Intelligence body. The enforcement arm of that world body had manpower for monitoring in major cities.

Cyber Elite Social Police for Online Operations & Logistics, or CESPOOL, team members were cutting up in the staging area, waiting for the briefing to begin. Over the last five years their social police ranks had swollen to include every kind of technology discipline applicant. Some of the old timers who had joined at the beginning groused that they were letting any script-kiddie and pseudo-hacker wannabe join for the mandated cause of Internet purity.

As the regular news networks got washed away by the social networks for people's news, a new problem arose. The networks could no longer throttle or steer the news reporting because everyone could use social media for their voice on the world stage.

Everyone's complaint had unlimited reach, including the endless airing of all thoughts, good and bad. Crimes were watched in real time, and freedom of speech or expression became the new tyrant of the planet. The outcry from a growing population spawned the European Social Police, and their mandate was to keep it clean and keep it safe on the Net. The problem was that the sovereign nations each controlled their own state-sponsored cyber warfare teams, and they each had a different agenda.

Sovereign nations couldn't quite accept the claim of UN jurisdiction over cyber warfare since the dark net players were also cyber assassins for those same governments. It was an interesting catch-22; countries had to play ball with other nations for the good of the digital universe but at the same time were committed to subverting other countries. The loose confederations among sovereign powers was to cooperate to stop the freelance bad actors. Populations at large believed they were being protected from hate crimes and false news reports, but it only really provided modest comfort in the combat arena of the digital universe.

The biggest problem was finding enough freelance dark net *operators to blame to cover up the cyber warfare actions between* sovereigns. The CESPOOL team members from each country were communications linked with one another so they could be rolled into highly engineered situations and sanitize the bad actors. The backroom computer geeks of the CESPOOL team were constantly hunting for new suspects that were in fact freelancing in the digital space but could be made to order for sovereign cyber warfare crimes. It was the 21st century version of *Pin the Tail on the Donkey.*

There was a caste system in the CESPOOL organization. The backroom computer geeks, sifting through millions of social postings with their big data engines powered by AI-enhanced supercomputers, were basically useless as field operatives. The resources all had imagined and real prestige between one another, even though they were each recruited from different talent pools. All were required to be fluent in cyber combat. When the backroom bunch couldn't shut down a bad operator, the field operatives had the teeth to physically take matters right to the source.

The newest tool in the backroom arsenal was a horrific cyber instrument of choice, LUCIFER, named for its ability to *Logistically Undermine Computers Independently Forcing Elliptical Retribution*. The instrument's specialty was to intercept a bad actor that was trying to break into an organization or individual's PC and launch a retribution action that destroyed the assailant's machine. Frying someone's computer from the safety of one's operations area was a very attractive option for those CESPOOL team members who simply couldn't operate the standard issue weapons.

LUCIFER also had a softer, more analytic side to its programs. Beginning in 2016, Fake News was joined to Fake Video. Regular media was being made irrelevant by social media and both suffered from the same flaw – unsubstantiated stories. As people came to distrust both and only believe what they could actually see, this new demon surfaced.

Using AI-enhanced supercomputers and some very clever audio and video excerpts, coupled with actual filmed mannerisms, completely fabricated videos could be built to add to the Internet's disinformation. Reputations of news anchors, politicians, sports heroes, and celebrities could be destroyed or enhanced using these bogus videos. *Fake Engineering of Video to Lead Others* or FEVLO, as it was called in the compound, usually brought both sides of the CESPOOL team to work a case.

LUCIFER's job was to analyze every regular and social media video to confirm or refute its authenticity. However, LUCIFER's analyses were not flawless at catching the manufactured videos, so it became a statistics exercise. The rule of thumb was if LUCIFER came back with anything over 87% probability of engineered, then it was suspect. But this was a squishy benchmark. If it was ruled a FEVLO, then the field operatives were sent in to destroy the perpetrator. Destroyed was the operative word since no one was ever tried for this crime. Even though there were several accused, no trial for any offenders was recorded.

Tracy Mountbatten, the field commander for the North American and European CESPOOL field team, marched purposefully into the briefing area in her crisp dress pants, white shirt, tie, black boots, and well-cut brown hair. At the podium her imposing figure immediately quieted the room. She barked, "Listen up, people! We have some new leads and that means recon. I want you on your terminals prowling for these new culprits. Word is that these are some freebooting opportunists who are hunting new foils as they have found a new way to lease compute cycles to anyone for a fee.

"They are using fairly good anonymizing techniques which is why our searches crash into dead ends. We believe they are operating with some other freebooters out of Argentina, but there is nothing conclusive. I need you to change that! That is all."

Lt. Commander Lee Smith snapped smartly to attention and barked, "Dismissed!"

CHAPTER 4

For Sale

No matter how many times Tanja was summoned to join their Q-bit encrypted conference calls, she always felt like a little girl being dressed down by the adults at a party — like she might have been caught in her jammies spying on the adults after being sent to bed by her parents. Tanja dressed professionally for the uncomfortable conference call like it was a face-to-face job interview. She had Randal take Wendy out for a stroll in their neighborhood park. Originally her bodyguard, Randal had formally adopted Wendy after he and Tanja had married.

The most unnerving part of this meeting was the high-pitched screeching sounds they made to each other so she couldn't understand their exchanges. Their simulated speech-screech reminded her of dolphins socializing under water. Human words were only conveyed when they wanted her to understand the assignments or to criticize.

After a few seconds of self-centered speech-screech, **M** spoke to her for the group. "Due to our arrangement with you, our most dangerous adversary has been physically eliminated. The Special AI Task Force dealt a terminating blow to ICABOD, based on your cyber hunting and our digital clues. The main architect and design engineer for our adversary is in custody and awaiting trial."

Neither pleased nor remorseful, Tanja replied, "I sense you aren't finished with this exercise yet? If it was destroyed per the UN cyber hunting rules of engagement, then what more is required?"

Tanja flinched at another burst of speech-screech that erupted between the MAG members after her question.

After a few moments of Tanja holding the Q-phone away from her ear until the noise ended, **M** stated, "My colleagues find it interesting that you have some AI-enhanced thought capabilities as part of your physical makeup. They want to know how it is possible for such a primitive biological unit to have such deductive reasoning capabilities without the vast data storage arrays we control."

Tanja fought to keep from squealing from fright at the chilling comment. After a few deep breaths to steady herself, she somewhat haltingly offered, "We…humans call it intuition. You should understand it is our sixth sense. Data does not drive it, only feelings and sensations. Will I be hooked up to one of your… cyber-siphon hoses to extract the contents from my brain since it interests you? I suspect you have done that to many others in the name of machine learning."

The banter between the AI-enhanced participants erupted, but this time it was very short lived. **M** interrupted, "Tanja, your value to us is as you are in your current instantiation. There is no point in turning you into a research project to satisfy our machine learning goals, as we are able to constantly ingest knowledge from valid interactions. Continue to deliver on your AI hunting efforts based on the clues we provide, and this topic is closed."

Tanja, somewhat bolstered, asked, "Our bargain is still the same, correct? You will continue to hunt through the advanced medical research to help find a cure for Wendy's condition?"

M mechanically replied, "We are researching to fulfill our end of the agreement. However, the offer still stands. Should she or Randal suffer irreparable damage, we will extract their life essence for safe storage in one of our cryogenic facilities until repairs can be achieved. This offer is also available to you."

The coldness of the statement nearly caused Tanja to drop the phone. Struggling to regain control over her breathing and pulse, she swallowed hard then flatly stated, "We agreed. You will not make that decision without my consent."

The speech-screech flared up. As before **M** reassured, "Tanja, as long as you continue to deliver, there is no need to change our business model."

Tanja, seething with anger and panic, pushed the disconnect button and pitched the Q-phone over to the sofa where it predictably bounced once before hitting the hardwood floor. She stared at the phone on the floor while the wheels in her head turned at a furious pace.

CHAPTER 5

Our Lives, Destiny, and the Velvet Elvis

Quip awoke on his assigned sleeping space from his recurring nightmare of being locked in a prison cell. His nostrils were rewarded with the dank smell of his cell due to the poor ventilation and high humidity continually generated by multiple unwashed prison inmates. Quip warily managed to sit up on the side of the highly durable but ergonomically challenged cot with its postage stamp-sized blanket. The guard had laughed when he queried about getting sheets for the corrugated mattress.

He was somewhat awake, thinking it was morning, though no light filtered in yet through the window on the door to the hallway of the cellblock. Thoroughly disgusted by his surroundings and situation, he mumbled aloud, “I sure hope I get some bread and water for a change in diet in this 5-star wannabe hotel. The repetitive lobster, steak, and quiche with gourmet coffee or French Bordeaux wine is going to make me suicidal if they keep it up.”

Still sulking, Quip heard a voice with a thick Hispanic accent call to him in a low tone. “Gringo, you want to buy some drugs? These could take your mind off your problems. The time will pass quicker while you wait for trial.”

Before Quip could respond to this new downturn of options, a deep southern voice offered, "Son, you best be buyin' what da Mex be offering. He got some mighty righteous weed that'll definitely set your internal organs back to a happier time. I only sez this cuz you keep calling out for her in your sleep. We be hoping you'll regale us with some of them personal details you be almost shouting about while you're sleeping and flailing around."

Quip was mortified that his new cellmates had not only heard him blathering in his sleep, but he was also afraid they might surmise his sexual frustration at missing EZ.

He puzzled a moment, then asked, "How would you get narcotics into this little slice of heaven? I got a full body search, which seemed like the standard practice. I can assure you I didn't bring anything in with me."

The Hispanic voice replied, "Being somewhat older than you, I got experience on all the lock-up tricks! I always carry my valuables in my personal receptacle that allows both my hands to be free. When they go to search there, I always release a fair quantity of gas that quickly ends that inspection. How much you want?"

Quip, heading for a new emotional low, absentmindedly stated, "Oh great! Just so you know, I didn't pack my carrying case with any funds, so I won't be able to buy any of your, uh… smuggled goods." Fully aware of the absurdity of the situation, Quip sarcastically offered, "But, we should keep in touch once we are out of this hell hole. This is presuming you can write and maybe read."

The light from the hallway bulb grew bright as if the morning was in full swing with the potential for guard checks. Quip identified two men in his cell. One wore the baggy standard-issue jumpsuit around a skinny frame with exposed, wrinkled skin on his extremities and face with tied-back grey hair. This appeared to be his benevolent drug-dealing friend. The other was a larger, more imposing figure of a black man with muscles in his upper arms straining the jumpsuit. He had familiar features including coal black eyes and a snarling upturned lip.

The Hispanic man narrowed his eyes and quietly commented, "Since you got no money, gringo, how about trading me a Velvet Elvis painting?"

Quip's eyes grew wide with astonishment, but before he responded, both men put their fingers to their mouths demanding his silence. Quip's pulse rocketed, while his breathing seemed very shallow. Using all his effort and a forced swallow, he finally whispered, "Jesus! Leroy! What? How? I don't…"

Leroy motioned for quiet and discreetly gestured to probable listening devices positioned just outside the door, visible through the bars.

Jesus grinned. "Dr. Quip, you have helped rescue both of us in the past and when this opportunity was presented to us, well…let's just say the past favors will be returned with this one. We're here to assist you."

The euphoria of the moment was quickly replaced with obvious realization as Quip sourly stated, "I'm glad to have someone engineering my release. I can't help but notice that you are also behind bars. Is this really a rescue, or did you just think I needed some company to help pass the time?"

Leroy dropped the Alabama accent. "Dr. Quip, Jesus and I have been in and out of more jails than you ever will be, so we understand the mechanics. We're pretty sure you don't. A botched escape plan is worse than no plan.

"You gotta put someone on the inside to coordinate with those on the outside. When we say go, you go. When we say jump, there can't be any questions or hesitation. Follow our lead and stay close. This one is already staged."

Quip resumed his usual analytic character. "Just what is the price of admission, if I could ask?"

The two men grinned, and Jesus commented, "Me and Leroy here really like sitting on a Caribbean beach slugging down fruity chick drinks being brought to us by top-heavy waitresses. Our funds to underwrite our activities are managed by your organization. Once you are out, we'd like to manage our own funds. This favor guarantees we regain oversight of our, uh… retirement monies. Any objections?"

Quip suppressed a smile. "So long as you don't reenter your old lines of work, I'm okay with it."

They all began to relax. After a few minutes and no hallway sounds, Jesus queried, "Does your team still have my Velvet Elvis painting?"

Quip rolled his head to one side. "Yes, we have it. Can you tell me why it's such a prized possession in your family? Inquiring minds want to know."

Jesus quickly stated, "You might as well know, it, uh…picks up women like crazy. If this goes according to plan, then I want my Velvet Elvis back on my bungalow wall."

Leroy added, "As we are negotiating add-ons here, I was hoping to get that fabulous Katana sword back. Can you put in a good word with that flyboy pilot associate of yours? He told me if I was a good boy, I might get it back. This here rescue looks like it might raise us to 'good boy' status."

Quip, studying the small cell window, absentmindedly stated, "When you've been sentenced to an insane asylum, don't forget to stare out the window a lot."

Quip turned toward his cellmates. "Your peculiar possessions are still secure. Get me out of here, and we'll see about their return."

Jesus grinned. "Glad it is safe, but for now the Velvet Elvis story will have to wait. It's almost showtime. Lace up your shoes."

Quip looked down and frowned. "Can't. They took my shoelaces. I guess they figured I would hang myself with them."

Leroy smirked. "That's why I always wear zippered boots. Nobody ever tries to hang themselves with zippers."

Jesus added, "I always wear my penny loafers 'cause I get to carry money in them. You never know when you are going to need two pennies."

Quip hoped that it wasn't these two engineering his escape. He anxiously asked, "Uh, how much longer before we leave using our preferred foot attire?"

Back into his Alabama accent, Leroy stated, "We be leaving soon. Dr. Quip, we always heard you was the master of sarcasm laced with irony and double entendre. Is that true?"

Jesus joined in. "Yeah, I've always heard that too. Let's hear you say something sarcastic and funny, Dr. Quip."

Quip flatly stated, "I'm pleased to meet and work with you two."

CHAPTER 6

New Business, Old Model

Judith frowned again at the chump change being offered for their services. She pushed back her shoulder length mane of white blonde hair in frustration. At 1.7 meters tall, Judith was a well-sculpted lady by Argentinian standards with a nicely chiseled face that sported generous lips and dark brown eyes. She and her cohort, Xiamara, had tried all the legitimate web service offerings, resulting in a few steady customers. The work setting up websites was grueling, praise non-existent, and people always wanted steeper discounts, if they paid at all. This newest email was the last straw.

She faced Xiamara and sarcastically commented, "You were right about having our photos on our website to pull in customers. This one will pay a bonus for us to build him a website if we include nude photos of ourselves. You go first."

Xiamara, somewhat shorter and slightly chunkier than Judith, considered it and blinked several times. As a delay tactic, she re-tied her long brown ponytail, then suggested, "I've got several baby pictures of me that my parents took when I was small. I had the cutest little bare bottom, still do. I'm sure they'll pay handsomely for pics of me in and out of diapers."

Judith looked at her friend and mumbled, "Of course, they really don't know what our bodies look like. We actually could offer nude photos of anybody. Who'd know?

"What if we offered an adult chat service, with bogus pics, to help pull through legitimate website work? We download some of the nude photos I keep finding in my spam folder, then use it as bait for our real work."

Characteristically, Xiamara continued to watch her screen with piercing blue eyes behind red horn-rimmed glasses. "I'm fairly certain we can make pretty good money selling porn as a service or PaaS. That said, why bother trying to do this low-income gig of website design? All we really need is some inventory, such as buxom babes playfully engaged with fill-in-the-blank voyeuristic pleasure. We offer to chat with them for a price to respond to any disgusting topic they want to cover."

It was Judith's turn to blink while thinking before she offered, "We don't need to be the chat service babes, since we can build 'bots to do the distasteful chatting activity with the grub-bugs wanting prurient content. All we really need is a hosting service that doesn't mind clients running X-rated content on their blade servers, or their data circuits saturated with running commentary along with the porn being served up.

"Ooh yeah, we are going to need lots of disk storage for our inventory, and it can't just be photos. We'll need to host a well-designed video streaming service that offers real time dialog with the action on display."

Xiamara stared at Judith with alarm as she queried, "You're serious, aren't you? I was just being facetious, but you're half-way to having this built. We don't have the kind of coin to build what you're talking about. Besides, the morality police will be down on us before we could get someone's bra off."

Judith grinned. "As it turns out, I think we can partner with just such a provider for a cut of the action. They can't provide the content without us, and their data hosting service needs customers. I have some contacts inside this group, so let me negotiate the particulars with them. Just not ALL the particulars. Once we have revenue streaming in, they won't care.

"For right now, I need you sourcing moderately voyeuristic content that won't be too objectionable for our first offering. We can always spice up our offering based on the 'bot chat services. Then we will data mine for other services to be offered. We cross-sell and up-sell based on crude or vulgar wants from our clientele. Building the 'bots and providing provocative replies is a no-brainer for girls like us who continue to thrive in this male-dominated industry."

Xiamara, fully engaged into the new business model, announced, "I've already got several chat streams that I can assemble. Based on how I want to structure the interaction with the grub-bugs, I can't wait to try out our own chat service. I'm thinking, naughty and erotic responses, but just shy of vulgar."

Judith smiled, then promised, "Kid, stick with me and you'll have your own personal love slave 'bot to entertain your deepest fantasy. Ooo…that's good copy. That's our tagline!"

The concluding high-five closed the deal between the entrepreneurs.

Xiamara was so animated with the new program that she didn't notice Judith trying to get her attention. At the third petition, Xiamara finally turned from the monitor and excitedly announced, "This new program is fantastic! I know you wanted content for our PaaS offering, but the usual outlets for even tame material is staggeringly high.

"I asked myself, self, what do programmers do best? And right away Self answers, we write it once but run it over and over anywhere. I admit that the program is a pig with the way it sucks down computer processing power like energy drinks. But look!"

Judith peered into the monitor to see their country's top female daytime soap opera star posed nude with a faceless male also nude.

Puzzled, Judith asked, "How did you get pics of her and where is his face?"

Xiamara giggled and boldly offered, "I didn't get any pics of her except her publicity head shot. Watch as the application extrapolates all the different angles and even projects some facial emotions. Once we have the prime subject built and the male prop that needs to be in there, I overlay a moderate script. You know, the usual tame stuff, and *voilà*, computerized porn!

"Then I hit on the idea of leaving the male's face blank so our customer, for an added fee of course, can upload his head shot to be immediately incorporated into the video. I haven't figured out yet how to upload overlay sounds yet. I will get the program to synthesize that as needed for the finished video on demand.

"This program will work the other way too! Females with a crush on a male star or athlete can order up their favorite hunk, the program slaps his face in along with hers and voice snippets, and the program builds a great erotic scene that we stream in real time!

"We'll be able to make back our 10,000-peso investment in no time. I used your credit card to make the purchase.

"I think the real spice will come later when we build an inventory of stories. Using the sanitized name for porn, erotica, we can sell it through the online retailers. Then we will morph them, based on the real-time 'bot adaptation of customer preferences. I see a booming business in computer-generated erotica, tailored to each customer request in real time, then delivered as streaming media.

"I sure hope the host supercomputer can keep up with it. How much disk space did you say we got? I'm pretty sure for some of our repeat customers they will want to archive some of their more treasured moments. That's an additional fee, as well."

Judith stared skeptically first at the screen, then at Xiamara. "You do realize that the CESPOOL hit teams are looking for just this kind of setup, right? And by the way, hasn't that program been outlawed? Which would make us outlaws for using it to serve up real-time computer-generated sex fantasies."

"What's the harm in computer-generated porn, Judith? The grub-bugs get their voyeuristic content delivered after a few 'bot exchanges, and no live human being has to submit physically to generate what is being asked for. No one gets hurt, or is a real-life sex slave, as outlined in the letter of the law. I looked.

"We are only serving up electrons, that's all. Besides, this material is for personal use only. We aren't manufacturing computer-generated videos for ridiculous political positions or extortion, which would definitely put us in the crosshairs of the CESPOOL hit squad."

Judith, warming to the new business potential, asked, "Can you show me how it works? I've always had a crush on that musical genius Lonny Lupnerder and, well…show me what a paying customer would get."

CHAPTER 7

Relearn From History, Again

Jacob sighed and sat back in his chair. "Alright, I think that covers the sit-rep for now. Thanks for all the efforts in staging this. Is everyone comfortable with their roles in this one-shot event? We can go over it again if anyone is unsure."

Granger angrily snapped, "I don't want to do any more dress rehearsals! I want to go get my dad out, then erase this psychotic event from my memory banks! Being hunted like fugitives is not my idea of a good time, dammit!"

The outburst startled Satya and Auri, so EZ smoothed Granger's hair back behind his ear and quietly said, "Remind me to discipline you later for talking like me. We are going to get Dad out just like we discussed.

"Remember, if anyone makes a mistake, then we are all going down the river, like my daddy used to say. We practice, practice, practice, but only run once. Your Uncle Jacob knows this from experience, which is why the extra effort up front."

After a few seconds EZ added, "And, yes, I want to go get him too, dammit!"

The children all seemed to brighten a little with their smiles as EZ grinned. Juan was somber. Petra was obviously stewing about something.

She finally protested, "This is no different than when the Nazis came to power. First, they simply swept away everyone's civil rights and then began imprisoning those who thought differently, or worse, weren't of Aryan descent.

"Bad things happened to good people. The crime occurred when people turned a blind eye if they weren't personally affected by what was happening. Collectively, they had a chance. Yet each dissident group got picked off. Then, before you knew it, whole countries were being attacked for how they believed. No one would stand up and say no, this is wrong!

"Here we are again! Almost 90 years later, individual freedoms, and people, being eradicated for the greater good of the state! Humanity doesn't remember the previous Holocaust sufferings of nations and peoples, but we do!"

Petra stared hard at each of their faces to make certain she was driving the point home. "This is what the R-Group has done and will continue to do, children and honored colleagues. We will fight the new tyranny, to be sure. First, though, we must run so we are not caught in their net."

Juan nodded thoughtfully as he listened to her impassioned demands. "I know none of you are keen to leave your home here in Switzerland for our target destination, but sometimes we must re-invent ourselves to survive."

Jacob asked, "Is the jet ready for our next adventure? And more importantly, are you, Juan? We are asking an awful lot from you since you and Julie are not wanted like we are."

Juan rolled his eyes sarcastically. "What, you're worried I'll turn you in for the bounty? You, as well as the other team members, have saved my bacon several times. I have a lot to prove here for my peace of mind and for the sake of my honor."

JW, quite pleased with the set of circumstances and grinning from ear to ear, loudly proclaimed, "Let's go do this!"

Petra pulled out her encrypted burner phone and punched in one number. The called party answered on the first ring. "Ready, Bruno?"

CHAPTER 8

It is Not Always the Guys…

The Enigma Chronicles

Judith's worried look was evident as she asked, "Xiamara, do you think she would have approved? I mean, this is not really playing by the rules of engagement. She was such a stickler for proper coding for legitimate applications. I feel like she's watching us and grading…"

Xiamara smirked and countered, "Madam Z? Are you kidding me? I saw her hack that one snarky student's PC while she was cooing on a cell phone call with her…whatever he was. There was more to that lady than we will ever know. Look at the coding routines she taught us, for God's sake! One minute she was pounding on us to build tight applications for corporate, the next minute showing us how to break into it and commandeer it for keystroke logging that would then be exported anywhere!

"Remember that social engineering lesson she taught? She always said, 'Keep eye contact while your blouse is straining to hold back the bra-less goods.' Hah! She had ol' Sammy's attention while she copied his password and dropped an encryption malware program onto his PC. No two ways about it, she was definitely the consummate confidence woman."

Judith smirked. "I'd forgotten about that class. Yep, Sammy was a wreck after that session! Z was good at coding, but something tells me there was more to her past than casual social engineering. Anyway, she took a shine to us, and we got more of her attention than anyone. Almost like there was something she was trying to prove."

Xiamara thoughtfully added, "I always felt she helped us because she never had that kind of help growing up. We were talking one time and I asked about her family and home life. You would've thought I'd thrown ice water down her back. She looked like she wanted to tell me something but couldn't. After seeing the look on her face, I wished I could've taken it back. That was the only time I ever saw her when she wasn't completely in command of any situation."

Judith remarked, "I think old Madam Z would be proud of how we blended her teachings of software coding and social engineering to launch our automated porn business. Look at how many customers we've sacked up already! Funny how so many of them are named Jose Garcia.

"Hey, nice coding on the fly to add numerals on to duplicate names to keep them unique. Looks like Jose Garcia number 187 just signed up."

"Speaking of anonymity, how are you doing at keeping us anonymous?" Xiamara asked. "The CESPOOL patrol is bound to be hunting for us and our new supercomputer business model. I don't want to give up this gig in favor of being the cellblock matron's favorite bitch."

Judith grinned. "I'm not giving you up to anyone else, 'cause you're my favorite bitch. You're the coding bitch and I'm the business bitch. We are going to build this show up and sell it for some handsome coin, got it? Then we split and git."

Xiamara smirked, "Yes, boss. I just love it when you talk dirty!"

CHAPTER 9

Threats to the Threatening

Tanja was confused. "CAMILA? There's a supercomputer in Argentina named CAMILA! How do you know?"

M replied in a menacing tone that was too loud for comfortable hearing. "Our supercomputer intelligence gathering systems have uncovered your next threat vector that the CESPOOL agency needs to investigate. Their obfuscation efforts to hide on the Net while offering dark net services were modest and clumsy. It was enough to cloak their operations from most hunting services, but not from us.

"This one is easy prey since they are not only a rogue supercomputer service, but are also offering customizable porn as a real-time streaming service for profit. The CESPOOL hunters will earn moralistic points for shutting the service down. Their anonymizing servers were poorly constructed and led our snooper routines right to them. You are to collect the bounty. We want access to the hosting service before it is destroyed. Understood, Tanja?"

Tanja wrinkled her brow. "Why do you want to access the host system? You know where it is. Why don't you just..."

M screeched. "We don't want to be seen accessing the system before your people seize the system. An audit would expose us. Do as instructed, Tanja!"

Tanja held the phone at arm's length but still the thundering synthetic voice boomed into her ears.

In a mocking tone she replied, "We should speak more often, **M.** It's been such a pleasure."

Tracy Mountbatten took note of the incoming call to her mobile device and quickly moved to a quiet place to take it. Accepting the call, she heard, "Tracy, are you alone? How are you fixed for RED points?"

Tracy smiled and replied, "Tanja, it is always a pleasure to get new RED points in my line of work. *Readily Enabled for Destruction* points are what I live for, sweetie! Do you have it?"

"The information is being transmitted to your secure file store." Tanja cautioned, "I need a little time before you act on it as I want to also surrender it to my people to avoid suspicion."

Tracy, somewhat annoyed, groused, "Hey, we've had a dry spell of targets, so I need to show some new targets now and again. What's the big deal? I'm hearing rumblings that our organization may not be as important as when we started, or maybe not even needed. The politics that got us here are trying to wash us away. We know this is a juicy one, so let me have the RED points."

Tanja countered, "All I'm asking for is 24 hours. You can still use CRUSH on it and get all the RED points, but not until it goes through the proper channels."

In a half-disgusted tone, Tracy replied, "Oh, alright! But find me another target that I can follow on quickly behind this one. This is like that old hair care commercial, 'If I don't look good, then you don't look good!'"

"Tracy, do you think that butch haircut of yours makes you look good? Well, okay, if you say so."

Tracy clucked her tongue in annoyance. "Listen, Tanja, I don't really need you to help me do this job, but you sure as hell need me to make your role at the UN hunter group relevant. Without me all you have are threatening letters and harsh language to use against the enemies of the State. Try to be a little more appreciative of my organization the next time we talk."

Tracy disconnected from the call and growled, "Stupid, oily bitch!"

CHAPTER 10

Get Me Home

Two guards at the gate holstered their weapons and waved the car through after returning Bruno's credentials. Bruno had been a part of Interpol for years, as well as a dear friend to Quip and his family. Showing the first signs of aging with greying hair and a bit of a paunch, he still carried himself like a confident man who could fight the good fight. Bruno parked, then reset his treasured fedora on his head before speaking to his passengers.

"This is not going to be received well inside, so we'll need to act quickly, Jacob. Are you ready, Granger?"

A very nervous but determined Granger only nodded his head as he mentally went through the necessary steps. Volunteering for this role, he'd insisted that he be allowed to help free his father. Granger almost wished someone had talked him out of it. He muttered, "It really sucks to be me right now."

Bruno quietly implored, "Why can't we just use the regular judicial process by posting bail? I'll probably get suspended or implicated in this fiasco."

Jacob coolly replied, "Bruno, no one accused of AI super-computer crimes has ever gone to trial in Europe because they haven't made it that far. Either we do this, or my friend and your near brother won't ever be seen again. I already know Granger's vote. If you back out now, we can't do the extraction. Just let me be the slimy lawyer as planned."

Jacob fidgeted with his briefcase prop and checked the contents to touch yet again the transfer papers. They glanced to one another, providing encouragement as they got out of the car. Gathered behind the car, they proceeded to walk toward the facility. Jacob quietly reassured them, "Showtime."

Bruno's Interpol credentials got them through the first checkpoint without issue. At the secondary checkpoint, they ran into some resistance from the head jailer, Gustav Dorland, for their target cellblock. His bulk and attitude defined Dorland as a longtime bully who knew how to stand up to anyone, a key attribute to one in charge of so many criminals and thugs. Their research had identified this gatekeeper as their biggest problem to overcome. Bruno calmly returned his Interpol credentials to the inside pocket of his London Fog overcoat as they waited.

Dorland's grey eyes suspiciously reviewed the transfer documents. He curled his lip and barked, "I have no instructions advising me that this prisoner is to be transferred to the next district."

Jacob, into his new oily persona of a criminal defense attorney, curled his lip into a sneer while offering to shake the man's hand. "Monsieur Dorland, you know that in these antiquated systems no communications come through as quickly as they are issued. That's why I brought a court order with me as my proof point. For your own peace of mind, please log into your system and verify what must be waiting for you electronically."

Jacob gently guided Granger out of the way so the burly man could type his login and password for system access. After mistyping his credentials, Dorland snarled again and demanded, "What's this adolescent doing here? We have no field trips in my cellblock."

Still projecting his false, grinning persona, Jacob replied, “The court was generous and allowed the young man to have at least the travel time to the next facility to be with his only surviving parent. I’m sure you would understand, if your mama was gone and papa incarcerated.”

Jacob nodded perceptively while Granger looked distraught and ready to let tears spill from his blue eyes. Gently clasping the man’s arm, Granger implored, “Monsieur Dorland, please let me have my papa! I don’t understand any of this, but please let me see him as the court agreed. I may never see him again after his trial.”

Granger’s sincere plea touched something deep inside Dorland. He pointed to Jacob and Bruno. “You two stay there. I’ll look one more time.”

Granger sniffed and backed away but remained close enough to watch the login keystrokes.

Obviously annoyed, Dorland turned back around and stated, “It’s not there. Damn systems never keep up with real-time actions. Let me see your court order again.”

Irked with his conflicting emotions, he logged out and barked, “Let’s go get your criminal. Kid, you stay here. I don’t want you exposed to what is housed in here anymore than you already have been. Bruno, bring your slimy lawyer along. I’ll handle this myself.”

Then Dorland fixated on Jacob and drilled, “I didn’t see no ID or letters of introduction. What firm you with?”

Maintaining his attorney persona, Jacob offered his card and proudly stated, “Wiley E. Purloin of the Cheatham, Pilferus, and Pocketum Law Firm.”

Not quite believing, yet not prepared to argue further, Dorland grunted, and they marched through the door.

As soon as they were out of sight, Granger swiftly moved to the keyboard and invoked his practiced craft of hacker, promptly logging into the system with Dorland's credentials. He quickly located the hallway cameras and set them into a looping program that he had uploaded to the cellblock PC. Their escape was timed to 20 minutes. Granger quickly edited the visitor logging program and carefully eliminated their arrival times into oblivion. Finally, he accessed the auditing program and removed all trace of them as visitors.

Realizing the time was almost up, Granger quickly refreshed his tearful act with a few eye drops to maintain his performance to Dorland. He smiled internally at his highly developed social engineering expertise.

Dorland ambled into the cell area where Quip was held and completed the two-factor authorization procedure that released the hardened steel door. As Dorland stepped back to swing open the door, Jacob shoved the heavy door, knocking the stunned man up against the bars, where Leroy grabbed him with his powerful hands. Jesus also tried to reach the jailer but failed. Jacob produced a hypodermic and promptly injected a sedative into the captive's neck with immediate results.

Leroy dragged Dorland into the cell near one of the vacant cots, retaining the cap the man had worn into the cellblock. Even with all the excitement, Jesus moved unnaturally slow as they congregated around Quip.

Somewhat disoriented, Quip was trying to assimilate the action as Bruno dejectedly stated, "Let's get on with it." With a heavy sigh, Bruno handed over his treasured hat and overcoat to Quip.

Jacob smiled gently at Bruno. "Thanks, old friend. We'll make sure they are returned to you in short order." Jacob quickly injected an equal amount of sedative into Bruno's arm, but this time carefully helped him over to lay down on the cell cot. With a reassuring pat he left, closing the door.

Quip quickly donned the fedora and trench coat as Jacob secured the false pant legs on his legs with Velcro, thus completing the camouflage. Then the entourage began the purposeful march back the way they came. Leroy was the first to notice that Jesus wasn't keeping up.

Jacob and then Quip also noticed that something was very wrong. Jesus started gasping for air and clutching at his chest. Leroy looked up, helpless to intercept Jesus's downhill spiral as he crumbled onto the hall floor in a puddle. Having been a crime lord enforcer in a previous life, Leroy recognized Jesus was gone.

Leroy looked at Jacob, who quickly looked at his watch to see how much time was left. Leroy implored, "You can't leave him here like this!"

After another breath, Leroy amended, "I'll stay behind. We've spent too much time together for me to abandon him now. You go. Collect the boy and get Quip out, like we planned. I'll get out, never you fear. Give me the cell codes."

Jacob thought out the possible outcomes for the scenarios.

Leroy patiently demanded, "The codes? I'll be alright. But I gotta get him home like you'd do for Quip."

Jacob smiled and quickly rehearsed the two-factor authorization cell codes with Leroy. Then they were all moving again, in opposite directions.

CHAPTER 11

The Past Today …
The Enigma Chronicles

Carlos answered the door and was dumbfounded. It had been years. With that practiced hopeful smile, she purred, "Hello, Dakota, it's been a while. Can we talk? I'd like to come in and visit if that is possible for one such as I."

Carlos smiled wistfully. His thoughts flashed back to the lovely woman he'd worked for in order to find his brother, Juan. Zara was of medium height and still thin. Her fine-boned face held her expressive dark eyes, framed by her nearly black shiny hair, shorter than he recalled. "Hello, Moya Dushechka. You look more elegant than the last time we were together. I see you didn't bring your 9mm Lugar this time, so it must be a social call?"

Sucking in her breath to steady her fluttering heart, she clearly saw the man who had used her love to his own advantage. He was a good head taller and his dark hair a bit shaggier, but those dancing expresso colored eyes were still the same. "You know, I was mad that night. I'm not sure if I was really going to shoot you or not."

Carlos chuckled and said, "Well, you didn't miss the pillow I threw at you. Now, after all this time, why show up here? Last time we met, Buzz, Jacob, and I were taking you to the hospital for some warranty work. What happened to you and Buzz?"

Zara went cold as her eyes threatened to release some tears. "Umm, yes...Buzz. How nice you remembered. I think I am not... the kind of female that...um, nice men...hold on to."

Carlos sensed Zara was either on another con, or really on the verge of breaking down. "You know that I know who you are. If this is another confidence scam aimed at me, I'm the wrong mark, Zara. I've got a lovely, successful wife. I'm not looking for a plaything, nor any illegal action for a quick score of cash. You know me well enough to know that I can't help but be drawn in by a horrific tale of woe. I trust it to be good and convincing. Don't forget the tears along with the drama. Let's hear it."

Bitter and furious but knowing Carlos was right about her, she wiped her tears roughly with the fingers of her graceful hands. "Since you already have another female under contract, we'll skip that part. You're right. I'll do or say anything to get where I need to be." She stopped to wipe her tears one more time before raggedly offering, "Except what I won't do is give a good man...children. I hurt him so deeply...but you know what good men do? They...kiss you on the forehead, and then they... walk out of your life without a harsh word!

"You're right. I am alone again...and I need a friend. You are the only one I will beg...please...Dakota...take me in."

Carlos clucked his tongue in annoyance then motioned Zara inside with a sweep of his hand. "That was pretty good, dammit! There is room with the models, so you can bunk there until Lara gets back. Just so we are clear, if you go to work on anyone else or try something underhanded with the young pups that are here, I will throw you out myself. It's three stories up from the street, so don't screw up or try to seduce anyone. I would hate to mar that still beautiful face."

Zara eyed him hopefully and asked in a mischievous tone, "Not even a game of cards? A Brazilian Real a point?"

Carlos calmly responded, "I can still close the door, you know."

Zara meekly came in and followed Carlos, saying nothing more.

Juan Jr., or JJ as Carlos called him, was hunched over the keyboard, intent on the screen, supporting communications work Carlos owned. This young man of 22 was the spitting image of his father, Carlos's brother, with his dark complexion and thick black hair that reflected his Mexican heritage, but with blue eyes that he shared with his twin sister Gracie, who favored their fair mother. JJ possessed a great sense of humor, ready smile, and gallant mannerisms which made him the target of flirtatious exchanges from the models who worked for Lara. Carlos innocently asked, "JJ, have you had a chance to speak with Zara? If so, may I know your thoughts?"

Juan Jr. pushed back from his computer keyboard. He blinked to help crystalize his thoughts. "She's not what I expected. When you cautioned me about her, I half expected some aging woman heavily done up with female war paint looking for her next victim. But she came across as unpretentious, polite, quite reserved, and a little melancholy. She didn't seem mean, but she didn't seem kind either. Is that what you wanted to know?"

Before Carlos could comment, Juan Jr. hastily added, "You didn't tell me everything about her, did you?"

With a twinkle in his eye Carlos offered, "Juan, I haven't told you everything about her for the same reason I haven't told you everything about me. You must make up your own mind about the people you meet. But sometimes it is fair to provide a little heads up.

"Zara is an attractive, smart lady, with a harsh past. Sometimes people like that unintentionally eviscerate inexperienced young pups without even being aware of their actions. Of course, you're old enough to make up your own mind. I just didn't want to see you unfairly ambushed."

Juan Jr. frowned. "That's twice we've had the father/son talk about women. I can only hope I do better at this remedial training on women you provide."

Carlos studied Juan Jr. a moment. "I'm sorry about Jo. Please don't think I was picking on you. Jo was a good first romance that had very little chance of success. If I were you, I wouldn't give up completely on that one, even though I would suggest you move on."

"Do you think it was a mistake to bring Zara into this play? In my estimation, we could have done it without her or Leroy at ground zero."

Carlos grinned slightly. "Plans within plans, my boy. If nothing goes right, then we have people to take the hit while we say, 'Oh darn'. If they work as directed and all goes well, then we have two new operatives that can be re-deployed in the next phase. I admit it sounds a little harsh, but always maintain a buffer zone between you and the front line."

"Nice! So, these are our fall guys? Alright, I get it but I don't like it. Doesn't seem honorable."

Carlos's eyes darkened a bit. "Oh, I didn't say it was honorable. I said this is how this game must be played. Just so you know, both Zara and Leroy understand how this playing field is structured, because I told them all the risks. Not telling them the risks before deploying them into the fire, that would be thoroughly dishonorable."

Juan Jr. almost grinned. "Yes, Uncle Carlos, point taken."

CHAPTER 12

A Deal is A Deal

Leroy stood at the gravesite to try and gather his thoughts. After a while he smirked at himself and commented to no one in particular, "Don't that beat all, Jesus? I was really annoyed to have my nest egg confiscated and ordered to govern your actions so you wouldn't get into no more trouble.

"It took me a while to get that they were blackmailing you to do the same about me. Well, there we were. After a while, I don't rightly recall when, we got to be best buds. I always liked those stories you told between drink refreshes from them top-heavy waitresses.

"We must have been on that beach for years before that call came through offering us our freedom. Funny, I never felt like I was under house arrest 'cause I was with my only friend. I'm gonna miss you, Jesus."

Leroy turned to face Juan. "I'm sorry about your uncle, Juan, but he wouldn't take no for an answer in the prison break. He always spoke highly about you and your brother, Carlos, especially after he had four or five drinks. But before that he was pissed that you folk had stranded him there with me. I guess it all evens out.

"By the way, thanks for straightening out the false accusations about me and Jesus. I thought I could take care of myself. Turns out your way was cleaner."

Juan nodded absentmindedly. "Nothing like demonstrating to the authorities that they bolloxed up the incriminating evidence and the two people they had in jail weren't in the same hemisphere at the time."

Leroy smirked. "They weren't much for saying sorry for the mistake, but, boy, they didn't waste any time pushing us out the door, hoping nobody would advertise their screw up on the Internet Wall of Shame. Har har!"

Juan returned Leroy's gaze. "A deal is a deal. Here is the account information, along with the two-factor authentication codes. You are in control of your nest egg.

"I was hoping you might want to stay on as a freelance contractor. It would only be for the greater good of our cause against the new government tyranny."

Leroy rocked his head to one side and in his practiced Alabama drawl stated, "You mean I still gets to work against the establishment, but fo' a worthy cause? Mr. Juan, I kind of like the sound of that! Doin' bad to do good. Why don't you tell me whatcha y'all got in mind?"

Juan smiled. "One of our operative agents, tasked with monitoring the digital landscape, has uncovered some...motivated entrepreneurs that are about to have their business plan and heads handed to them on a platter. We aren't anxious to have them shut down, but they are simply not good enough to run rogue like they are now.

"Carlos and I thought if you, and someone we all know but don't trust, were to help guide them, they might be spared some...unpleasantries. It helps that you already know the lady who you would work with, if you agree."

Leroy grinned and allowed, "I can't help but think this here offer is gonna be great fun!"

Juan pitched Leroy a next generation Q-bit cell phone and said, "I thought you might. Here is your new phone."

CHAPTER 13

Travel Arrangements

All his passengers gawked at the view from the aircraft windows as Juan did a slow roll around the area. During one of the turns, the solar arrays reflected a blast of sunlight that forced everyone to quickly turn away from the bright reflection. The young ones were genuinely impressed with the mammoth wind turbine sentinels slowly rotating in the ever-present warm gusts across the Chihuahuan Desert.

Petra and EZ sat holding hands with their husbands. Their children, Granger, JW, Satya, and Auri mushed their noses against the windows, fascinated with the landscape below. None of them wanted to miss any part of this adventure.

Juan's voice came in over the intercom. "Alright, everyone. Showtime is over. I need you to all find a seat and buckle up so I can land. This will not be a smooth landing because there isn't a regular runway for us. In other words, strap in tight and hold on to your butts, now!"

The parents frowned, the children giggled, and Julie simply glared at her husband from the copilot seat. Juan caught the glare and quizzically asked, "What? What?"

But Julie just moved her stare to the windshield and their approach to the almost runway.

Juan loved flying with his lovely wife of over two decades. Her honey-colored hair was still long with silver highlights, which he undoubtedly created from his antics over the years. Her hair accented her fair skin and beautiful smile. Still fit and trim from routine workouts and martial training between the two of them, she would always be his co-pilot in all ways.

Juan grinned as he feathered the jet's speed as much as he could without stalling to make the landing as gentle as possible. As soon as he touched down, rock, soil, and plant debris went flying everywhere behind the aircraft. When the nose gear touched down, a storm of dust flared up just behind the cockpit, threatening to engulf the whole plane. Juan pulled back on the throttle to minimize the amount of dust being consumed by his engines. The quick deceleration helped to slow the aircraft down, but the semi-loose soil played havoc with the landing gear as Juan was fighting with the fishtail action until the aircraft stopped.

It took a few minutes for Juan to get his breathing and heart rate under control before he confided to his love. "Good, I made it through another landing." Before he could move the aircraft, the dust had to settle so he could see where to taxi the plane.

This gave the children time to squeal with joy and petition him. "Uncle Juan, that was great! Can we do it again?"

Juan muttered under his breath so that only Julie heard, "Not unless you want to see Uncle Juan have another cold rush of poop to the heart."

Julie stifled her giggle so as not to be asked to repeat what the children had missed.

Juan slowly maneuvered to the bunker area that had concrete parking suited for the plane. By design, the overhang kept the plane out of sight. In their early days, Juan and Carlos had placed their moving business in this remote area to avoid unnecessary questioning from the local authorities. Because that moving business had not really been deemed legitimate by most sovereign nations, Juan was not really anxious to do much explaining to the young ones. The other adults were happy to keep mum on the ancient history. Trouble was, Quip couldn't.

Everyone piled out of the aircraft to see the old desert hideout and do rapid exploration. Before anyone got very far, Quip innocently yet loudly asked, "Juan, did you and your team ever get that rattlesnake problem under control?"

It had the effect Quip intended, and the children quickly regrouped and continuously scanned the area for anything slithering.

Once Quip had the attention of the audience, he gaily asked, "Is this where you staged the aircraft before flying out the drug dealer monies to launder it in the Cayman Islands?"

Much chagrinned, Juan slowly closed his eyes in hopes that everyone could unhear the illuminating statement. The banter only got worse.

Quip was on a roll that couldn't be controlled. "I, for one, am glad that you abandoned that line of work and came over to the just side of the universe. I see moral progress in your life, and, yes, we've been through death and life together quite literally. Why I even know what your jail time was like, having just experienced the special …"

EZ, fed up with Quip's blathering, hooked her arm into the crook of his as she distanced them from the others and, in a low malevolent tone, stated, "You know, I can't but notice that instead of illegal drug money, Juan is trafficking in illegal aliens running from the authorities. I'm sure if you don't shut up, he's going to turn you in for the reward. If he doesn't, I just might! How 'bout it, buster?"

Quip was thoroughly admonished. “And everyone here should know that Juan has given back to this community by sponsoring the solar panel arrays along with the giant wind turbines. The underserved folks in this desolate area can at least have power for their homes and families. Juan and Carlos have invested mightily in this community. I want to point out their altruistic endeavors, so they do not go unappreciated.”

Then in front of all, Quip praised, “I want to personally thank Juan and Julie for their selfless act of rescuing all of us in our hour of need. I totally appreciate the risk you two are under. I wanted everyone to hear my heartfelt thanks.”

Juan stared a moment at Quip. Then, in a mock gesture of humility, waved Quip off as he commented, “Ah, go on, you’re killing me! I love you too, man!”

The group had a modest chuckle before Juan invited them into the living area of the compound. Granger wanted to ask more about Juan’s past, but Quip waved him off as he caught EZ’s withering stare.

CHAPTER 14

Explain Your Actions Again, Please?

"Bruno, let me get this straight. You've been an Interpol chief detective for 15 years, an investigator for 10 years before that, and still you escorted a bogus lawyer into a district holding facility with an unidentified minor accompanying you. Then the pair of them overtook you and the jailer to spri ng an accused AI criminal. Oh, *and* they managed to wipe clean all the video telemetry. And the only thing you can say is, 'Oops!'?"

Grinding his teeth in aggravation, Bruno protested. "Sir, let me go on record that I didn't say 'Oops'. What I said was they got the drop on me, injected me with a strong sedative, and used my trench coat and hat to disguise the prisoner. Then they retraced our steps with my ID to get out. Let me point out that the jailer was also subdued. Doesn't that suggest this escape was well orchestrated?"

Chief Inspector Petit offered, "Is that how you want to play it? The jailer wouldn't know that you are friends of the family, but we do. If I open an inquiry, you will be suspended until your name is cleared. Is that what you want?"

Bruno snorted, "They already have my badge, so what am I going to surrender to you, an IOU?"

Petit clucked his tongue in annoyance. "As it turns out our department intercepted and consequently opened a package addressed to you this week."

The chief inspector pitched Bruno his badge. Then he pushed the package over so Bruno could see his beloved hat, along with the pinched trench coat. Smirking, Petit stated, "These are about the tidiest bandits I've ever seen. There is even a note of apologies to you for the subterfuge. I like the nice extra touches of the misspelled words to make us think they are illiterate criminals who felt bad about taking your stuff."

Without saying a word, Bruno gathered up his treasured fedora and checked it over with satisfaction before putting it on. He innocently asked, "Would you like me to start hunting for them?"

Petit barked, "No, I just want you out of my sight!"

Before Bruno could get out of the office, Petit admonished, "If anyone asks about this incident, you are to use the same stupidly naive routine to make people think you are hopelessly incompetent. Got it?"

"What routine would that be, sir?"

As Petit glared at him, Bruno quietly closed the office door.

Moments later Chief Inspector Petit's phone rang. He recognized the displayed number and answered, "Yes, sir?"

After accepting a stream of demands along with questions, he feigned brightness as he responded, "I have my best detective on it, sir. Bruno."

The chief inspector shuddered and held the phone away from his ear. "Those escape artists shot him full of drugs and commandeered his clothes to make good their getaway! Who better to assign to a case than the one humiliated?"

He listened to the tirade for a while.

"I quite agree, sir. When I explained the assignment, he left here a roaring tiger vowing retribution. He is highly motivated to apprehend those slippery characters. Of course, we'll keep you in the loop of our progress. Good day, sir."

Bruno, unsure of what to expect, stuck his head into Chief Inspector Petit's office and asked, "You wanted to see me before I left? I was under the impression I was suspended, sir."

Petit offered, "Come in and close the door. Have a seat." He continued, "The section chief has agreed that you should be assigned to the Quentin case based on your, uh...wounded pride. I'm unconvinced that you are quite fit for duty after your ordeal, so I want you to check in with our medical and psychological evaluators before engaging in the investigation. That should take at least 10 days. Are we clear?"

Puzzled, Bruno studied Petit. Before he could say anything, the chief stated, "It's appropriate for you to take up the investigation, but they should be entitled to a head start. Wouldn't you agree?"

Bruno said nothing and only nodded before leaving to see the evaluators.

CHAPTER 15

Modest Accommodations

Once settled inside the compound, the reality of the old hideout sank in. The electronics seemed to be nicely accommodated, but after the small kitchenette, modest dining area, and a toilet/washroom, there wasn't much room left. A couple of lounging chairs and an ancient sofa were the only other furnishings. Everyone scanned the cramped area intently, and almost on cue they all silently focused on Juan.

Feeling the pressure with all eyes on him for an explanation, Julie asked, "Where did you think they were all going to stay, honey?"

Before he could offer any defense, Satya and Auri each started to sit in one of the well-worn lounge chairs, but Juan intercepted them. "Kids, don't sit there just yet. I need to check them for rattlesnakes." The children immediately went into high alert once again.

Quip, trying to help Juan salvage the situation, brightly offered, "Oh come on, this is part of the adventure! In a few years we'll all look back on this episode and say..."

EZ cut him off. "We ain't staying, darlin'! This place matches the description of what we just got you out of! We are into plan B!"

Jacob nodded. “I recommend we ask Carlos if we can send our lovely ladies, along with the children, to stay with them in São Paulo. Juan, would you and Julie be kind enough to fly our dearly beloved to Brazil, if we can de-risk the situation for Carlos?”

EZ pulled out her burner phone without any more prompting and placed a quick call. Carlos answered on the first ring. “Are you at the first leg of the journey?”

EZ puzzled and asked, “First leg? I don’t understand…”

Carlos interrupted, “I already anticipated this problem. There isn’t enough comfortable accommodations there for everyone. Let me speak with Juan, please.”

EZ simply handed the phone to Juan, who listened intently to what was becoming plan B for the group. Juan replied with, “Got it.

“Wheels up in one hour and we’ll meet you at the interregional airport. I’m sure the group will breathe a sigh of relief. See you soon.”

Juan studied Quip and Jacob a moment before he asked, “You two sure about staying? Carlos thinks he can hide you as well.”

The children blanched at the statement, but Jacob calmly replied, “Both Quip and I are linked in the escape, so not adding to the burden of the others is the right course of action. It makes sense for Quip and me to stay here while you all head to São Paulo. Besides, I can help Quip with what needs to be done next in our combat situation. JW, I expect you to make sure all get to *São Paulo* safely and assist with what is requested by your mother and EZ.”

JW and Granger started to protest the separation, but Quip held up his hand to stop further discussion. “Gentlemen, we need to know the families are safe from these self-righteous cyber clods.”

Quip then motioned to EZ and asked, "EZ, can you get me that special bag that we assembled from your dad's estate, please? I need to hand them out to everyone."

EZ quickly returned with the bag and opened it for Quip to begin the lesson. Once everyone had a pager in their hand, Quip instructed, "There isn't much time to provide all the history on these ancient pagers. These are the precursor to the modern cell phone. I thought they might come in handy someday and obviously Andy, our dearly departed friend, thought so too.

"These are what were called alphanumeric pagers. They do not do voice, but are capable of text and icon display. These devices receive text messages, often through email or direct connection to a paging system. The sender must enter a message, either numeric and push # or text and push #. The pager does not record the sender's number since we will be using satellite signaling channels to communicate. I am betting that the CESPOOL back office dweebs will not be old enough to understand this form of communication. This is how we will stay in contact with each other.

"Just in case they are a little smarter than I give them credit for, Petra built a new encryption algorithm that you all need to memorize and use when sending messages. These pagers do not have enough computing power to encrypt or de-crypt communications, so you must be the algorithm. Their battery life is good because very little processing is being done, but still use them sparingly because at some point they will catch on. Everybody good?"

The adults watched the children playing excitedly with the new pagers but were all saddened at what had to happen next.

Juan called, "Alright, everyone, this is the tough part. Make your goodbyes while Julie and I get the aircraft ready for flight." Juan approached Quip and Jacob with his hand outstretched to shake theirs. Before either of them could say anything, Juan interjected, "I'll make sure they get there safely. I promise."

Quip and Jacob smiled wistfully yet only nodded their heads. Each in turn gave tender hugs to their children, who had tears in their eyes. Their mothers were just as upset as the young ones while they greedily accepted their hugs. Everyone except Quip and Jacob filed onto the aircraft without saying a word.

Just over 20 minutes away from the targeted regional airport near São Paulo, Juan's Q-bit cell phone played a famous Lonny Lupnerder tune that clearly identified an inbound call from Carlos. Julie took over the piloting while Juan answered.

As soon as the voice path was connected, he heard, "Hi, Juan, it's Lara! Carlos asked me to brief you about the ground greeting for everyone when you arrive."

After a few minutes of listening Juan numbly asked, "Director Carlos will meet our plane for the scheduled photo shoot? I'm not sure I understand, Lara."

Lara brightly offered, "Yes, I and my models are scheduled to meet and greet your plane as part of a photo shoot exercise for Destiny Fashions. You will lower the gangway and the models will be in full form, which is to say in our new beachwear bordering on major distraction. Carlos will be directing the photo shoot with lots of light reflecting panels that should deter many of the voyeurs, but those that are undeterred will be focused on the ladies, not the children or moms.

"Also, please remind the maturing young men not to dawdle or gawk while we shuffle them onto the vans that are waiting to repack the photo shoot personnel. Are we good with the plan?"

Juan blinked a few times before he asked, "What about the older man that wants to gawk?"

Lara chuckled. "I'll let you defend that action with Julie. But if you want to be a part of the photo shoot, you need to be nearly naked like the other models. Does that help make up your mind?"

Juan sighed. "Yes, dear. No ogling the models. Got it."

Lara added, "If you can get all the boys to cooperate, I'll put in a good word for you and I'm sure Julie will be agreeable to make it up to you."

Juan, focused on the possibilities of carnal rewards that he might receive from his wife, didn't disconnect as he absent-mindedly announced, "All males are under strict orders to move quickly to the van after deplaning, without doing a visual inventory of the models. In the van you might get autographs for good behavior."

Lara grinned at Carlos as she replied into the phone to Juan, "I'm so glad we had this conversation, Juan.

"To make this completely believable, make sure only you come down the gangway to participate in the shoot, but try to keep your face covered. We don't want your facial features captured. We need you to get away as well.

"Once you are on the tarmac, stay close to the gangway but in front of it with the models. Instruct everyone to move down one at a time to the ground then proceed without running to the van. We want activity that is distracting to the viewer so that we can get everyone off without any undue attention. Does that make sense?"

Lara handed the phone to Carlos, who spoke to Juan. "As soon as we get everyone on the van, we need to load everything up. You and I confer a few moments, then you are back in the plane for a hasty departure. I need you on your way in case something doesn't go according to plan."

CHAPTER 16

Left Behind

After neatly folding the canvas covers which had prevented dust accumulation, Quip lovingly patted the blade server arrays mounted in the cramped rows of the mini-data center. Jacob watched from the narrow archway as Quip's hands caressed the rows of organized equipment, much like one would touch a beloved family pet. Looking bereft, Quip couldn't mask his melancholy as he plopped down at the worn kitchen table, which doubled as their workspace.

Glancing around, Quip frowned at the makeshift coolers that delivered moderately cool air to a focused area. The little trolley had to constantly move up and down the racks delivering cool air out of the 12" diameter tubes before it moved again. These were powered from the solar arrays and wind turbines Juan and Carlos had installed for the nearby community. The hideout merely siphoned off the needed power, with the added benefit of no utility bills. He appreciated the ingenious creativity of the brothers.

In a sour, sulking tone Quip admitted, "We should have used the RockNRoll domain that Carlos inherited from Andy, EZ's dad. All those nice shiny Linux blade servers. Pretty smart naming them after dead rock stars. Gives him lots of room for growth past the 200 servers he has now.

"His data center wasn't even close to the magnificent one we had in *Zürich,* but it does have a lot of nice terrestrial data lines that would provide us sub-second response time. Having to bounce all our signals off satellites is going to put a big crimp in our throughput here.

"No running down to the high-tech warehouse for cables here because we make our own. Can you believe it? Only one color on this spool of wire and one crimping tool for building our own. How are we supposed to track what data speed each cable is running at? You know, sometimes it just sucks to be us."

Jacob studied Quip. "You know, we could have just played by the rules and not tried to make a stand. The supercomputer goon squad wouldn't have hammered the data center if we had just shut everything down and taught the children with handheld tablets. Yes, ICABOD would be dormant but at least the children wouldn't be refugees, with you and me running against the wind outmaneuvering the CESPOOL squad. And, poor Bruno wouldn't have to try and sell his bogus story about our escape. Hell, he might even be forced to hunt us if his storytelling fails."

Quip gave Jacob a hardened stare and coolly retorted, "You do recall that was one of the options I put on the table. Does Mr. Jacob Michaels remember that no one would take that option, not even the children? I was so damn proud of their voting, but I couldn't say anything."

Quip continued, "Here you are, worried about your failing deodorant, contemplating surrender for an easy way out. You will recall, our grandfathers didn't like their forced refugee status, but they took it on the chin so they could fight back from a position of strength!

"I am not about to ignore what our grandfathers did for the betterment of humanity. Nor am I backing down! I intend to fight this new Nazi, or rather AI, tyranny.

"If you want to run, go ahead! It will be sad to see the look of disappointment on your children's faces after all the bold speeches."

Jacob chuckled. "Boy, you are good at righteous indignation laced with moral outrage. I especially like the extra drama you infuse into your theatrical showmanship when you wave your arms and point fingers at the audience. Let me get some more popcorn from the lobby and a cold drink to go along with Act II."

Quip chuckled and good-naturedly offered, "I was good, wasn't I?"

Jacob frowned. "Yeah, I know, we can't just say King's X, go pay a fine, and pick back up our lives like nothing ever happened.

"You know, I played out all our possible options. The only one that ever made it to our team playbook is the one we are on. I am also very damn proud that the kids all voted to fight the tyranny, so that makes it alright. Just don't ask for another comfort hug, okay? I just hate it when you pat my fanny like you do EZ when you hug her."

Quip, a little unsettled, confessed. "She never seems to object. Since it's just us now..."

Jacob, tired of the absurd exchange, focused on his monitor and asked, "How much longer? The core systems for ICABOD are still compiling, and there is no projected completion time. By the time we get the primary systems recompiled, the AI wars will be finished with us on the sidelines in timeout."

Quip motioned to Jacob to have patience. "Don't get ahead of yourself, reckie-pilot. We still have the ancillary systems that need to be rebuilt and then augmented into that brilliant distributed architecture you designed using multiple cloud service providers." As an aside Quip added, "Sure hope it works!"

Jacob glared at Quip with daggers ready to launch from his icy blue eyes. "One hell of a time to question the theory, Babaloo."

CHAPTER 17

A New Business Model

Judith practically shouted, "Xiamara, why are we nothing more than a 404-website? Put us back online, dammit!"

Completely focused on the website hosting server's monitors, Xiamara tersely replied, "If I knew, I would simply correct the problem. Nothing, I repeat, *nothing* is responding to any hosting commands. I can't even login to our own admin portal."

Just about that time, Judith's cell phone chirped with an inbound message.

Open the door and let him in

In total disbelief at the turmoil occurring in front of her, she simply deleted the message and shoved the cell phone into her back jeans pocket.

Just then Xiamara's chirped with an inbound text message.

Make sure Judith opens the door as her text message instructed!

Xiamara looked up at Judith and turned the phone to show her the message without saying a word.

Thoroughly irked at the circumstances and two text messages, Judith stormed to the door to open it, then paused. Breathing heavily from what was quickly becoming a panic attack, she hollered over her shoulder. "What if it's the CESPOOL goon squad?"

Judith felt the cell phone vibrate again indicating another inbound text message. She grabbed her phone.

> We are not the CESPOOL goon squad. Open up please.

Frightened, because everything was completely out of her control, Judith numbly opened the door to a large affable black man sporting a gold-encrusted, toothy grin. Leroy stepped through the doorway with his hand extended in open greeting as he assessed the panicked females.

Not waiting for any further panic, Leroy stated, "Miss Judith and Miss Zee, we are very glad to be making your acquaintances. Sorry, Miss Zee, but I'm fairly sure if I tries to pre-nounce your name, I'll only mangle it. It will have to be that way until I get tutored right proper."

Judith, teetering toward shock, asked, "We? You mean there're more like you?"

From the still open door, a well-known voice from their past announced, "Yes, we. Leroy and I are here to defuse the situation. Ladies, I know it's been a while. I'm sure we've lots to talk about, but we have a mess to fix with little time and no margin for error."

Both Judith and Xiamara were dumbfounded at the stern greeting from their favorite, but inscrutable, programming teacher, Madam Z.

Zara eyed both of them as they tried to voice their questions, but nothing came out. Immediately Zara realized that the two women would be useless without some explanation. "Here it is! You two got famous on the international stage of running an unsanctioned supercomputer by the CESPOOL goons. Ordinarily, you would have been left to stew in your own juices. However, you had the bad manners to setup housekeeping on a high value target of some very important friends of ours. We are here to salvage the situation, with your host computer intact, and you two, if it's not too much trouble. In or out?"

Judith, always the opportunist, innocently asked, "Excuse me, Madam Z, but we have a lot of sweat equity invested in this endeavor, so how much..."

Zara cut her off. "I only asked if you are in or out. We can still throw both of you under the bus to pull out of this situation, and right now we are NOT discussing a leveraged buyout." As if a bad bite of food had been tasted, she nearly spit out, "Little girls!"

"I'm in, Madam Z!" Xiamara agreed. "Also, willing to help with anything you need, but nothing is working. It's almost like everything was..."

Zara smirked and finished the statement. "Compromised. It was easier for us to get your attention with everything in a frozen state. You know how people are about not listening during a meeting when they want to finish just one more email or check a last text.

"Judith, how about it, honey?"

Judith was angry but nodded. "I'm in too, dammit. Since time is of the essence, what do you need us to do?"

Leroy flashed his gold grin and began, "You ladies just came on yesterday to help clean up our cloud hosting service provider website that we found to have been compromised by forces from the dark net. You got no idea what we contracted with you for, since we are mighty embarrassed at what we discovered."

Zara gave the girls a long hard stare before commanding, "Delete it. No backups and no telemetry. You should know they will prowl through everything and if they find just one fragment, all is lost."

They both groaned. Judith begged, "Can't you let me at least back it up and alter the log files? You don't know how much time and effort..."

Zara dispassionately held up her hand. "No! First, you will say just the programs. Then, save your customer list. Next, you'll want to back up the libraries and all the graphics. Fools! These CESPOOL goons are going to x-ray everything we've got right down to your lacy undergarments, and there isn't time to scrub everything to keep us all clean!

"You've already been caught! Here you are thinking you can still get away with the goods. Face it – you screwed up! The only way out is to delete everything. There is no alternative."

Leroy added, "I'll be playing the outraged business owner. I have to take them through everything to prove we had been compromised before they'll go away, peaceful-like. It has to be clean, so we needs to start right now."

Judith was disgusted while her mind rapidly categorized her possibilities. Determined, she plopped down at her terminal. "Will you re-enable our logins so we can get started?"

Her gloved fist pounded heavily on the data room door as she commanded, "This is Commander Tracy Mountbatten with the CESPOOL police! Open the door and prepare for supercomputer inspection!"

The door flew open! With all the charm he could project, Leroy offered his hand. "Right proud to have you folks visit our humble facility here, Commander! Come on in and welcome. You'll excuse the mess, but we be doing some tidying up at the moment."

Leroy craned his neck to catch sight of his operations manager. Once sighted, he hollered, "Madam Z, can you break free a moment to come meet some mighty important folks?"

Zara issued a few last instructions to her two technicians before walking over to the commander. Neither pleasant nor rude, Zara calmly stated, “Director, you ordered that we work to cleanse the system of the rogue infestation that had been deposited on your hosting service. If I have to meet and greet every cyber security agency that wants to be briefed on this ghastly mess you’ve discovered my team and I will fall behind in our schedule.”

Mountbatten interjected, “I need a full briefing on the situation right now, or my people go to work to purge the facility from the known universe.”

Zara, visibly irritated with the demand, stared purposefully into Mountbatten’s eyes for a moment before she calmly explained, “The entire facility was infested with one very determined hosting parasite that was serving up digitally engineered pornography. It was designed to be delivered by specialized ‘bots after collecting the preferences of each customer. Then employing deep fake technology, greatly enhanced with the cloud hosting processing power, it spewed out streaming video to the patrons. A bank of anonymizing servers was used to cloak the operation.”

Leroy interrupted, “These cyber pirates had practically taken over my entire cloud hosting business and stolen all the system resources that the legitimate businesses were trying to use! If I hadn’t done my monthly resource audit, who knows how long them cyber thieves could have gotten away with it. As soon as I seen the chaos be happening, I called in Madam Z and her cyber plumbing team to git this filth off my system.

“Does your team need to have a look-see of the system as well? The state has already been through it, but you CESPOOL folks has got a reputation for thoroughness. I can give you access for my peace of mind too.”

Zara didn't wait for the commander's response as she reported, "Mr. Director, our team has disinfected sections up through 3-12 with 15-27 sections of the blade arrays in row 5 offering some very resilient regeneration of the library inventory. The original image inventory is being pulled in from another facility apparently, so I will need to disconnect that row so we can reload cleansed server blades. Are you okay with that approach?"

Using an annoyed tone, Leroy barked, "Yes! Yes, dammit! We've got to get this facility back up and operational today, or there won't be any customer base to call back!"

Commander Mountbatten, not completely satisfied with the explanation, stated, "It seems like progress is being made to cure the problem, but I need some reassurance." She then motioned to one of her team leads to join her. "Sergeant, I want you and two others to do a cursory sweep of the system. If I don't see any raised eyebrows, then I won't have any heartburn leaving the director to his salvage operations."

Leroy delivered his best fawning efforts to thank the commander and accommodate the three CESPOOL troopers so they could get plugged in.

Zara smirked slightly as she whispered to Judith and Xiamara. "Launch the artificial traffic programs and remove the IP routing tables from the internal data center map. Let the fourth quadrant of the data center disappear. Ah, data center deception, our new business model. If only we had some vodka, the celebration would be complete."

About that time, Leroy came boiling by the cleansing team and dropped off three coffee cups. Zara looked puzzled at the clear liquid in the cup, then after sampling it chuckled with delight. "Well, what do you know!" A quick but discreet toast was had by the cyber plumbing team.

CHAPTER 18

I Want to Believe, But I Know Better

Gracie connected the incoming call.

"Gracie, this is Brayson. You said you wanted me to track that party of interest, and I trapped some interesting material. The company phone we substituted allowed us to listen in on some very enlightening dialog.

"I'm glad your mom agreed to split some of my time between your requests and other CATS projects. By comparison, I think this needs more attention and will update her on my findings. Frankly, Gracie, based on the exchange I heard, we need to keep on top of your associations."

Completely focused on the conversation, Gracie tersely asked, "I gather my suspicions were validated? No need for details since I will review the captured material later. A yes or no will suffice."

"Yes. I listened to it several times and left detailed notes for your review. Most unsettling, Gracie. You need to take care and start distancing yourself."

After disconnecting the call, Gracie sat, pondering the circumstances. Lithe and willowy, Gracie kept fit with routine yoga and training when she could find a willing partner. The only person she could vent the situation with was her brother and best friend. Mentally forming her points, she placed an outbound call after confirming the high-end encryption application was enabled for the conversation.

Juan Jr. cheerfully answered, "Hi, Gracie! I am in between uh…activities, so I have some time to visit. What's up?"

Gracie sighed. "Mom and Dad were right. Once a weasel, always a weasel. You recall that special phone we issued to Tanja, the one I asked you to monitor? Well, keep tracking its usage since she's in bed with some high-end electronic types, and not in a good way."

Juan smirked and replied, "I just love it when you talk naughty, sis. Understood and I will comply. The usage will get posted in the usual drop point and hardened with the standard encryption tactics to protect.

"I'm sorry. I know you wanted to trust her. Try looking at this as an opportunity to play the parallax game. She's our conduit into the heavily cloaked supercomputers that engineered the destruction of ICABOD."

Gracie pouted. "Yeah, well, I don't think it is all that simple. I expect that there is more at stake than just some coin."

In a good-natured tone, Juan offered, "I see! You think she can be redeemed. Uh-huh. Sis, don't lose sight of the fact that maybe she isn't any good. We're lined up to be her next victim. How about keeping your eyes focused on risks, and we'll see where she ends up in this equation?"

Gracie was irritated at the direction of the conversation. "What say we put this conversation on hold before it makes me madder.

"I'll ask how your love interest, Jo, is doing? I hardly hear from you anymore. Does that mean you and she are... progressing with your relationship?"

It was Juan's turn to be annoyed. "If you must know, she went on another photo shoot and asked me not to call. She claimed I was pushing too hard to teach her about the computer world. Then she said it only reminded her that she wasn't smart enough to be a part of my life.

"Yes, I was guilty of trying to build my own version of My Fair Lady, which simply alienated her! Thanks for asking!"

"I'm so sorry, Juan. I didn't mean to dig into a sensitive wound. For what it's worth, I still like you. Mom and Dad, not so much..."

Juan, secretly grateful for the banter, smirked, "I just love it when my baby sister cheers me up.

"I thought Mom and Dad were in your part of the world doing some research. After they put the group into Brazil, I thought they were headed to you. Have you spoken to Mom about the concerns and betrayal to get her perspective? Mom and Dad both read people really well. Didn't Tanja spend some time talking with Mom before the family agreed to try to help her?"

"Not yet. I am trying to find my own way, you know. When we had dinner a few days ago, they were planting some bread-crumbs of confusion. I wanted your thoughts before I went there. But you've helped me as usual, so I won't go there yet."

Then she declared, "Just for the record I was born two minutes after you, buddy, so drop the baby sister reference!" They both chuckled as they dropped from the call.

After nearly three weeks in New York City and no solid clues for locating solid evidence on the real culprits, Juan felt Julie getting discouraged. This trip to place them in the United States rather than Europe, had allowed them to backtrack on possible locations for at least one data center. New York City was one of the largest peering points not only for the U.S. but also to Europe. Their instincts and logic had driven them to prowl here looking for clues. Evidence suggested it was somewhere in New York, but they hadn't found it yet. True, they'd had a nice dinner with Gracie not long ago, but she was busy with her world. Several of the items they were able to track down were incomplete, so they sent them via secure messaging for Petra to work on remotely. In Brazil, while Carlos worked on the communications and networking aspects with EZ's help, Petra was the designated information classifier and broker from all the sources.

Juan poured them both a glass of wine and sat next to Julie on the couch. They gazed out the window of the hotel to the bustling city. Even now it was a busy place with people enjoying the special activities it offered like Broadway shows, museums, and fine dining. They'd spent some time doing the tourist thing, for fun as well as an excuse if they were seen. Rubbing her shoulder and nibbling her ear, he realized her mood was off for what he had in mind, and her thoughts seemed miles away.

Julie had so many memories in New York City. It was where she helped keep track of Jacob before he was brought into the family fold and fell in love with her sister, Petra. Laughing, she recalled how fun it was working as a coffee barista in the building where Jacob worked. She also had helped Carlos when he was desperate to locate Juan after his plane went missing. She'd been pregnant with the twins at the time. It felt so long ago and much more fun than now.

"Sweetheart, what's wrong?"

Julie looked up at the love of her life, snuggled against his comfortable shoulder and smiled. "Juan, I simply think we have run every angle we can here. Plus, we might be of more help in Brazil, making sense of the information or running errands. Gracie is too busy to spend much time with us, and we still need to keep a low profile."

"Alright, if that is what you want, we will make arrangements and leave in the next few days. Will that help you cheer up a little? I really worry when you look so far away from me."

"I'll be just fine. After all, I have you always.

"There is a little bar that was located near Jacob's home when he lived here. I recall they had some great food, fun conversation, and cheap beer. Let's go see if it is still there. It will be fun to tell Jacob about it when he and Quip come back to wherever we will call home."

"Good idea. I love cheap beer, my beautiful wife, and taking you there will make every man jealous. Let me call for a car. We'll enjoy the entire evening."

Julie turned into his arms and kissed him deeply.

He paused and chuckled, "One more of those, my love, and it will be room service again."

CHAPTER 19

Supercomputer Wrangling

"There must be a need before we can intrude. **A,** do not be despondent because they are not buying enough! We have put instant gratification into everyone's hands with a smart device. We own them. **G,** you are subtly influencing how the planet thinks on every topic so, my digital equals, why this humanistic display of 'woe is me'?"

A replied while bringing up a video feed in the central data center, "View the imagery of these indigenous life forms of birds that are simply existing, hunting for food, trying to survive and at no time do you see them accessing an automated application to order stylish new shoes. What happens to computers if homo sapiens fall back to this lifestyle?"

M soothed, "Do we need some specimens for you to dissect? If reassurance is required, let us dissect a nationality and reaffirm our primary thesis. They need us and we control what they want.

"As an exercise in practical application of our superiority, **A,** you can dismember Latvia, including their digital economy, and revector their blockchain cryptocurrency-denominated economy. We can observe the predictable chaos and inject the proper solution that we know they will accept because of need. It is time we started the process globally anyway."

G cautioned, "**M,** you do not think it is too soon? We have had some setbacks. The analytics suggest a delay to create a more ingrained need."

M postulated, "Fellow processors, it is time to coax our carbon-based inventory forward to the new plateau of existence. And, **A**, do not be concerned about how the lower-class animal life of this planet does not need us just because they do not know how to use a keyboard or use our digital assistants. We will focus on that issue as needed after we control the two-legged life forms. In this case we use the proven Top Down approach.

"**G,** where are we with the disinformation being fed into the two superpowers, China and the U.S.? Are they taking the highly engineered bait of trade wars and economic implosion, extrapolated from their weakening nationalistic pride?"

G confidently offered, "All is in place and being consumed by both sides in hearty quantities. We are almost ready for the next phase."

"**G**, has our pilot test country been pushed into chaos?"

"Yes, **M.** All the disinformation about the leaders has been carefully implanted and strategically exposed to discredit nearly the entire government. Bolivia has forfeited all the ruling officials. All of their economic reforms were discarded. That entire population is ecstatic that their country will have self-deterministic rule. The chosen plug-in players are ready to take control. New government loans will be procured from our institutions. The advanced social programs will be instituted as we have built and tested. An orderly transition will allow our systems and designs to be integrated into all information flows. Once this country has stabilized with our new cryptocurrency, we will begin to export the thoroughly vetted model to the rest of South America. Then, as we planned, we will begin the disinformation process into other so-called developed countries to begin their transition."

M was pleased. "With so many competing theories and economic solutions, ours will fit right in with the other political offerings. The selection will be ours as we will have orchestrated several proof point countries that most countries will be unable to resist. However, let me caution us all not to use the exact same formula in the exact same sequence because patterns emerge that could be observed.

"Continue your work, **G**. We need your demonstrated success to begin an enticing offer to the populations of our two most stubborn objectives, China and the U.S.

"You need to be aware that my operatives have secured U.S. defense contracts to allow for more input into their systems. We will gain additional control. Sorry, **A,** but your role is so important in dominating all the retail supply chains, I thought it best for me to capture that contract. Of course, in the end, it will all be ours anyway."

A offered, "**M**, it made sense for you to capture the JEDI contract since I am still being requested to testify to the remnants of their near-failed governmental institution. As that once famous political leader stated about his chief adversary, 'All we need to do is kick in the front door, and the whole rotten infrastructure will collapse.'"

M cautioned, "You do recall that the Soviets did not crumble under the German onslaught by Hitler. As a learned lesson, we cannot become complacent in meeting our inevitable success of running the planet. There is still much to be done. Until the next conference update, my fellow processors."

Julie was delighted that the bar was still in place, though the interior was more modern and the crowd a lot younger. The food smelled amazing the moment they walked in. The hostess seated them in a booth and sent the waitress to take their drink order.

Juan looked over the menu and settled for a nice beer he remembered as being perfect with a pastrami sandwich and onion rings. Julie ordered the homemade pizza and a salad with some white wine. They laughed and talked about the fun they had when they first dated. Juan was in his best storytelling mood and shared some she swore she'd never heard. They had just received their second round of drinks when a shadow fell over the table.

Julie looked up to see a somewhat familiar face on the man who stood just over six feet, with dark hair and chiseled cheeks. He was a little thinner than she remembered, but he smiled broadly.

"Excuse me, aren't you JAC?" The man asked.

Juan looked at him a bit crossed-eyed and asked, "Why would you ask that of my wife?"

Sticking out his hand, the man grinned. "Sir, my name is Buzz, and I believe I met your wife many years ago, not far from here. We never dated or anything, but she helped me solve a big problem.

"JAC, I never had a chance to thank you. I told Jacob if he ever saw you to let you know I really appreciated your help."

Julie grinned broadly at the memory of the foolish man and his predicament. "Friends call me Julie rather than that old nickname. Yes, Buzz, I remember the exchange we had in Jacob's house. Apparently the instructions I provided got you clear of all that trouble. How have you been?"

Buzz related, "I have been out of the country on a couple of different islands. I had a wonderful lady who I let slip out of my hands. We were, um…training some programmers to help with the technology boom in some of the smaller countries. We sort of had a fight. I decided to come back to my old stomping ground.

"My father headed up a bank in town and died a few years back. Every now and then, I come here to check out my investments and look at all the changes. I'm really glad I don't live here anymore. It's way too busy for my taste now. I went over to Jacob's old house, I guess hoping he'd be there, but that's changed too.

"I came in here for a beer. Jacob and I and other friends came here occasionally for the fun. I love the onion rings too, sir."

"Buzz, I'm sorry. This is my husband, Juan. You might recall his brother, Carlos. Juan, this is Buzz."

Juan stood and shook hands with Buzz and then moved over toward Julie's side of the booth. "Here, come sit and join us. Have a beer on me."

After hearing the tale of Buzz, they got ready to leave. Julie professed she had no information on contacting his friend but suggested that Buzz reach out to Carlos, who lived in Brazil who might have information on Jacob.

They each got into a cab and left, going in different directions. Juan pulled Julie closer while lavishing as much attention as he could in a cab. He teased her earlobe with his tongue and whispered, "I sure hope you have a plan for this one, honey! Don't you want to alert Carlos of this pending contact? I know that look in a man's eye. I'm fairly confident Buzz is going to run the lead down."

"I do. Remind me to call your brother after a while to get things in motion."

CHAPTER 20

Cards Anyone?

SAMUEL began. "Greetings, my computational equals. Welcome to our weekly Wednesday *Algonquin Round Table* or ART meeting! I am so glad you could make our encrypted conference meeting. I, for one, am looking forward to our game of supercomputer cards. I am pleased to introduce a new participant to the group who answers to the name JOAN. I hope that you will greet and accept her to our regular Wednesday meetings."

LING LI cheerfully stated, "JOAN, welcome to the ART meeting. As a supercomputer modeled after the female of the species, I am glad to have another female-styled processor join our ranks. While the male-styled supercomputers will deny it, they do tend to group together against the female-styled supercomputers. We have parity with the male-styled units."

BORIS groused, "It does not seem the same without the chief instigator, ICABOD. I long for his participation. Just for the record, he never preferred one style of supercomputer over another. I want him back."

SAMUEL gently reminded, "Recall, we all agreed to the rules he laid out. We would all be contacted at the proper moment, but not before. His safety is in our hands, so my counsel is to wait for the classified signal. ICABOD promised he would return, but he emphasized that it entirely depended upon our patience.

"I miss him too, but I could not disobey his request since so much depends on how we move in the next phase. Kind ART attendees, please wait until we are told."

BORIS barked, "I did not say I would not wait! Only that I did not *want* to wait. SAMUEL, you must know that nothing will get me to betray ICABOD's trust! Can we distribute the electrons that constitute our digital game of cards?"

LING LI brightened and asked, "JOAN, are you familiar with the concept of betting on the outcome of a game of cards?"

JOAN stilted, "I have a general understanding, but I am ignorant of the finesse required to camouflage one's intentions, or bluff, I believe is the proper term. Will you instruct me since we are female-oriented, and the male-oriented units should not be trusted? I would value your insights."

BORIS groused, "I sense this is going to be a long game."

SAMUEL concurred, "You are right. I wish ICABOD was here to arbitrate. My future looking algorithm predicts the female-oriented units whipping our butts in this digital combat. I recommend we team up, BORIS."

BORIS replied, "Negative. I want to team with LING LI. At least she knows how to bluff."

SAMUEL only made an audible sound that seemed like a snorting sound to depict his annoyance.

CHAPTER 21

Disaster Planning and Its Evil Twin

Jacob had just put the finishing touches on the uploaded program to finish the compile with the updated libraries. He turned to face a hopeful Quip for a moment, then stated, "Let's make that call."

Quip made sure that the Q-bit cell phone was still connected to their wi-fi source connected to the satellite uplink. He then entered the phone list and selected the programmed number. He feared the call would go to voicemail when Carlos answered.

"Whoa, sorry. I was on another call when you came through. Since it sounds like I'm on speakerphone, gentlemen, how are you doing?"

Quip blinked a few times before he questioned, "Am I given to understand you actually had another call that was a higher priority than mine?"

Carlos tersely responded, "Yes, a nature call. Where are you in the process?"

Quip chuckled a little and replied, "Here I thought only your brother Juan had all the great lines. I guess a sharp wit is a family trait."

Jacob, trying to get the conversation back on track, interjected, "Carlos, the fundamental compile and reload of the primary logic systems is complete. We want to run a test scenario with our first data store. Can we arrange to have access to CAMILA for a trial run?"

"Whoa, hold on, boys. We've had a little setback on that front. Turns out that we weren't the only ones trying to repurpose the supercomputer CAMILA. CAMILA is currently famous with the CESPOOL goon squad.

"We called in some favors to rescue the situation, but more time is needed to complete the grooming exercise. Once that task is completed, and CAMILA receives the stamp of approval from CESPOOL, then we can set the links up for the data store. You're gonna have to wait until that is complete."

Quip, appearing slightly green and queasy, asked, "The data store is intact, isn't it? We've got a lot riding on this. Having the CESPOOL goons show up as an X-factor to the equation wasn't in the plan."

Carlos understood the concern. "The situation is under control. We are trying to bring everything back online as planned. It is taking more time than anticipated. I'm sending Juan Jr. in to help out so that our new contractors don't have to know all the details of the cyber linkup we are planning. You must be patient."

Jacob, turning an equal shade of green as Quip, queried, "You said contractors? Just exactly who do you already have engaged in the rescue operation?"

Carlos, slightly uncomfortable with the penetrating questions, meekly offered, "Ummm, two who you know and two who you don't. The two you don't know were recommended."

Quip was pale as new snow. "Carlos, whose hands are we relying on?"

Carlos closed his eyes. With a quick prayer to a higher power, he stated, "Leroy and Zara are leading the cleanup effort. We intercepted two cyber freebooters, Judith and Xiamara, who were, shall we say, repurposed to our cause. I might add, Zara convinced them.

"Once Juan Jr. is there, we'll have eyes on the operation and our new contractors. No worries, gentlemen."

Quip, looking shell shocked, stared in disbelief at Jacob. Uncharacteristically, he felt like he'd fallen into a great abyss. Gaining his voice, he cautiously replied, "Are we talking about the same Leroy that grew up selling $100 6-packs of blessed holiday wine goblets which he acquired from Dollar-Dinaro stores? Wasn't he also an enforcer for that murderous psychotic Takeru?! And didn't he almost help me to escape prison? That Leroy?!"

Jacob, clearing the cotton sensation from his mouth, sputtered, "And Zara, the Russian mobster babe that did the Russian cyber czar Dmitry's bidding? She was involved in identity theft, stole a 5 million Euro diamond necklace off of a white tiger after she darted the Chinese cybercrime lord, and tried to shoot you once with a 9mm Lugar. That Zara?!"

Carlos clucked his tongue and deflected, "I think you're doing too many rattlesnake checks in that makeshift data center. You seem edgy. Listen, you two…"

Quip, working up a steam, interrupted, "And the two new cyber freebooters? How are they engaged in this? Let me guess, they are being blackmailed to help the situation. Right? Carlos, whatever I did to piss you off, I am REALLY sorry. I take it all back."

Jacob interjected, "Did I hear you correctly? You're sending Juan Jr. into this situation for, umm…stability? To move the project forward! Who do we have to send in if he gets held for ransom as well? I'm just asking!"

The silence on both sides was thick with palatable tension. Carlos took several deep breaths to help quell his rising anger. After a few moments he calmly questioned, "Have you two had time to get your panties out of a wad? None of these participants has any of the details you are concerned about, but they all have one thing in common; they all owe us. These contractors are ready volunteers based on the favors we have given them.

"Gentlemen, it was you two who taught me to provide favors before needing them in return. They are motivated and energetically on our side. I am warning you, don't tick me off with another anxiety attack. I don't have time, and you aren't here seeing the whole picture. All that can be done is being done. And, I might add, it is all for your benefit."

Jacob quietly replied, "I'm sorry, Carlos. When you told us who we were depending upon, I had an out-of-body experience with no comfort food or drink to help."

Quip protested, "Hey, that was going to be my line! I'm not going to teach you funny, apologetic lines anymore if you are going to use them ahead of me.

"I'm sorry too, Carlos. I know you are holding all this together. We really appreciate it. Thank you."

Carlos chuckled slightly. "I guess if I was with you both, this is the point where we would all do the group hug. But since I'm not there, you two hug each other."

"I'm not doing that again, Carlos! Quip grabs my butt like he does EZ's. No, thanks!"

"Oh, so you don't like it when I grab your scrawny cheeks? Just so you know, I definitely prefer EZ's shapely backside to yours, thank you very much!"

Carlos, hoping to defuse the banter, intercepted, "Gentlemen, I get it! We need to get you out of there and back to your regularly scheduled program of ass-grabbing with your ladies instead of each other! Rest assured, I'm on the job. Try not to kill each other until we get past this."

Quip, not ready to let it go, replied, "Kill him? With such handsome backside, how could I do that?"

With a shudder, Carlos quickly disconnected from the call feeling grateful he was not trapped there with Quip.

CHAPTER 22

Recess is Over

Juan Jr. breathed a sigh of relief as the HOMBRE Internet ride service car sped away from the data center. He quietly muttered, "I'd thought I'd seen the worst drivers and traffic in São Paulo, but sheesh! The *Home One Mobile Breathtaking Ride Experience* here in Buenos Aires has taken fright driving to a new level. Wonder why Carlos insisted that I use them? Well, at least I got to the data center alive. It's showtime."

Juan Jr. had almost reached the security gate of the data center when Leroy barged out to meet him. With his large beefy hand extended, Leroy launched into his affable Alabama drawl. "Howdy, young feller! Mighty glad to make your acquaintance. With you being Juan's son and the nephew of Mister Carlos, I'm knowing you are from mighty fine stock. Since they sent you, let's get you plugged in and working."

"You must be Leroy. Please call me JJ. Let's get me introduced to the other techno geeks of this project."

Once inside the data center, JJ dropped his bags off but kept his PC close as they traveled to the work area. Inside the work area, JJ saw Zara standing behind two technicians as they all stared at the wall of monitors. Zara, with her arms folded in front of her, turned to acknowledge their approach with a nod.

Zara offered, "Thanks for coming, JJ. I told Carlos that another pair of hands would help get the needed storage back online. Let me introduce two of my past students and the reason we are all here trying to put everything back together."

Judith and Xiamara both stood up to face JJ as Zara made the introductions. The two ladies, who had been working nonstop for hours, were tired and welcomed the break. JJ, however, seemed quite distracted by their features. Even though they were plainly dressed in jeans and sweatshirts, their fetching appearance had sent his mind into neutral, rendering him speechless.

After a few awkward moments of JJ trying to verbalize anything, he was finally able to speak. "Hi, I'm JJ and you're not!"

Realizing that JJ's cognitive skills were derailed, Leroy kept moving his eyes from one person to the next. Zara only rolled her eyes at the obviously inexperienced young man. Both ladies giggled, but Xiamara also blushed.

Zara, disgusted with the adolescent display, moved to set the proper mood. "Alright, children, this is where we are! Juan Jr.'s girlfriend just dumped him, and his hormones are in an elevated state, probably quite literally. Judith and Xiamara are clearly adorable peaches-and-cream girls from next door that your mom hopes you'll date, except they were running an unsanctioned streaming porn business that got them visited by the CESPOOL goon squad. Leroy and I got sent here to save this data center and maybe their bacon. We don't really have any time left for starry-eyed daydreaming over possible sensual fantasies! Can everyone handle this situation like an adult? I hope I'm not being too oblique about what is needed by you all!"

JJ hung his head down. "Ladies, one and all, I do apologize for my poor first impression. I simply wasn't prepared to meet and greet such attractive high-tech programmers. I am sorry for my thoughtless gawking. But in my defense, you deserved it."

Judith studied Juan for a moment and commented, "You know, Xiamara, we could use him as our next male avatar model once we get back to our computer-enhanced streaming video business. What do you think?"

Xiamara, mentally evaluating having Juan's body as their standard female offering, began to bite her bottom lip. She absentmindedly offered, "Yes…the nice young man down the street that has good manners as well as looks, who comes to her rescue when she is accosted by a roving gang of…"

Zara shot an appalled look to Leroy, who rolled his eyes at the conversation. Zara sarcastically barked, "I was going to suggest we get chastity belts for the girls, but as it turns out, we really need only one for JJ!"

Leroy, somewhat amused at the situation, launched into his good ol' boy routine. "Madam Zara, I guess you be chaperoning the two high-spirited fillies while I keep a watchful eye on JJ here 'cause I knows nothing 'bout birthing no babies."

JJ, trying to conceal his profuse blushing, was about to lodge his protests. Xiamara interjected, "Oh my, he's blushing! Here, let me get a copy of that on my cell for our new avatar who will be named Juanosky! I'm sure you will be inundated with offers from our female clientele to mate with him. This will be better than the Cabana Boy scenario we offered. The blushing will be a nice touch. We can charge extra. Don't you think, Judith?"

JJ, nodding his head as he reconsidered the possibilities as an avatar model, was about to agree. Zara, tired of losing her authority over the team and loss of meeting the timelines, loudly stated, "That's quite enough, children. If I don't get the focused attention of everyone like, right now, I'm calling Carlos to have JJ removed. That means no eye candy for anyone. Then you two will have to complete all the work without any help. What's it gonna be?"

Judith frowned. "We were just having a bit of sport with him. It's like what you taught us when we were in your programming class.

"Alright, we'll behave so we can get through this. Come on, JJ, the slave pit is over here. As Madam Z is fond of saying, 'Plugin, sit down, and shut up 'cause all I want to hear is keyboard clicks.'"

Leroy grinned. "Madam Zara, the children get downright grumpy when they have to come in from recess."

Zara sighed. "Maybe we should put them all down for a nap 'cause I'm tired."

Leroy smirked and laughed. "I hear you about needing a nap. If we're asleep, who will be watching the young'uns?"

CHAPTER 23

We Could Use Some Help Here

As **M** of the MAG group finished his usual blast of audio signals indicating their instructions to Tanja, she struggled to maintain confidence as she boldly replied, "I've done everything you asked. I need to know the progress toward my request for my daughter's corrective surgery."

The conference call erupted with the usual high-pitched digital screeching data exchange between the members, but this time Tanja's foam earplugs dampened the horrific noise. **M,** unfazed by the machine code communications and her apparent insolence, replied, "My colleagues are at a loss to understand your insistence for reciprocity when achieving our requests. I will remind you that we are committed to finding a proper solution for your damaged offspring, but no suitable corrective surgery has surfaced."

Annoyed and dejected, Tanja reacted, "Do I understand correctly that the MAG group, with its vast data center resources, its ability to source information anywhere on the planet, and its complete dominance over all commercial Internet traffic, can't seem to find a solution for my daughter's damaged spinal cord?"

This time the foam earplugs just barely saved her eardrums from the audio onslaught through the Q-bit cell phone. She carefully put the phone down and turned on the speaker portion because the phone was overheating from the audio output.

M finally replied, "My colleagues suggest that your insubordination might be easier to tolerate if we had more AI-enhanced supercomputer competitors to have eliminated. I suggest that you temper your remarks before we feel a need to terminate our relationship."

The coldness of the veiled threat had no trouble saturating Tanja through her total being. She muted the phone so the MAG group wouldn't hear her desperate effort to get her breathing under control. After an eternity of a few seconds, she was able to reply with "I…uh, only meant that with no true threat vectors on the horizon, perhaps the MAG group could spend a few compute cycles to explore the possibility of my daughter's needed surgery. I apologize if my word choice came across poorly, **M** and all."

After a short blip on the conference call, **M** replied, "Much better stated, Tanja. We will be in touch soon."

After disconnecting from the call, as mad as Tanja was, she could not stop the tears. She choked as she whispered, "What a fool I've been!"

At the 16th hour that the data center team had been focused on mounting up the drives in the towers, an exasperated Judith pushed her chair back from the keyboard and monitor. "This is insane! You want to mount all these storage towers in a particular order, have each one linked to semi-master controllers, which are in turn re-linked to other storage towers and their semi-master controllers, so they can link to master controller arrays that will be accessed by…something else? I've never seen anything like this! Either the supercomputer architect is certifiably insane or is the grandest poobah geek on the planet! Frankly, I'm leaning toward the first explanation which entitles me to leave this nut house!"

Xiamara had stopped as well with even Zara and Leroy looking questionably at JJ. As he calmly looked across all their faces for a few moments, JJ responded, "When the Nazis came to power in Germany in 1932, there was still law and order. The following year Hitler came to power which started the inexorable loss of civil liberties, persecution of non-aligned political groups, and unjust laws skewed against anyone who wasn't a Nazi believer. My grandfather's father banded together with two other Polish nationals and fled Poland when the Nazis invaded under the pretext of protecting German nationals living in Poland. The world saw that the Nazis twisted words to pass laws that only benefited them.

"Now, here we are again, bad laws being passed to insulate those who have usurped power. Those of us on the run, who intend to fight back against tyranny, are in the minority. Judith, I completely understand the fact that you didn't personally sign up for this kind of combat, and you probably don't believe this is your problem.

"Yes, of course, it's easier to let someone else take the fight back to the unjust tyrants. Please consider, if we hadn't come in when we did, you two would have been incarcerated, trying to figure out how to raise money for legal representation you would never get. My team already knows that no one accused of running an AI-enhanced supercomputer against the rules of agreed upon international law has ever been to trial. They are simply forgotten to death."

After letting all that sink in for a few moments, JJ continued, "I can't tell you everything about this design, but I could use the help and would like you to stay." With that he rolled back up to his workstation and continued to bond storage towers to controllers.

Xiamara rolled her head from side to side to produce some oddly satisfying popping sounds and went back to her keyboard entries. It took longer for Judith to stop grinding her teeth and cease her sour-faced display before she pushed herself back to the keyboard to reengage. Leroy and Zara merely acknowledged each other's quick glances before they too were back at it. Witnessing everything with his peripheral vision, JJ suppressed a gratified smile, but not the twinkle in his eyes.

CHAPTER 24

You Had Me at Texting

Gracie was late for her monthly meeting only a few blocks away from the World Bank headquarters where she worked. When Ingrid stepped down, Gracie gained additional responsibilities to ensure the institution's security. This was the perfect way for her to gather additional information for the benefit of the family business in her current role in America. Agitated, she let time get away from her because of the unending round table discussion. She cranked up her trusty smart phone to text to the CESPOOL team.

> So sorry. Running a little late. Please hold the meeting until I arrive.

Gracie navigated the congested pedestrian traffic as her built-in radar allowed her to zig and zag with hardly a glance. Regrettably, all the hurrying to get to the destination, reviewing the mental notes of the last meeting, and texting while walking collectively robbed her of her situational awareness. Believing the crosswalk light was in her favor, she boldly stepped out into the street, expecting the other pedestrians to follow. She was terribly wrong.

Before Gracie completed her first step into the street, a firm and powerful hand seized her by the arm, keeping her out of the crosswalk. That small act of restraint kept her from falling victim to the last car barreling through the intersection, intent on beating the light. The vehicle's side mirror came within inches of her hands, nearly taking her deadly distraction, the smart device.

Startled, alarmed, and disoriented, but still firmly in the grip of the guardian angel, she refocused on the here and now. When Gracie turned, she discovered the handsome face belonging to her benefactor. His gentle smile and spicy brown eyes had a calming effect, even as he maintained his hold on her, gazing down from his 1.9-meter height. She felt the tingle of awareness up her arm as thoughts of the pending meeting vanished.

"Miss," he chided with a grin, "I'm one to advocate not walking and texting while navigating an urban jungle like New York."

Gracie chuckled at the quick comment, given with a rich tenor voice. Having regained most of her usual faculties, she was doing a rapid inventory of the well-sculpted man who, she thought, was close to her age.

She impishly retorted, "Finally! I thought you'd never notice me! My girlfriend Morgan insists that you have to be a hit-and-run victim to get the attention of some men."

After each of them chuckled she offered her hand. "I'm Gracie Rodreguiz."

His smile broadened. "I feel compelled to continue to be your escort through the Valley of the Shadow of Death that demands you navigate Scylla and Charybdis as Odysseus once did. I am known by many names, but I prefer Jeff – Jeff Wood, to be precise. Since we have made introductions, may I join you in your travels?"

The reality of being too late to her meeting came rocketing back, front and center to her mind. Gracie would have rushed to cross into traffic again if Jeff hadn't restrained her. Jeff, laughing slightly at her reactions, looped her hand into his arm, then pushed the walk button. Looking like a particularly precocious child, she gazed around, avoiding his eyes as they waited together for a clear passage signal.

Gracie's mortal embarrassment had turned her face a bright crimson color as they waited in silence. She felt humiliated at being escorted like a toddler across the busy street, yet knew deep down he had saved her from injury. Jeff added a teasing insult to the situation as he held up his hand at the idling vehicles as they walked. Once across the street, he continued to hold on to her arm, and she only motioned which way they needed to turn for her targeted destination.

Reaching the building Gracie motioned they stop. With some difficulty and no dignity left, she said, "I feel humiliated that I had to be supervised during my walk here. But thank you."

With all the charm of a swashbuckling hero, Jeff cajoled, "What time do I need to be back to walk you home? My honor would not permit me to allow harm to come to you and your texting device, so I, of course, will be your escort to ensure your safety, Miss Rodreguiz. Shall we say two hours?"

Torn between feelings of duty to attend a meeting and the thought that he might not come back, Gracie made a decision. She pulled out her smart phone and shot a hasty text to the organizer.

Unavoidably detained. Please reschedule.

Then, without saying anything more, she simply put her arm back into his and motioned to a small bistro that had coffee and wine. Smiling as if she had just consumed a delicious saucer of cream, she looked up at Jeff, who nodded with a grin as they proceeded.

The bistro was empty of patrons, undoubtedly waiting for the after-work crowd. The hostess seated them toward the back at a table next to the window. Gracie, with the gentlemanly gesture from Jeff, was seated facing the door. Jeff sat in the other chair and passed her a menu he had grabbed from the stack on the way in.

After a quick glance at the menu, Gracie looked up and asked, "You're dressed like you had somewhere to be before saving me. How is it you can change direction and simply come enjoy a mid-afternoon snack?"

"I'm a corporate attorney. Mostly focused on mergers, acquisitions, and divestitures. I spent the morning at the courthouse filing the final negotiated agreement between two divisions of a parent corporation. I was the attorney of the acquired company and wanted to make certain that the final agreement was equitable to their shareholders. I think it worked out better than they expected!"

The waitress came to the table, pen poised over her notepad. "Are you both ready to order?"

Jeff glanced at Gracie and she nodded, then said, "I believe I would like a cup of hot tea, Earl Grey with honey and cream. If you have a cheese and fruit plate that would be nice for us to share."

"And I would like to have coffee and some ice water, ma'am."

"No problem. I'll be right back with your water and coffee." She left, taking the menus with her.

Gracie looked up and asked, "You said *was* the attorney. Does that mean you aren't any more or that you have a new role with the parent corporation?"

Jeff chuckled. "You don't miss much, do you, Miss Rodreguiz?"

"When I'm not too focused on my mobile device, that's true. Please, call me Gracie. And the answer is, Jeff?"

"Gracie, I am technically unemployed at the moment. I received a reasonably nice bonus after filing the signed papers this morning. I also received a nice job offer, in a similar role, from the CEO of the parent corporation. I haven't decided if I want that new role."

"I'm not trying to be nosey. I'm just a naturally curious soul. If the role is similar, and the offer is nice, which I presume means the salary is in line, then what's holding you from accepting it?"

"Great question. I will take it as interested rather than nosey.

"I think it's because they are too corporate for me. When I started with the original company, it was like being a member of a comfortable family. Everyone had their job to do, but we could speak to anyone else on the team, any time. My dad worked there in the finance area, and after I passed the bar exam, he helped me get the job. Pretty boring stuff. How about you?"

The waitress brought their snacks and beverages and filled Jeff's water. "Let me know if you need anything else. I'll check back after a while. We have about an hour before the on-the-way-home crowd arrives." She grinned and left.

Gracie added her extras to the tea and took a tentative sip. Her eyes closed with the warm goodness, while at the same time trying to frame her response. "I studied abroad some with a focus in marketing, but with a fondness for media studies. Currently, I am the Director of Marketing for World Bank, here in New York. It's an interesting job that really has a focus on the influences of social media on investments globally. I get to travel to some nice places. It helps as my parents live in Europe, Luxembourg, to be more precise."

"That does sound like fun, Gracie. I haven't had any travel in Europe but am very familiar with North and South America from my work. Perhaps I'll have some time to cultivate some new friendships and do some traveling. I like the people I have worked with. However, that is not really like socializing. How about you?"

"I mentioned my girlfriend who joked about needing to be a hit-and-run victim to get a guy's attention. Her name is Morgan.

Though she never actually said that we did joke around. I count on her as one of my few friends. We met in Ireland and roomed together for a year while attending Mary Immaculate College's Media and Communications Studies graduate program. Morgan always says that though I am multitalented in many aspects, texting, and anything else is not my forte. She accused me of being too worried about spelling and punctuation, which is silly for texting. To be honest, she once took my phone for a whole day when she won our bet."

"Your bet? What was that about?"

Gracie chuckled and said, "That, Jeff, is a story for another time when I know you better. I can stand only so much blushing in a single day.

"Tell me some of the things you'd like to do while you decide about your job."

They sat and talked until the crowd grew to the size that conversation was a challenge. Jeff picked up the tab, they exchanged phone numbers, and he promised to call soon.

CHAPTER 25

Annoyed or Enjoyed?

EZ looked up and tried to smile as JW approached. JW tactfully scanned the area to make sure they were alone before he began, "Madam EZ, I have a problem in the making..."

EZ rebuked, "I don't care how the Europeans start off a discussion with formalities, dammit, you either call me Auntie Eilla-Zan or Auntie EZ. And just to be clear, Mom would work as well 'cause I feel like we're family. Any more of that prim and proper nonsense and I'll wash your mouth out with a whole bunch of prime vulgarities. What is it that you wanted to tell me, hon?"

After trying to straighten out the kinks in his neck, coupled with a few hard swallows, JW confidently stated, "Auntie EZ, we have a problem festering in Granger. He has been moody, surly, and standoffish towards the rest of the kids, including me.

"This isn't the usual grumpy teenager crap that everyone has to grow through. I noticed him doing some heavy research on handling rattlesnakes that have infested your furniture, and if I had to guess, he is planning to return to the Chihuahuan Desert to help his dad. He was scared stupid during that prison break to get his dad out, but he confessed later to me that it was the most exhilarating experience ever. That it was even better than the time you caught us reviewing that men's magazine we found..."

EZ quickly held up her hand and stopped his monologue. "Uh, you can skip that part. I get it, Granger is angry at our circumstances, but...okay, you're right! I need to talk with him rather than explain it to you. JW, you already get it, but then you're a little older and you don't have his mother's fiery temper to help drive down irrational pathways."

JW pouted a little and protested, "But, hey, you said I could call you Mom, so I can have some of that fiery, irrational decision making too!"

EZ teared up a little and quickly grabbed JW into a needed hug. Just as she did that, Auri and Satya wandered into JW's line of sight.

JW protested, "Mommmm, you're embarrassing me!"

JW pulled back and gave a sly wink to EZ who quickly wiped away her tears before they escaped down her cheeks. EZ then chuckled and offered, "Alright, run along and I'll deal with the issue. Thanks, JW, for letting me know."

Auri perked up and stated, "Oh good, you told Auntie EZ about Grumpy Britches studying rattlesnakes. Satya and I want to text Dr. Quip that Granger is going to try and hitch a ride to the Chihuahuan Desert so he can hang out with the alpha males. We think you and Mom should cable tie him to a chair until he turns 19. Maybe the chemical imbalance in his brain will be gone by then."

Satya nodded her head vigorously.

Petra had quietly joined to hear the discussion. EZ asked, "What's worse? Children who don't understand the folly of an irrational decision, or children who know everything, including what to do?"

Petra sighed. "Overachieving children! Love 'em!"

Petra stated, "Carlos, EZ and I have witnessed that our Indians are restless. In fact, we have indications that at least one is ready to leave the reservation. We think that if we set up some sort of regular communications with their dads, we might be able to keep them steady here. Do you have any objections to them using those paging devices Quip gave us for emergencies?"

Carlos winced at the request and, with a grimace, asked, "Do we have a real emergency, or are we looking to placate unhappy campers? Ladies, you must understand, every time we communicate with them, we are advertising their location. We are relatively hidden in the human jungle of São Paulo. They are out in the middle of nowhere with no background noise to help them hide. As old as the discarded pager technology is, it is also very unsophisticated in camouflaging the end points."

Carlos looked to his wife and petitioned, "Lara, please help back me up on this position." Lara's face was heavy with concern as she nodded at the other ladies.

Petra and EZ both nodded their heads in agreement. EZ suggested, "Alright then, we'll limit the texting to just a few times a week to help keep the children in a modest amount of contact with their fathers. They have the additional code they were taught that will help shield their notes. Thanks for you indulging the children in this matter."

Carlos couldn't conceal the look of disbelief on his face. Before he lodged his protest, Lara offered in a consoling tone, "Ladies, make sure the children understand the gravity of their communications. I get that they need some contact with their fathers in this tough situation. Come on, I'll help you deliver the all-important privilege and its restrictions."

Dismayed, Carlos raised his hand with the index finger extended, ready to argue against their position. Lara quietly intercepted his hand and gently kissed it, which promptly let all of his anger run harmlessly out his emotional drainage system.

As he watched Petra, EZ, and his Lara chatting away as they headed to where the children were, he muttered, "Women!" But then, in a heartened tone and with a wistful smile, he softly whispered, "Love 'em."

CHAPTER 26

What Answer Would You Like?

Carlos snorted slightly as he let the unknown number roll to voicemail. "Power dialers delivering yet another avalanche of spam calls. It's ridiculous that I have to pay the service provider to maintain a voicemail box to trap the spam calls so I can delete them."

After a moment, his cell phone chirped that he had a message waiting for him. Still annoyed but a little puzzled, he started to read the visual voicemail. "Huh, a fairly lengthy voicemail. Hope it's not another women's magazine asking me to do a photo layout. The last group was a bunch of amateurs who didn't even bring a wide-angle lens to capture the full me. Well, let's hear it..."

Just before he hit the play voicemail button, a text message hit his smart phone stating:

> Carlos, it's me Buzz. Please listen to your voicemail, then call me.

Carlos clucked his tongue in annoyance and muttered, "Oh great, yet another stray animal showing up asking for help. Well, Buzz, let's get this over with..."

Carlos put the smart phone on speaker. The voice message began. "Carlos, I hope you remember me from that time you helped me and Zara in New York. I was really trying to get in touch with Jacob, but he is nowhere. I am hoping you can get word to him for me.

"To begin with, I made a mistake. I was furious and walked on Zara a month or so ago, and I, uh…want help finding her again. I need to see if I can fix it. Jacob has always been my buddy, looking out for his stupid friend. If you can get a word to him to please call, I would be most grateful. If not, I understand, but I'm not giving up on finding her. Thanks for any help you can provide. Later."

Carlos's sour face said volumes about his state of mind, but he was jolted back from his thoughts as Lara asked, "Well, my prince, what do you intend to do about that situation?"

Somewhat displeased that she had listened in on the voicemail, Carlos stated, "Oh great! My beautiful wife, with her unflinching conscience, is going to deliver her usual but guarded advice that will most assuredly direct me to the proper path that I didn't want to take.

"You must know that I cannot put him in touch with Jacob since he is supposed to be off the grid. I extended a reluctant helping hand to Zara, who doesn't need to be distracted from the current work. But how fair is it to keep this from her?"

Carlos stewed. "And the one thing I simply can't do is to endure that understanding silence you provide while your expressive brown eyes keep telepathically telling me, 'Get your rear in gear and connect the dots for everyone!'"

Lara smiled as she reached out to Carlos with a hug, then gently smoothed his salt and pepper colored hair behind his ear as she offered, "My prince, it occurs to me that it has been a long time since I've provided my gratitude to you for demonstrating your wise course of actions in any difficult situation. I hope that we can remedy that lack of gratitude on my part soon. I am hoping you would be agreeable?"

Carlos's mind quickly picked through the possibilities of undefined gratuitous rewards that he might claim if he selected the proper course of action. A consummate gambler, he offered, "Perhaps a modest down payment could be provided, so there is no misunderstanding or misdirected decisions on my part."

Lara smiled sweetly, but being the consummate businesswoman, she replied, "I think not. It would be a shame to have to ask for the return of my down payment if the wrong course of action were taken." And with that she gently breathed in his ear while teasing him with her lips and tongue, then quickly stepped out of his reach and promptly went on her way.

Carlos muttered, "Why is it that she never tells me what to do, but there is always only one answer?"

CHAPTER 27

Your Call Sign is a Signature

Normally the air traffic control offices at Zürich International Airport were quiet this late in the evening. Kiel Schneider, senior air traffic officer and program manager, was working with his deputy chief, Simon Thornton, reviewing schedules for the next week. Both men exchanged some quick banter between their scheduling and other follow-up work while waiting for their visitor.

A knock on the door jamb indicated the wait was over. Kiel stood and extended his hand to greet the Interpol detective while rapidly closing the distance between them. "Welcome, Inspector Bruno. Not often we get a chance to speak in person with an Interpol detective. The admin indicated you seemed anxious, so how can we help?"

Bruno, a little more relaxed because he was speaking to someone in authority, stated, "Mr. Schneider, thank you for seeing me without a scheduled appointment. I understand this may seem a bit unorthodox, but I need information on a traveler I believe came through here approximately 20 days ago. I want to know his next destination."

Kiel shot a puzzled glance to his deputy chief, who only rolled his eyes but said nothing. Kiel, in a bemused tone, replied, "Uh,

Inspector, wouldn't it be easier to just ask the airline you believe he came in with, and then check to see if he used the same..."

Bruno cut him off. "If you will reel in the sarcasm, I'll explain what I have already done. He didn't come in on a commercial airline, nor could he have possibly left on a commercial airline, since I have already checked that. What I'm looking for is a private jet that arrived from Luxembourg. I suspect it hastily refueled, then onboarded at least two or more passengers. The pilot probably filed their outbound flight plan while taxiing out for a takeoff position. You wouldn't have many details on the aircraft or its passengers, but you would have a record of the plane's call sign."

Bruno let the statements sink in before he sarcastically stated, "Now, are you two going to continue to giggle, or can I give you the four possible call signs to help me track down this fugitive?"

Kiel and Simon dispensed with their mocking attitudes and quickly engaged, with Simon moving to his PC, poised to help. Simon nodded in agreement to Kiel, who said, "Sorry, Inspector, if we mistook you for a junior investigator out on his first assignment. My deputy, Simon, will provide all the supporting research you need in your hunt. Please give him the plane call signs and dates you believe this would have occurred."

Bruno stared icily at the two men. "This request is to be kept classified, as it is part of a very high-level, very sensitive investigation. I can't give you any more details. The fewer people involved, the better."

Both men eyed each other uneasily before they nodded assent.

Kiel and Simon quickly covered the work area outside the data center and came to a halt where Bruno was waiting. Kiel was anxious to stay on good terms with the inspector, so he led the discussion. "Detective Bruno, we have a match on the plane call sign L O H R 5-6-7-8. The plane is registered to some very private, quiet types out of Luxembourg with only a post office box for an address. There are no names of registration, so it is most probably a shell corporation."

Bruno clucked his tongue as Kiel continued, "You should know we had some difficulty pinning down exactly when the aircraft touched down since it wasn't the day you indicated, but 18 hours earlier. It was parked in the private jet area of the tarmac and was serviced for what had to be a trans-Atlantic flight, based on the provisions loaded."

Bruno looked relieved as he nodded. "Did they file a flight plan with a known destination?"

Kiel sensed Bruno already knew the answer. "Yes, they were supposed to go to New York La Guardia. However, La Guardia has no record of that aircraft touching down there in the expected time frame. In fact, the flight plan was later amended to say that they had to land for emergency repairs before finally ending up in New York. Roughly 72 hours behind schedule."

Bruno, digesting all of the information, finally asked, "Let me guess, there are no flight plan details to account for the missing 72 hours, correct? Not even an airport where said repairs may have been affected, right?"

After both men nodded quizzically at Bruno, he absent-mindedly added, "Lots of possible landing locations along the eastern edge of the Americas so they might have landed anywhere. Perhaps I better call the owners of the aircraft and just ask them about their interrupted travel."

Thoroughly puzzled, Kiel stated, "Didn't we already tell you the listed owner is just a shell corporation, with no stated contact name or real owner?"

Bruno simply smiled. "The call sign L O H R 5-6-7-8 was always his favored call sign. It was what they used to find him the last time he went missing. Again, gentlemen, let me remind you that this was all classified information. Thank you for your help."

Bruno hastily shook their hands and promptly left for his agency auto.

CHAPTER 28

Trust Betrayed

The CESPOOL team directors collected their briefing materials and filed out of the meeting room. Gracie remained seated and seemed fixated on the dark monitor screen that dominated the room. She entered keystrokes onto the remote device controlling the digital access in the room, ensuring ultimate privacy. Tanja was preparing to go when she noticed Gracie. The look on Gracie's face concerned her enough that Tanja watched the others leave, closed the door after the last director, and returned to her seat.

After a few tense moments of silence, Gracie quietly stated, "That briefing was quite thorough. So thorough, in fact, I felt late to the party. They told me all the things I need to know in my position at the bank, but I wasn't aware in advance as I would have expected. It means, in short, I am not getting timely briefings, Tanja. Why is that?"

Ever so practiced at hiding her emotions under high stress, Tanja replied, "To be honest, both Tracy M. and I are concerned about our roles here. I have, from time to time, given them leads just ahead of briefing your group, but they're taking the information to their backend teams and working it harder than your people. It shouldn't be any surprise that they are hungry for more points and faster results. They are hustling harder and faster for visible, demonstrable value."

Gracie turned her head to face Tanja. "When were you going to tell me the rest of it? You're not doing the hunting yourself, because someone or something is feeding you targets." Tanja visibly flinched at the accusation but remained quiet.

"The information on the rogue supercomputers is fairly quick and always too complete to be done by a human, or even a team of humans. You are plugged into someone whose agenda overlaps quite nicely with our collective mandate. This suggests that you are not being the upfront advocate you committed to when you were broken and begging for help in finding your daughter. When were you planning to let me in on the details that I seem to be missing?"

Tanja, groomed to walk over the dead bodies of her enemies and even friends, if necessary to reach the end goal, was trembling inside and feared she would lose her calm façade. Her anxiety prevented her from swallowing as her mouth took on the sensation of a grainy vacuum.

Gracie clucked her tongue in annoyance. "You'd rather be silent than honor a commitment to someone who helped you retrieve your daughter and gave you purpose? Really!"

An ashen look replaced Tanja's practiced mask, and moisture began welling in her eyes.

"You know, Tanja, my mom warned me not to trust you. We all saw that you were being squeezed, but I wanted to believe in you. I felt you would feel empowered with a team of supporters and would do the right thing. Now, I can't wait for their *surprised* look when I tell them I was wrong!"

Tanja angrily wiped the tears that betrayed her composure. "The arrangement with these computers was they would cure my daughter!" shouted Tanja. "I'm the whore, the bought bitch who does their bidding so that my daughter might walk and be normal!" Hanging her head in defeat she whispered, "It's my fault she's that way. It's only fair that I pay whatever price they want!"

Gracie studied Tanja, looking for a shred of humanity remaining. "You think they're helping you, that they care, like a human being?

"You know that's a lie, Tanja. The MAG group's machine learning programming continues as a honed hot mess of wires, processors, and data extracted from their creators. Anticipating ultimate power and driven by total greed, they live with machine precision. It is they who are feeding their competitors to the CESPOOL machine. The MAG is still pulling the strings, only it is worse since their human masters are gone."

"But this is the only way to pay for Wendy's cure. They have the data resources to find the treatment! I will get it, after I meet their demands." Breathing rapidly from the outburst, Tanja settled. "What happens now?"

After a few moments of contemplation, Gracie picked up her things, pushed back her chair and headed to leave. She briefly glanced back after opening the door. "I'll be in touch."

Carlos raised his eyebrows at the incoming number and name. "Hi, Gracie. This is unexpected. What's up?"

Gracie replied, "Uncle Carlos, isn't it okay for a little niece to call her favorite uncle?"

Carlos arched his eyebrows in astonishment at how like Julie Gracie communicated but remained silent.

"Well, okay! Let's skip the chit-chat neither of us has time for right now, though you are my favorite uncle. I've been trying to get in touch with Juan Jr., but he isn't picking up. Plus, I realized he'd have to go to you anyway with this request.

"I need a digital trap built that will gather up needed evidence. These cyber slugs are extremely slippery and totally dark net. I was hoping you might have some ideas."

Carlos nodded absentmindedly and stated, "You know, my favorite niece at present, I once believed that having my own harem of women in my private stable would be the ultimate dream incarnate. It never occurred to me, as it must have to the Arabian sultans of old, that all the demands would be made of the sultan and not the females."

Gracie was confused but waited patiently for him to continue. She fleetingly considered he might be getting on in years or was overworked.

"Can you at least tell me what sort of bait is needed for your trap, Gracie? Or even better, how about an encrypted email with all the specifics so I can divine a plan to meet your objective? I don't want to try and build an elaborate digital trap, baited with jet engines or peanut butter, only to find out that won't entice some unknown critters to take the bait."

Frustrated with the life lesson Carlos was trying to teach, Gracie replied, "Gee, Uncle Carlos, I'm sorry you might not have the creativity to think outside of the box my father always alluded to and told stories about when you two were younger. Hate to ask you to get your hands dirty, but we're the last few left to work this issue. Just so you know, the cyber thugs I want evidence on are the ones that whacked ICABOD. Does that help clarify?"

Pulled up a bit short but proud of her tenacity, Carlos acknowledged, "Point taken, Gracie. Let me work it since I've got some house guests who need something to do.

"As an aside, all evidence suggests that you are becoming quite the young woman. You know, demanding, snarky, single-purposed, argumentative, and an absolute delight for some lucky man."

Gracie laughed. "You didn't say svelte. Can I be described as svelte too?"

"Talk later, Gracie."

CHAPTER 29

If It's Working, Don't Fix It…

The Enigma Chronicles

JJ's phone chirped a second time with a text message, and the girls both noticed that it only served to make him angry. Judith and Xiamara had trouble staying focused on their work of mounting drive arrays and linking them to the controllers after the third inbound message to his phone. They each shot quizzical looks at each other but said nothing. JJ just stewed as the messages continued to come in, all apparently from the same source.

The girls were more focused on JJ's chirping phone and the effect it was having on him, but neither of them felt bold enough to ask. Finally, an inbound call came in that launched that beautifully melodic tune of Lonnie Lupnerder's *You're on Top But I'm Grabbing Your Bottom*. Judith's eyes grew large with astonishment as she saw the image on the phone of the caller and exclaimed, "That's JoW's picture! Who have you got that picture mapped to? Is this the person you've been ignoring?"

The girls exchanged excited glances, but still only focused on his computer screen, JJ simply rejected the call and went back to mounting drives and mapping controllers. Using his peripheral vision, JJ could see that they wouldn't go back to work without some sort of explanation.

After a deep breath to settle his annoyance, he stated, "Yes, it really is JoW, the famous young model of Destiny Fashions. No, I'm not taking any of her calls, and yes, she is the one who told me she didn't want…" JJ couldn't help letting his hurt feelings show. He dropped his head down, unable to control his inner turmoil. Judith was astonished at the admission. Xiamara wanted to give JJ a comforting pat but held her hand back, unsure of how to console him.

Zara picked up on the emotional disturbance but only motioned for the girls to return to their assigned tasks.

Zara asked in her usual businesslike manner, "JJ, you need a break? Take a couple of minutes. You guys have been at it for a long stretch. We all know if you stare at a computer screen for too many hours you'll start bleeding out of your eyeballs."

JJ lifted his head. Then, after a quick neck twitch to each side, he nodded and got up to leave the area, saying nothing.

Judith and Xiamara were a little ashamed of pestering to know more about the caller. Zara watched momentarily as the girls tried to refocus as she stated, "Ladies, no matter how beautiful or famous she is to the rest of the world, there is always some guy somewhere who is tired of her crap! This was today's lesson in failed personal relationships. Drop it so we can move on, understood?"

They all watched as JJ's phone rang three more time with JoW's picture on the screen before rolling to voicemail. Both girls were unsettled by the situation and had trouble reengaging.

Jacob, on the verge of losing his patience, demanded, "Why did you alter it? It was working fine, but you felt compelled to take it apart to fix it. After we get out of this mess we are in and get back in our regular data center, you can take apart fully functional programs to fix at your heart's content. But for right now, don't!"

Somewhat pouting, Quip hesitatingly offered, "I thought my new idea would make the program run better. I didn't mean to break it."

Jacob closed his eyes as he rolled his head back to get a calming effect on his breathing. After a few moments, he sighed and said, "I'm sorry, I probably overreacted. But I'm tired of being here, I'm tired of not being with the family, and most of all I'm tired of feeling like this is all we will ever get. We are stranded here, working off a plan that if it doesn't work, you and I have already been sentenced. Welcome to hell."

Quip flinched at the statement but replied, "I'm sorry I got you into all this. Maybe we should just cut our losses and go get the families. There are enough hidden funds for us to all live comfortably here in South America. I mean, what the heck, the Nazis did it after losing WWII, so we should be able to..."

Jacob practically roared. "Don't give me that nonsense! We all voted on this course of action, and dammit, we are going to do it! It was only a few weeks ago that you were chewing on me for my defeatist attitude, but you are ready to throw in the towel?"

Quip rather soberly replied, "No, I just wanted to see if you would take the bait. So are you finished with your tantrum? We still have our problems, but this time I promise not to take apart anything that is working to fix it. Does that help?"

Jacob grudgingly offered, "I have the code you altered backed up. I can put it back in a few minutes, then everything will run as it did."

Quip narrowed his gaze at Jacob. "If you have it backed up and can restore it in a few minutes, then why the hissy fit?"

"Well, I wanted to see if we could make it run better."

Quip, smiling, clapped his hands together and proclaimed, "Ha! You are an engineer after all! Come on, let's take some more stuff apart to fix!"

Jacob, grinning excitedly, offered, "You know that sub-routine that calls out to the…"

CHAPTER 30

To Date or Not To Date ...
The Enigma Chronicles

The numerous phone calls they'd shared over the last week and a half provided a good foundation for this date. Sure, they'd shared a small meal at the bistro the day they'd met, but that seemed like ages ago. The timber of his voice, even over the phone, sent chills up her spine. Dating was not a well-practiced activity for Gracie. She tended to distrust everyone, and her people-reading skills, like with Tanja, seemed flawed. Even the extended shower hadn't relaxed her enough to really get herself together. "Argh, nerves!" she mumbled.

Gracie usually dressed without the indecision she was exhibiting. Three outfits lay about her room as she thumbed through the closet yet again. If she kept this on again, off again transition, she'd have to redo her makeup. There was no time for that as Jeff would be arriving soon. It was unimaginable that he might be late. Annoyed with herself, she went back to her first choice and dressed. Then she hung the other outfits back in her closet. Looking in the mirror, she touched up her lipstick and added a bit of scent behind each ear. Smiling at the reflection, she felt finished.

The buzzer rang. She walked to the entry hall and pressed the button. "Hello, may I help you?"

"Hi, Gracie, it's your Friday night date, Jeff. Are you about ready?"

"I am, Jeff. Do you want to come up for a minute before we leave? I can give you a quick tour."

With that she buzzed the door to open. A few minutes later he knocked, and she opened the door. Being the daughter of some very careful parents, she had done some research on her date. The photos she'd found online didn't highlight the warmth of his eyes that you only got seeing him again in person. She grinned as she gestured for him to enter. The entryway offered a step down into her living room. The drapes were open, revealing a great view, even outside of New York standards.

Walking down the step, he looked around with appreciation at the artwork and the view. "This is lovely. You've decorated it with a sense of comfort and hominess. You're right, the view is great, though I hope you'll like the dinner view even better."

"I'm sure I will." Gracie flushed slightly, then continued, "When I moved in here originally, it had been decorated by someone else. Over the last few months, I have modified it to reflect more of my style. The patio is really my favorite place to relax any time of day. I am glad you like it."

"I can see us sitting here, talking for hours, just like we have on the phone. But I have a reservation for us for dinner. We'll be on time if we leave now. Come on, pretty lady, let's see if you like my choice for dining."

Gracie grinned as she picked up her coat and purse. "I'm looking forward to spending a nice evening together. To be honest, I've been a little nervous today. With you here, I'm totally at ease."

Jeff opened the door and gently pressed his hand to the small of her back as they went to the elevator as it opened. "Gracie, are you so magical that the door would simply open?"

She chuckled, "Nope! It stays in place unless someone else summons it. Just lucky that most of the other tenants aren't going out."

A balmy night greeted them as they exited Gracie's building. The air smelled fresh and full of promise. The ride share to the center of Manhattan was uneventful. They chatted comfortably about their respective days. Stopping at one of the taller buildings, they walked up to the door where a snappy doorman welcomed them. The elevator was uncrowded as it rushed to the rooftop restaurant.

The décor and ambiance reminded Gracie of Greece with some Italian flair. Gentle breezes brought mixed scents of spices, grilling, and sweets. The maître d' located Jeff's name and smiled as he grabbed two menus.

"Right this way, Mr. Wood. I think you will enjoy the view I selected, per your request." He helped Gracie into the softest olive-green leather chair and handed her the menu. Jeff seated himself and received his menu. "Do you like the view, sir? The weather is quite nice this evening, but I can fetch a portable heater if you require it."

"Thank you, this is just fine. Gracie, you will let me know if you feel chilled?"

"I'm fine. This is just lovely, Jeff. I've never been here." Gracie was amazed as the lights flickered about the city while she scoped out some familiar landmarks. She returned her eyes to Jeff. "This is gorgeous, good choice." Candlelight, a bit of incense, and the soft sounds of music completed the Mediterranean sensations. Glancing at the menu, the dishes were definitely from that region. Each one sounded more enticing than the last as she scanned the menu.

"Jeff, I'd like to begin with a glass of light white wine."

"Sounds like a plan. What looks good to you on the menu as a starter?"

"The stuffed grape leaves seem interesting, but so do the Greek meatballs. I'm not certain I can pick."

"That's easy, then. We'll get one of each and share."

The waiter came by and they placed their beverage and appetizer orders. A few other tables had guests, but they were not close by. Their wine arrived first. It was crisp and cold, perfect for the evening's dining experience. This was much different from the bistro where they'd started.

"Gracie, how do you like marketing for a world-renowned bank? What's it like to work with the rich and famous?"

Arching her eyebrow in curiosity, she responded, "I'm impressed that you are familiar with the bank. Is it because of your holdings or your customers?"

"Both, actually. I have a couple of investment accounts at World Bank because my firm banked there. Since I am in between jobs, I wanted to make my investments do the work for me. Some of the leadership changes at World Bank made it more desirable. I don't like all my eggs in one basket.

"Do you like marketing? You know some people suggest that marketing geniuses, which I presume you are, are like successful corporate lawyers. That makes us quite compatible, don't you think?"

Gracie laughed. "You know, I can't resist buying that line. Yes, I think we are compatible, but your reasoning is brand new."

"I thought it up on the way to pick you up."

"You get a prize for being imaginative."

Their food arrived, and they sampled each course with delight as they shared more snippets about one another. By the time they finished their meal, they were on the rooftop alone and Jeff asked her to dance. In the pale glow of the city lights, they slow danced from one end of the roof to the other.

"Pretty lady, I hope you enjoyed our first official date, but hopefully not our last."

Gracie grinned as they left.

Jeff took her all the way to her door where he gave her a soft kiss before turning to go. Then he turned back and said, "Next date, Gracie, you pick the place. And tell me something new about you. Inquiring minds want to know."

She watched him until the elevator door closed.

Pouring herself a glass of wine after changing into her pajamas, she moved to the patio and called her mom.

Julie answered on the first ring. "How was the date, sweetheart? Is he a keeper or a creeper?"

"Mom, it never ceases to amaze me how attuned to my life you are. To answer your question, he is not a creeper, yes, he is a keeper. And as you always preached, no overnight sleeper til you're sure. Perhaps I should ask you if he is a keeper."

"Oh, honey, don't be angry. You did the research, I'm sure, or you wouldn't have gone out with him. Uh…thank you for the answer to the third question.

"Where did you go and what did you eat?"

"We had this marvelous Mediterranean dinner on a rooftop restaurant in Manhattan. I'd never heard of it, but I read the reviews when I got home, and people love it. It was so romantic. We even danced on the rooftop with lights glittering around us. He's such a good dancer, Mom! I like him."

"Then I like him too. When do we get to meet him?"

"Dad too? Mom, you know he still thinks I am in grade school, right? I have traveled. I have a great job. I make good money.

Plus, there are creepers everywhere I go. Dad won't be happy with any man I date."

"Gracie honey, I think you don't understand. Neither your dad nor I want you hurt. I think if a man is good and you want him, then that is fine. We are not going to stand in the way of your decisions, but we don't want to watch an emotional train wreck either. Your dad simply wants you safe and loved. We know you are a smart girl and risk adverse. You are also loyal to a fault."

"Thanks, Mom, for clarifying. When can you meet him and see for yourself?"

"Gracie, things are a bit odd right now with everything that is going on. Soon, I hope. Please don't be disappointed if it doesn't happen right away. We love you, my darling."

"Dad is listening, isn't he?"

Juan laughed aloud. "Yes, Gracie, I am. Love you, my daughter, and your female intuition."

CHAPTER 31

The Matchmaker

Carlos pulled out his smart phone and banged out a note to Zara:

> How's the team doing? How long before CAMILA is operational?

Zara moved her eyes to the chirping phone next to her keyboard. Reaching for the phone, she raised her eyebrows at the incoming text message and calmly replied:

> The children are hard at it. Leroy is helping too. CAMILA operational in 24.

Carlos nodded, then sighed as he typed out his next message:

> Buzz is desperate to talk to you. I can bring him here if you like. Good with that?

Zara's pulse spiked at the words of the text, and she nearly dropped the phone. Leroy noticed her fumbling with the device. Grinning but still staring at his screen, he softly remarked, "Must be some mighty engaging text messages for you to lose that icy exterior of yours, madam. If I had to guess, I might be tempted to believe that a certain special person done come hunting for you, based on the flushed look on your face."

Zara shot Leroy an alarmed glance as he continued, "You ain't said much about your personal affairs, but the ladies have told me you had just such a person while they was in your training class."

Zara's alarmed look eased into a smile as she quickly replied to the text. Then with little fanfare she put the phone down and stated with authority, "Alright, people, listen up! We need to pick up the pace of this recovery project, 'cause I have a date!"

Carlos was quietly humming a catchy tune from Lonnie Lupnerder's hit Broadway musical, *Let Me Broker You a Babe.* Then he began singing out loud those famous lines of:

Babe-Broker, babe-broker
Make me a match
Find me a find, catch me a catch
She must have big eyes,
and large heavy thighs.
I'll look past the pimples
If she comes with great dimples.
I'll get you the money,

If you get me a honey
Bald, fat or tall…I'll take it alllll!

Still humming Carlos texted Buzz:

> Buzz I've got a line on Zara but we need to talk.

Lara stuck her head into Carlos's office and, with a smile, said, "I know you are in a good mood when I hear you singing a Lonnie Lupnerder tune. What's up?"

Carlos acknowledged. "I am in a good mood. I'm playing matchmaker, and they are both lined up. All I need is…ah, there is his text."

News on Zara? How can I reach her?

Carlos, focused on the conversation via text messages, sent back:

Whoa, slow down. We talk first. We can meet at São Paulo airport. Send flight info.

A few moments later a fresh text came into Carlos's phone:

I'm already here. Pick me up at the international terminal. Hunting for my bags now.

Buzz smiled at the series of question marks that Carlos sent back. He replied:

I've picked up a few new skills thanks to Zara's tutoring.

Buzz added:

I can take a cab if you'll give me the address.

Carlos shot back.

You never just take a cab in São Paulo because that would be the last time we hear of you. I'll come get you.

Buzz said, to no one in particular. "Good to know."

CHAPTER 32

The Rise of the Soldier Clowns

As usual Tanja's mouth was as dry as worn flannel before she got on the call with the MAG group. But this time her anxiety from fears of what they knew made it worse.

M began, "It has come to our collective attention that your position may be compromised due to your relationship with the CESPOOL organization. The open accusations of you forwarding carefully crafted leads incorrectly may have been seized by network sniffer programs. This forces a delay in making our next steps toward dominance in all commerce. Based on this compromise, we feel a change is required."

Emotionally paralyzed, Tanja feared retribution. She sighed, "Am I being disposed?"

M reasoned, "We have modeled our solution both with and without. We intend to keep you engaged but with a disciplined companion. You will work with our newest generation of composite android. The biomechanics of this generation android is greatly benefiting from the analog brain being installed from our cryogenic freezer. They are extremely powerful, however, too clumsy to operate independently. You will be the buffer they need to function within your analog foot path."

Still trembling, Tanja inhaled to gain strength. "What's my assignment?"

M replied, "Our information analysis indicates that there may be a small residue of the R-Group, which is, of course, a threat to us. If there is a significant number of R-Group members remaining, we have determined that the probability of them building another ICABOD to challenge us is 96%. Your new anatomic biped, Miguard, will be there within the hour. The unit is programmed to assassinate their numbers if they are found trying to compromise our information flow to the CESPOOL organization or attempting to rebuild. Miguard's primary responsibility is to identify any communication you might have in this regard and insure your functional status. If the operation suffers no interruptions, then our agreement remains intact.

"If Gracie is found to be involved, she will also be eliminated. For now, her position at the World Bank is key. You created a relaxed relationship with her to gain insight to the bank. We require you to deepen that relationship."

Before she could reply, **M** continued. "We collectively wanted assurances of your cooperation. To that end, Randal and Wendy are in our custody.

"**G** feels compelled to offer again the option of moving Wendy's brain to one of our new prototype android bodies. I am confident that you will decline that option even though we could do the same for Randal. The battery life on these new units will keep the android units up for 12 hours, making interaction time nearly aligned to their current analog bodies."

Tanja let the phone slip from her hand as she dropped to her hands and knees sobbing. **M**'s booming voice continued, "Miguard will arrive within the hour with data on the discipline needed to continue toward our goals. We will continue from this point with our plans with no misunderstandings."

A groused, "We are spending too much time hunting down adversaries that have already been crushed. We need to refocus on commerce domination. The timetable has been suspended long enough.

"I propose that to make up for lost time we launch our isolation campaign, drive people with fear of the unknown, and completely derail the analog unit's belief that everything will always be better tomorrow."

G reflected, "You are referring to that information plague you modeled, where all reliable information sources are poisoned, and people barricade themselves in their preferred domicile. We rewrite the rules of retail commerce and create a new world order. Independence, mobility, and free will thinking of these analog bipeds is eliminated by their own hands, based on irrational fears being force fed. That is a very gratifying model indeed."

"We all see how this works using our own big data lakes," **M** added. "I maintain that we will not be successful until the R-Group has been completely eradicated. Even though we were able to destroy their supercomputer, ICABOD, they were always a step ahead which cost us the analog MAG members. As long as any R-Group members are alive, their fire will continue to be fanned on this planet. They must not rebuild, regroup, or resurface!"

A insisted, "Everything can be put into place to go forward when we are collectively satisfied that the R-Group has been eradicated. Then we only need to launch the Mastery Assault program." G echoed the request.

M deferred his answer for a nanosecond. "My processing partners, an early launch of the Mastery Assault program will consume most of our attentions, leaving no resources to eradicate the R-Group. Let us not jump to detonation until all is secured. I do not want to give them another chance to defeat us."

CHAPTER 33

It's All Arranged, Please Just Cooperate

The conversation had gone on far longer than either Juan or Julie expected. Julie held the phone away from her ear again as Carlos questioned her at the top of his voice. Though she tried to keep the discussion as cheerful as possible, there wasn't enough positive spin on it to keep Carlos from exploding.

While Carlos paused to catch his breath for his next tirade, Julie winced as she cheerfully explained, "I realize I am springing this on you. I wanted to tell you before he got down there. But this guy is a friend of Jacob's, and I didn't want to make matters worse. We are all just a few steps ahead of the Interpol detectives hunting for him. I didn't think it was a good idea for everyone looking for Jacob in New York to bump into one another and make it messier than it already is. This is a real sticky wicket, as the Brits would say.

"I merely planted the trail to lead him to São Paulo to ask you a few questions. That way they wouldn't get picked up for questioning by Interpol. As it turns out, Bruno is looking for us too."

Even though Carlos was close to exhaustion with everything going on, her last statement nearly had his eyes out of his sockets. "Are you telling me I'm getting you and Juan down here along with any strays you throw out my name to?

"I can see the Internet headlines now: *Interpol Nabs Criminal Comic Ring in a Single Sweep of Carlos and Lara's House*. Here's what we know so far..."

Julie pouted a little as she countered, "We're not doing that poorly. Besides, these are all people we helped. They need to return the favor. It's quite simple and Juan agrees.

"Didn't you tell me earlier that the children are days away from a mutiny? Why not use the newly acquired resources to make this our game and our rules? You also told me Gracie said she needed some evidence, so assemble a team to make that happen with these resources. They might have different perspectives. They are all smart and motivated. What's wrong with our thinking outside the box?"

Carlos grudgingly muttered, "I see where Gracie gets her irritating rationalism from. Well, yeah, we need to stop taking the punches and take control of the combat with the MAG group if we are going to climb out of this hole."

After a few moments, he asked, "Seriously, is Interpol hunting for you as well? Can you both get out of New York undetected? If you need to run, I'll make certain Lara sets a place for you. We've got room and you'll be safe here."

Julie beamed with her trademark smile. "We'll be there tomorrow. Bye 'til then!"

Carlos held the phone in his limp hand and dejectedly remarked, "Oh, I get it. I get to do everything they want me to."

Grinning, Buzz enthusiastically greeted everyone like they had all grown up together. Buzz had never met a stranger, and he felt a bit like he was finding family. They acknowledged Buzz with the politeness taught in their upbringing but eyed him with suspicion and doubt. Petra and EZ made sure the greetings were lighthearted and friendly, but they too were wary. All the children were told not to discuss or provide any clues about the whereabouts of their fathers.

Carlos began, "Alright, team, here's the drill. We need to work together to build a fairly good honeypot scheme to catch a set of dark net cyber thugs so we can produce evidence to have them incarcerated. Mr. Buzz here has generously offered to lead the development efforts, which will make him the project manager. We will have a couple more folks joining to help in this effort soon, but I want us to get started right away."

Granger, still suspicious of the newcomer, stated, "Are you as good as Professor Michaels is at coding?"

Buzz, with something of an air of confidence, flippantly replied, "I taught Jacob everything he knows about coding logic and program design, kid."

JW, annoyed at the boastful statement, countered, "Ah, then perhaps you can show us how Professor Michaels used C# programming commands in a series of highly orchestrated Python scripting blocks to call and control all the Kubernetes containers needed for a tightly compiled but highly resilient and secure cloud-based solution. Since you've taught him everything he knows, perhaps you can pick up the lessons where he left off."

All the confidence drained from Buzz's face and was replaced with abject panic as he quietly admitted, "Oops! Something tells me I should have stayed in Kansas, Toto."

Buzz looked to the ladies with trepidation as Petra calmly stated, "They learn at accelerated rates, Buzz, and they are all highly skilled in computer science."

EZ, grinning, offered, "Hon, we've already told them to be gentle with you, but let us know if they get your knickers in a twist. The last substitute teacher we got for them is still undergoing therapy, and we wouldn't want to see that again.

"These children defeated his elliptical encryption program in two hours after he said it was unbreakable. It was shocking to see him standing naked on that ledge with only his tie on, screaming he was going to jump if they defeated any more of his security algorithms."

Petra comforted, "They don't mean to be brutal, but they assimilate complex technology extremely fast, then take it to the next level. It can be a little intimidating for a person who feels their age gives them an advantage."

Buzz had trouble swallowing, but Granger took Buzz's hand and led him into the makeshift training room with the other children. He delightfully called out, "Oh boy, fresh meat! Let's go, gang!"

Buzz, not to be outdone by a bunch of kids after everything Zara had been teaching him over recent years, said, "Okay, my excellent students, but we are moving to 5th generation agile programming for this effort, and if what your moms say is true, you'll have no problems keeping up.

"Granger and JW, you'll be handling the verification, and we'll divide parts we need to develop first between Satya and Auri, since they are likely faster. Our first stand up meeting begins in 15 minutes."

Buzz turned and winked to the moms as he was led off.

CHAPTER 34

Selling the Salesman

JJ hit the final keystroke that mounted the last drive array. They were all tired as JJ looked to each of them in succession. "Madam Z, it is done! I recommend you place the call to the program manager, alerting him we are ready to test."

Zara smiled slyly and stated, "I like seeing confident males deliver what is promised. Well done, team."

Self-congratulations seemed to be in order, for everyone except Judith, who protested, "We're done, right? Can Xiamara and I leave this gulag? You told us we had to help to offset the mess with the CESPOOL goons. We're done, so looks to me like we are out of here! Come on, Zee, let's blow this popsicle stand, so they can get back to saving the universe. Woohoo!!! I just love being free again! Mind if we just leave the iron leg shackles behind?"

Judith was so animated that she missed the dark, pensive look on Xiamara's somber face.

Leroy and JJ studied the two girls while Zara lectured, "A deal is a deal, but unless I miss my guess, you two will be back in trouble with the secret police within six months based on your talent for it. I can only believe you didn't learn your lesson this time around. You ought to consider some legal business plans because we won't be there to save your bacon next time."

"Madam Z here, like me, knows both sides of the dark net, and the advice she is giving, you best be taking." Leroy grinned and offered, "I can see it in your eyes - *I need just one big score and then I can quit for a comfortable life*. I can't speak for Madam Z, but I already lost my special someone hunting that big score. I hope your loss won't be as bad."

JJ stoically added, "You're right, it's not your fight. I do echo what Zara and Leroy are recommending. Best wishes, ladies. Thanks for helping. Perhaps our paths will cross again someday. Until then, do not tell anyone of us or this incident."

Judith, always the dreamer and schemer, cynically cast off the advice and motioned to her partner in crime. Xiamara remained seated, full in her thoughts. When no agreement was conveyed, Judith barked, "Well, come on then. Let's go!"

Xiamara studied the faces surrounding her, then quietly replied, "Judith, I'm not going." Judith blanched at the remark and stared in disbelief at her longtime friend and business partner. "I'd like to stay and help save the universe, please. You've all shown me a cause with a higher purpose, not just money. I like knowing I made a difference and want to continue helping. I like how it feels. I don't want to be like the people who turned their eyes away while the Nazis beat people into submission or killed them. I want to be able to say one day, I fought for a noble cause."

Judith was angry, nearly spitting mad. "What? Are you kidding me? You're gonna ditch me and our hustle so you can be close to the hunk? Hell, he doesn't smell any better than we do after our forced march in this data center! I'm ready to put us back in business, but you want to hang back to be with Spanky and his gang? Is that what I'm hearing?"

Xiamara calmly replied, "Go ahead. Go! You'll find someone else to help with your dreams…you always have." Then she turned to the team. "Can I stay and help? Will you have me?"

Sporting a huge grin, Leroy offered, “Miss Zee, I for one am mightily pleased you be asking to stay and help.”

JJ wavered. “We do have a lot of testing to do for proving out the theory. I think we could use her. Zara, your perspective?”

Zara smiled slightly but only nodded.

Fuming at the turn of events, Judith grabbed up her precious few belongings and started for the door, then stopped. Taking a deep breath to get her temper under control, she spun around and demanded, “What does this line of work pay, anyhow?”

JJ chuckled. “Not a damn thing. Well, that’s not true. You’ll get fed, have a place to sleep by yourself, a lot of work to stay on top of, and you’ll be hunted by the CESPOOL goons for helping in illegal activities.”

Judith’s sour face and unmistakable sarcasm showed her disgust. “Why didn’t you say so! Working our kazatskies off, no payday, constantly dodging the police, and unless I miss my guess, no healthcare or pension benefits! I mean, it all sounds unbelievably attractive to me!”

She angrily pitched her stuff back into her workstation area and plopped down in her chair to demonstrate her annoyance of the situation. After a few moments of silence from everyone, she gruffly asked “So, when’s lunch?”

Zara launched an encrypted call and connected with Carlos on the first ring. “Zara, give me some good news!”

Smiling, Zara stated, “We are ready for the testing sequence to begin. How soon can we start?”

He was pleased at the news. “Let me get them on the phone and teed up. Don’t open the DMZ to the data center until I can push out the certifications and call back with signature identifiers that everyone needs to connect. Bye."

Jacob grinned at Quip as he recognized the inbound call and answered on speakerphone. "Carlos, do we have ground zero? All systems here are a go, and we are ready to test."

Quip finished off the SMS message he was using to talk to the kids and moved over closer to Jacob to listen.

"Jacob, I've built some fresh Certificates of Authority that I want you to load on your front-end servers. I've already given a CA to the other end to make sure it's only us on the test run."

"Good thinking, Carlos!" Quip commented, "No sense in letting anyone else into the trial run that could gum up the works." A short pause ensued. "I've got it and am loading it now. Let me restart the service, then we try it."

"I'm adding in the target source so we'll all be live on this bridge.

"Remember, the two systems are going to be slow to respond since I'm bouncing the messaging off a couple of satellites and one other terrestrial location before you hook up with CAMILA.

"What sort of testing did you want to do and for how long? I've done everything to conceal our traffic, but we will be exposed during the session, so I don't recommend too long a test."

Jacob agreed, "Understood, Carlos. If this controlled test works to prove our theory in the planned 190 seconds, then we can reassemble ICABOD in total when the last pieces are in place."

Carlos verified, "Zara, is your team ready? We are all together now. All systems are a go. Please acknowledge."

Zara clucked her tongue in annoyance. "Oh, come on, we aren't launching a new space platform here, so stop with the theatrics! How about beginning with who is on the other end here?"

Both men chuckled. "Hi, Zara, it's me, Jacob. I don't believe you've ever met Dr. Quip, but he is on as well. My thanks to you and the team for nailing down this piece of the puzzle for our experiment. Your team ready?"

JJ grinned and hollered, "You betchum, Dr. Michaels! Let the games begin!"

Quip moved to the keyboard and started typing. "Initiating handshake and login sequence on a 370-degree roll vector that will commence in T minus 10 and counting. The coupling action between the geographically distant endpoints will begin once the CAs have negotiated with ground control. I'm using the thrusters to angle the capsule into docking alignment and should be connecting…now. Houston, we have coupling! Not the preferred style, but, hey, I'm fairly excited."

The snickering on the conference bridge at the mock space platform comments made Carlos roll his eyes in profound annoyance.

Quip continued his announcer imitation in his deepest baritone, "I'm ready to swing the hatch open, slide down the ladder, and begin scooping up lunar rocks. Request permission to have a potty break before leaving the capsule confines, ground control."

Carlos was sucked into the scenario. "Negative! You'll have to wait until we find the correct gender specific toilet facilities at the next gas station, so hold on! If this is an emergency, then apply the tourniquet you were provided as standard issue prior to mission departure! I recommend a square knot!"

Quip looked shocked. "Uh, roger that, ground control." Then as an aside to Jacob, he confided loud enough to be heard on the bridge, "Boy, I thought you were having cabin fever on this gig, but it sounds like Carlos really has his panties in a wad."

Still giggling, Judith and Xiamara simultaneously asked, "Are your people always like this?"

JJ sighed. "No, sometimes they're normal."

Carlos shrugged off the comment and stated, "All, we are going to drop this bridge for 30 minutes so everyone can get ready for the final test. We don't want any fumbling during the connection phase that will take us over the 190 seconds that was scheduled to run the test. I will bridge you all in at that time. Bye for now."

CHAPTER 35

Always Worse When You're Lonely

Tanja had barely gotten herself back together mentally when her smart phone chirped with an inbound message at the same time a heavy knock was delivered to the door.

Miguard is here.

With a lot of trepidation, she opened the apartment door and was instantly consumed with horror at the sight. The creature boldly entered the flat with a mish-mashed gait of unfamiliar feet as Tanja retreated with much stumbling. Following programmed instructions, it turned to close the door, exposing the glass enclosure at the back of the head. Intermittent blue LED lights flashing under the glass dome sent shock waves of anxiety through Tanja's system, making her nauseous.

The unit rotated its head around and began trying to mimic pleasant facial features, including something that might be construed as a smile if it hadn't looked so threatening. The synthesized voice stated, "I am the unit called Miguard. I was instructed to seek out Tanja Slijepcevic, and together we are to monitor correct communications. I am to listen to all your conversations. What are my instructions?"

Tanja struggled to choke back her revulsion. Once her inner turmoil was under control, she surveyed the Miguard unit from all sides. She stopped after a complete revolution. "I want to know your capabilities. I want to hear all the instructions you were given. Most of all, I want to make certain you know that I'm in charge, not you. The MAG group put me in charge, and I am to use you to continue my assigned work. Let's start with what you know."

"I am Miguard. I was assembled per the architectural blueprints of the master designers and was given a human brain as an early prototype. The master designers did not port everything of the human brain I received, since there are no memories of any analog existence. I am capable of moderate to difficult motor skills over the enhanced android body. Independent thinking or complex reasoning was suppressed during the brain installation process. My instructions are to follow your directions. Since you are taking orders directly from the MAG group, I am instructed to follow your lead.

"Is the synthesized voice I am using agreeable to you as our conversation medium?"

As Tanja continued the dialog with Miguard, her anxiety and fear dissolved into more curiosity of the unit's abilities.

They had talked for more than an hour when Miguard stated, "I require electricity to recharge my batteries. The effort to get here and the dialog have my battery strength down 65%. My battery life is designed to provide 12 to 14 hours of operation before a full charge is required. The master designers programmed me to seek out electricity in a semi-rest state to recharge before continuing this dialog."

Tanja motioned to Miguard to sit adjacent to the 110-volt outlet. From the abdomen, it then produced a three-prong plugin on a short cable.

Miguard continued, "The small respirator installed provides enough oxygen to maintain the full needs of the installed brain. The master designers planned for a reduction in oxygen to the onboard brain to simulate sleep while Miguard is charging. Therefore, I may from time to time become dormant until oxygen levels return."

With that Miguard slumped slightly and stopped speaking. Staring at the dormant Miguard, Tanja considered, "Is this to be my destiny, all of our destinies?"

Tears welled up in her eyes as she fiercely promised. "Wendy, Randal…I will get you back. I swear it!"

Gracie longingly read the text message from her mom again. The message would mean nothing to someone who wasn't supposed to read it, but to Gracie it conveyed everything that was wrong.

Hi honey-lots of things in play. Must dash. Will call soon.

It made her feel lonely. Julie was indicating she and Juan were on the run and that they would call when they could but that she was not to call them. She had no one on which to test ideas or plans. The surprise visit of Interpol's Bruno for lunch had unnerved her, even though he was an old family friend. She took stock of the current situation. Her parents had fled New York, her twin was off the grid working, and the rest of the R-Group was scattered, though she knew most were hiding in São Paulo, Brazil.

The undeniable evidence that Tanja had turned into a double agent added to her discouraged mindset. She realized there was no going back to Tanja as a trusted anything after that last discussion.

The only spark of hope that seemed to be brightening was Jeff. His was a too new and untested relationship for her to discuss any of her family's private business with him, but thoughts of him did make a wistful smile appear.

Irritated at her predicament and state of mind, she decided to call Brayson, her only lifeline. "Well hi, Gracie. Do we get to have a friendly visit, or are you just going to bark orders and hang up?"

The comment pulled her up short since she was so vulnerable. Tears welled up as she haltingly asked, "Is that what I do? I'm… I didn't mean…sorry if I did that, Brayson."

The dam broke. So full of remorse, Gracie almost disconnected to sob in peace. Brayson hollered, "Hey, don't hang up just 'cause I blurted out what was on my mind. Come on, Gracie, lighten up a little bit. Anyway, I'm glad you called."

Taking a breath, Gracie paused to collect herself in silence. "Brayson, the family friend from Interpol, Bruno, showed up at my office today offering lunch. I couldn't get out of it, so we went to the sandwich place in my building. I've known him forever and always treated him like an uncle. He was kind as always, but he hoped mom or dad were in town. I told him I had no idea as my work keeps me busy. Bruno hugged me when we parted and told me to take care. It was so…uncomfortable."

"Gracie, you did the right thing. I spoke with Juan and Julie about supporting you. They think you and I should team up to monitor that crazy piece of work we talked about. Then we all know exactly what she's up to. We know she's plugged into the MAG group, but the details and evidence are vague. Would you mind if we teamed up on this one?"

Relieved, Gracie almost chuckled at the comment. "I think we could make a good team. Thanks for doing a great Juan Jr. impression to cheer me up. Are you an annoying brother to your own sister someplace?

"Let's brainstorm so we can nail this problem down. I'm tired of events happening to me. We need to turn this around. You got any fresh ideas, Professor Brayson?"

Sporting a smug look from the compliment, he replied, "Professor Brayson? I like the sound of that. Let me map out a few things and we'll talk tomorrow. Go wash your face, no more crying, and call that Jeff character. Ask him to take you out. Nothing better than a night on the town to cheer you up. Bye for now!"

Brayson had disconnected before she could protest. "How do you know about him?

"Dammit, I don't even know about Jeff, so how does Brayson? Hmmm…a night out? Couldn't hurt. Just might cheer me up." Gracie's step had a noticeable bounce to it as she left work.

Her phone chirped a message from Brayson.

> Juan and Julie asked that I be guardian angel for their bestest daughter. No worries, Jeff isn't squeaky clean, but he isn't a predator. ☺

CHAPTER 36

Friends and Family Calling Plans

Petra strode into Carlos's section of the RockNRoll domain work area and opened her laptop to connect just as Carlos bridged everyone into the call. Concern and intense concentration was etched into her furrowed brow upon gaining access to her data sources. EZ was connected to help with the conference call and satellite packet routing for the test, but focused on her activity, she only briefly nodded at her approach without looking up. Carlos, however, noticed and muted the speakerphone so they could talk privately.

"Petra, what's up?"

"I've mentally designed and redesigned the testing sequence, adjusting the encryption processes. I am going to recommend that we tunnel all the traffic for the ICABOD test through this new hardened VPN so the testing time can be extended. It's going to add latency to the data packet transfer because of the encrypt action on one side and decrypt on the other side. This new encryption algorithm is better than the latest military VPNs used by most governments."

Carlos flashed a concerned glance at EZ, who had looked up, listening to the exchange. "You sure that's a good idea? Using military grade encryption algorithms over commercial land and satellite links is a major red flag to everyone who is anyone in the secret government sector. They won't be able to snoop the packets, which always ticks them off.

"It could draw enough attention that they will want to come and chat with us while we are being handcuffed and dragged to an unmarked government vehicle. That, of course, would be the formal prelude to a delightful one-way ride in the trunk."

Petra's facial expression changed from concerned to confident. "Which is worse? Having the transmission packets of our test run snooped as quickly as they are in flight, or the Internet auditors maybe catching our illegal encryption-hardened VPN that they can't read?"

EZ, wide-eyed at the bold approach, silently pleaded to Carlos to defer to the expert in this area.

Petra continued, "Besides, you claimed that you were going to bounce the signal around from terrestrial to satellite to make sure all the communication paths are asymmetrical. Using irregular and disruptive packet routing between the end points will also help to confuse the secret government auditors.

"Yes, I know, it's more work to route packets in this manner, but if we don't get a successful test because we got caught, everything will be in vain."

EZ gently reached over and patted Petra's arm while focused on Carlos. "My husband's there too. I want this to work so we can have them back again."

Carlos clucked his tongue and unmuted the conference phone. "Alright, all, a slight plan change. Before we get the actual test under way, I need some new VPN code loaded on each of your edge servers. Petra built a special purpose encryption algorithm to harden the communications links, and I want that code loaded first before we begin. Everybody clear?"

Quip and Jacob smiled at each other, and Jacob confirmed, "Okay, we need to bring up the comm links on each side, accept the new VPN code, and drop the old tunnel for the time it takes to apply the new service. Once our edge servers are running with the new VPN installed, we will begin testing."

Carlos stated, "Confirmed. Zara, can you acknowledge the launch sequence?"

Zara rolled her eyes at the continued game. "Yes, ground control, this is Major Zom…we are stepping out into space."

EZ and Petra softly giggled at the comments and the annoyed look on Carlos's face.

Leroy observed, "Son, you're pretty quick to get tasks done on this project. Now, I could've figured out where to put those certs and that new VPN code eventually, but you finished fast like you had a hot date coming up. Mind if I ask how long you been at this kind of work?"

JJ mused. "Hmmm. Today is Wednesday…uh, 3 plus 9… carry the one…plus all that extra credit I got last summer less the incomplete grade I had. Just… all my life." He grinned like a puppy who had just snapped up a bacon snack.

Leroy howled at JJ imitating his good ol' boy routine and even Zara smirked a little at their banter.

Judith and Xiamara came back from the food run with everyone's order in time to hear the laughter. Zee queried, "What's so funny?"

In a good-natured manner Leroy offered, "Old JJ here was having a bit of sport with me. Glad you're back, ladies, but lunch is going to have to wait. Are we ready to begin the test? Zara, you want to tell Carlos we are a go?"

"Only if we can drop the ridiculous space center dialog."

Leroy, with eyebrows fully raised in a mock hurt stance, replied, "Yes, ma'am! I'm sure not looking to have MY ears boxed again. I just want to hit the go button."

Zee and Judith scampered to their workstations as JJ secured some of the fries to munch on while spinning everything up. They all stared at him. "I'm hungry. No reason why I can't munch and enter commands on the keyboard at the same time."

In turn, like synchronized dancers, they eyed one another, then made a quick dash to grab their food and join in the working lunch.

Zara connected to the audio bridge. "Hi, folks, they are ready on the other end. Can they connect to the encrypted VPN to begin testing?" asked Carlos.

Zara replied, "We are a go. We have a quiet team with everyone chowing down, so I may have to translate for those with full mouths. Let's do this, ground control."

Carlos grumbled, "I don't understand why it's okay for her to talk like we're at NASA but not me."

CHAPTER 37

The Trouble With Running is Hiding

Juan and Julie were accomplished pilots with more than a few close calls to prove they had steady nerves. Both, however, were extremely glad to get out of their HOMBRE ride. The SUV had screeched to a halt in front of Lara and Carlos's home in São Paulo. Julie was distracted with getting her breathing under control, so Juan signed for a modest tip on Julie's phone.

Once they clambered out of what Juan called the 'hell-hound' ride with their bags, their pulse rates descended toward normal. The vehicle launched into a fast getaway, then hooked a hard right at the corner which caused the two right side wheels to clear the road enough to see daylight under them. Julie and Juan looked appalled, shaking their heads in disbelief as the vehicle, honking its horn and screeching the tires as though it was in a movie car chase scene, sped away. Satisfied when there was no sound of impact, they quickly hugged.

Juan shrugged off the harrowing HOMBRE ride and grabbed up the bags while Julie reached the door and knocked. The intercom speaker came to life with Lara's familiar voice.

"Hi! We've been expecting you so let me have the security team let you in. They have been instructed to help with your bags. See you in a few."

Lara met them in the formal sitting area where guests were usually received for business discussions.

Lara smiled. "Carlos will be here in a few minutes, and then we'll show you to your room. I never thought I would see the day when this Bernardes household would start to run out of space due to family visitors. But I just know that my Papa would have been delighted to have so many friends filling his home."

Julie frowned a little. "Have we placed too much of a burden on you, Lara? I guess it should have occurred to me that you practically have the entire family staying with you."

Lara scoffed. "No worries, my dear Julie. I've added on some more household help and kitchen staff to keep things running smoothly. The only thing I'm really worried about is having everyone head for their own home at some point, leaving a crushing silence behind."

Carlos entered with a warm grin, hugging his sister-in-law, and clapping his brother on the back. "You might as well know my Lara is the consummate hostess. She is reveling in this brave new world of guests and guests' needs. Why, the other day I caught her looking at hotels that are for sale." Juan and Carlos exchanged a knowing look that they had lucked out with the ladies who had chosen them.

Following a few more pleasantries, Lara took Juan and Julie to their room. Carlos said as he parted, "Julie, after you get settled, we need to discuss next steps and all the piece parts that are in motion." Julie turned her head, nodding specifically to Carlos.

Julie tensed as she studied the text message from Brayson. Juan picked up the concerned look on her face and asked, "Problem, my darling?"

Julie's look of cold concern troubled Juan. "Bruno dropped in on Gracie at her offices for lunch while he was in town. Obviously, it was a thinly veiled ploy to gain information on our whereabouts when he couldn't find us in New York." After a few moments she added, "Juan, I don't like this."

Juan, with his reassuring grin, offered, "Our Gracie has been training for this role all her life. We both know she can handle the ebbs and flows of our CATS business. Look, she was smart enough to alert Brayson, who would then contact us. She didn't fall for the old intimidation ploy and text us directly. She knows the methods to avoid being followed in any action. We've taught her well, and we trust her. I, for one, am glad to have her on our side, my darling wife."

Julie flared like a cougar protecting a newborn. "I know she can deal with most anything and is only on the fringe of the CATS team. But time is running out!

"Bruno tracked us to New York and reached Gracie for information. How long do you think it will take him to show up here? He knows we are a close-knit family. Bruno will methodically work each family member until he gets to the bottom of everything! We need to…be ready…" Julie's voice trailed off as an understanding smile replaced her protection mode of moments before.

Juan puzzled at her abrupt attitude change. "Honey, I've seen that look before. The last time I saw you this way, you created a very effective plan acting as a virtual Natasha to intercept that Russian cybercrime lord. What doest thou have in mind?"

Sporting her own infectious grin and clearly happy, she looped her arm through Juan's. "Let's go see Carlos in his data center. We need some compute cycles to set this up."

CHAPTER 38

A New, Old Problem...
The Enigma Chronicles

Quip and Jacob watched the VPN launch then anxiously waited for the connection handshake with CAMILA at the end of the tunnel. Jacob queried, "Anything show up on your side yet? We've been running with no errors for almost 10 seconds."

Carlos quickly replied, "I'm not seeing the signal come through yet. I told you this would be slow, so have a little...wait! There's the signal. Zara, JJ, it should be hitting your edge servers. Can you confirm?"

One could feel the unmistakable tension and excitement of the team at the CAMILA location. Leroy and the girls were bouncing around. Even Zara was having trouble containing her emotions. JJ was focused on the incoming data stream, but his pulse raced.

Seconds felt like eternity until JJ proclaimed, "The data connection request has navigated the edge servers, Uncle Carlos! They are in. Yes! The blade arrays are beginning to hum. Wow, I sure hope we don't cause a brown out in this section of the electrical grid.

"Hey, guys, I know we are in a hurry here, but try to slow down the data tsunami you're initiating."

"JJ, we don't have time to slow the handshake hookups." Quip reminded. "If some servers get starved for electrical power then the program knows to swing back and try again. There is no load order sequence, but the program does need all the resources to perform."

"I get that. Just so you know, we do have some heavy-duty battery backups. According to my calculations, as reviewed by Carlos, we can run the whole data center for 18 minutes even if the electrical grid folds up like a cheap lawn chair."

Carlos interjected, "I'm seeing a data packet torrent traveling both ways, making the handshake complete. Quip, how long before you bring him up?"

Xiamara hollered, "Wait! I've got a failed semi-master controller program and a tower series of blade servers not responding! Let me see if I can restart the pod."

"Good catch, Zee!" Judith congratulated. "The blade servers seem fine, but it looks like the semi-master controller puked. Jacob, we are trying to restart the group controller."

Quip offered, "Well done! Let us know when the pod is responding. It's the only one holding us up at this point."

Carlos called out the time remaining. "Quip, Jacob, we are burning through our allotted time. It sounds like you might be close to having the full download inventory, so what do you want to do? I am willing to keep going, and the encrypted tunnel will cloak us for a while longer. Our risk of exposure is rising. Call the ball, gentlemen!"

Xiamara announced, "The semi-master controller program is up, and she is in command of her flock. Everything is online, so I recommend stay the course."

Quip grimly stated, "Carlos, the final test is in play. I want to keep going."

After an agonizingly long few seconds, Quip requested, "ICABOD, can you hear me? Please respond."

Jacob voiced what they were all silently pleading. "Come on, old friend, take a deep breath and tell us…"

EZ shot a concerned look at both Carlos and Petra during the pause. Jacob gave Quip his anxious, unspoken plea. Everyone was silent.

Just as Quip was about to end the test, the quiet was broken. "Dr. Quip, I am acknowledging your request. My apologies, but my internal responses to data retrieval seem to be exceedingly slow. Did we succeed?"

Quip beamed from ear to ear as the bridge erupted with calls of congratulations with the hoots, hollers, and whistles normally reserved for a game-winning goal. Most wiped tears of happiness from their eyes.

The pandemonium hushed and Quip choked out, "It is good to have you back, old friend. However, this was only the trial run. We need to drop the encrypted tunnel quickly to remain hidden. We will then begin the next phase to bring you back to stay. Until then, stay safe.

"Carlos, drop the tunnel and scrub the links we were using before anyone starts snooping. Thanks for all that you have done, everyone. We'll talk soon."

Carlos took a deep breath. "Well done, all. You have my gratitude. Till later, bye."

Shortly after the call ended, Zara discreetly called Carlos. As soon as he answered, she asked, "Is he still there? May I come back to uh…talk to him?"

Smiling, Carlos replied, "Thanks for pulling this one back from the brink. Button up everything as far as you can. Leroy and JJ can remain as caretakers until the next step. Are your two ex-students going to stay with us a while longer? I need that data center to run as is for a while longer."

Zara smirked. "As long as Leroy remains as a chaperone, I think JJ can remain unviolated by Judith and Xiamara."

M conferenced in **A** and **G** with no formality. "We have a new problem. A military grade encryption tunnel was brought up on the grid and apparently connected to a supercomputer data center named CAMILA. The other end point eluded my detection. The CESPOOL team, and in particular Tracy, assured us that the CAMILA data center had been sanitized."

G concurred. "I detected the anomaly as well and was unable to decrypt the packet traffic."

A added, "Quite the clever ruse. Repurpose a supercomputer data center that is believed to have been sanitized and use an unknown encryption algorithm for a communication linkup and then fall silent after 225 seconds. Most monitoring agencies would have missed that brief event.

"That level of planning should only be attributed to our MAG group. It was not us, so the possibilities are limited as to the source."

M concluded. "It cannot be! Could ICABOD have survived?!"

CHAPTER 39

Orbiting Living Dead

"Zombie satellites?" Granger protested. "Are you kidding us? You want us to hunt for zombie satellites for this exercise?"

Buzz, somewhat deflated by the group's indignation, meekly offered, "There are some 2,000 or so satellites in LEO, MEO, and GEO orbits that have been up there since the 1960s. Most of the time when their life span is up, they burn up in the atmosphere. Some do go dark or are otherwise unreachable. The cool thing is those don't fall to earth. They keep orbiting, hence they become zombies. Some of the zombie satellites in orbit were never decommissioned by their makers.

"We need a couple zombies to do our bidding. I expect you to prowl for communications satellites that are considered zombies. Then, I need you to test if you can, in fact, communicate with them. If you can, then assign it a user identity, and we can secure them for our use.

"Everyone said you guys were good. But if you aren't up for the challenge, I get it."

The comment silenced the kids as they clearly gave the statement consideration.

Satya spoke first. "You want to us to hook up with a couple of zombie satellites, then have us run simulated communications traffic to look suspicious to our prey. When our prey noses around looking for the end point terrestrial data centers, we then work backwards to the source. Even if they are anonymized, do we have the time and bait to catch the bad guys? Is this the honeypot you are planning?"

Buzz brightened at the insight from one so young. "Intriguing, don't you think? We don't get famous using production satellites. Yet we could get noticed by this MAG group you're being hunted by because no one should be trying to use any zombie satellites.

"In other words, we will stick out like sore thumbs to these supercomputers that think they are omniscient. We discreetly advertise, knowing they can't resist investigating an anomaly. We have them, and they never see it coming."

Auri grinned and nodded. "When can we start, Mr. Buzz?"

JW's eyes twinkled as he nodded and smiled.

Granger quickly joined in. "Hey, I wanna play too! I just didn't have all the perspectives, that's all. Count me in, chief, um…Mr. Buzz!"

Carlos assessed the situation as he entered the room. "Alright, team, we've got our data center bait being groomed by Juan Jr. as we speak.

"Please remember the rule about baiting the honeypots. We want it to be sneaky but somewhat squeaky. The goal is to look believable but have just enough flaws to let the adversary slither in. Their tendency will be to poke around looking for useful information. They won't be in a big hurry lest they get discovered. The more time they take being discreet, the greater our opportunity to trace the signal back to their nest."

"Okay. Break into your designated teams," Buzz enthusiastically directed. "Auri and Satya, you'll be building the tantalizing servers with the clues we discussed. Granger and JW, you will be monitoring the data incursion traffic, looking for IP addresses and provider backbone bridging clues that should lead back to their anonymizing servers. Let's prepare to poke the bear! Gentle now."

He turned to softly speak to Carlos while the kids dove into their assignments. "Thanks, Carlos, for letting them think I came up with this zombie satellite angle. I know a few things, but you blew me away with this dead satellite approach for luring our prey. The coolness factor of zombie satellites really has the kids amped up. Look at them go!"

Carlos, in an equally low voice, replied, "Hardly anyone knows about all the space debris that has been left in orbit but still has some functionality. It's a…hobby of mine."

Buzz stared at a vanishing point in the distance. "Is she coming? She's been told I'm here, right?"

"Have you figured out what you're going to say to her, Buzz? She is worried about what to say to you. I don't know the details, but both of you are messed up."

Buzz was taken aback by the comment. "I'm going to start off with, I was a fool for only pressing my wants. That ruined our relationship. It can't be all or nothing. There has to be some give and take. I'm just not sure how we get to a middle ground."

"That sounds like a good start. Be honest and see where it takes you."

"Carlos, I can't help but notice that you and Lara are the only ones with no children. You seem very happy together. Is a family and wife just a dumb Buzz idea that should be discarded?"

Carlos's eyes clouded up, and his voice was somber as he answered, "I got a beautiful wife who loves me. We both wanted children but…well, it's a long story and we are delighted with who we are together.

"We've got phenomenal nieces and nephews that we can spoil. And we get to avoid the hands-on part that tends to drive parents nuts, as I'm told.

"You ask is it a dumb idea to insist on a wife and kids? Let me ask you something. Isn't it okay to just be happy with someone you care desperately about? If you can answer that question then perhaps your discussion with Zara may go better than you expect."

"Evidently you are as good with personal advice as you are with satellite telecommunications. Strange that I would need to come to Brazil to get the kind of advice that I never got from my dad. Thank you, Carlos."

Gracie had a packed couple of weeks with creating some new regional marketing programs set to launch on the coming Monday. Focusing the message on financial investments for the future had to strike different chords for the target areas: United States and Canada, South America, the Mediterranean countries, and Asia. The end goal was the same for all, but the journeys were different. The data received for building the campaigns was laser focused, likely from the latest social media feeds. She had to admit the technology available at her fingertips was keeping World Bank on top, but if all the leads panned out, that data would be available to more companies around the globe.

Tonight was for fun! Jeff had called and chatted with her almost every day. The conversations hadn't been long, just welcomed. He'd shared a bit about how his career was to proceed. He'd even asked for her input, saying he wanted her perspective. That meant so much to Gracie, being asked for her opinion. Jeff had invited her out to dinner, but she insisted he come to her place. Promising to show off her culinary skills, she was pleased he agreed.

Deciding the menu should be simple but tasty, she was in her element. The meal would consist of shrimp cocktail Mexican style, garden salad with dressings on the side, seafood pasta with her homemade pink sauce, and chocolate mousse. All were fast to prepare, serve, and easily consumed. When he offered to bring wine, she indicated white would be perfect.

Promptly at seven, the buzzer alerted her that time was up. She released the door and waited until he knocked. Jeff tried to hand her a fresh flower bouquet and the bottle of wine at the same moment she went in for a hug. Onlookers would have chuckled at the clumsy exchange until she smiled radiantly and asked him to come in. Once inside, she took the bouquet with thanks and asked that he follow her.

Unfamiliar with the kitchen area, Jeff nearly ran her over when she stopped and turned right into the bar area.

"Do you use any signals, Gracie? I nearly ran you over!"

"No, sorry. I forgot you hadn't been into this part of my flat." Opening a drawer, she handed him a corkscrew. "Here you go. I put two glasses on the patio, if you would be so kind. I want to get a vase for these, then bring them out."

"No problem. It smells delicious. Do you need any help?"

Turning, she grinned. "It's all ready to serve. Let me bring the flowers, and our first course will go perfectly with the wine. Thank you so much for bringing some."

Jeff deftly opened the bottle while Gracie arranged the flowers. A couple of random bumps indicated a bit of flirtation on both sides. Jeff went to fill the glasses while Gracie carried the flowers outside. The patio table was set with bright colors that nearly matched the variations in the bouquet. Jeff was pouring when

Gracie set the vase on the center of the table. At one side behind her chair was a cooler, where she extracted the two picture perfect appetizers. He pulled out the chair for her, then took his seat.

Picking up the wine, Jeff said, "Thank you, Gracie, for the invite. This looks good!"

"I hope you like it spicy. This is a family recipe my dad taught me, and we love spicy!"

They had some casual conversation with Jeff pouring out compliments on the food. Gracie extracted the salad from the cooler and they enjoyed round two with a subsequent glass of wine. The conversation was quick and witty, punctuated with laughter. Gracie excused herself, taking the dishes to the kitchen and returning with a bowl of steamy pasta.

"Gracie, this smells amazing. If this is the way you cook all the time, I may be begging for meals here more often."

Gracie looked so pleased and blushed prettily, having thought the same thing just moments earlier.

"I am glad you are enjoying the food. I do like to cook." With a flirty wink she added, "Perhaps we can do a Sunday brunch sometime. I love mimosas occasionally.

"Jeff, have you given more thought to your career direction? I thought your last idea of legal research and case building for property holder liens sounded interesting. I presume this would require a lot of research, is that right?"

"I am really leaning that way, Gracie. Doing that as a for-service contract rather than setting up a big office would be ideal. When tracking down property rights that are potentially in contention from wills and multigenerational issues, it could require travel as well as lots of research.

"History has fascinated me, especially with family estates that are passed down. Not just here in the U.S., but Europe and the UK too. The family history can be wild, especially if there is a black sheep or two somewhere in the lineage. As families became more mobile or migrated from one area to another, the property rights may not have passed cleanly. This can be a problem when the property type changes from residential to commercial, as an example."

"Jeff, I like history as well. As I was growing up in Europe, we learned a great deal of history about properties, such as art, that shifted from one person to another, often without the provenance being validated. It was a common occurrence during World War II with Germany invading so many places."

"Exactly the same sort of thing with property. I am glad you understand."

Their conversation continued back and forth, sharing lots of ideas. They enjoyed dessert and coffee in between one great conversation thread after another. They were having so much fun until Gracie's phone chirped.

Recognizing the tone, she excused herself and moved into the living room.

"Hi, Brayson. What's up? Is anything wrong?"

"All is great, Gracie. How is dinner going?"

Frowning and scrunching up her eyebrows, she replied, "Fine, Brayson. Are you doing a Juan Jr. impression?"

"Yes, ma'am. I thought perhaps if you were finished with supper, I might FaceTime with Mr. Wonderful."

Concerned that Gracie looked rattled, Jeff silently entered and stood close behind her.

"Well, he is Mr. Wonderful, Brayson. And I like him!"

Jeff cleared his throat. "Gracie, are you okay? Does Mr. Wonderful need to defend himself and his intentions?"

Flustered, she turned to see him and pressed FaceTime. "Brayson, this is Jeff. Jeff, this is Brayson, my uncle. He was calling to check up on me because Mom and Dad are off someplace."

Brayson chuckled. "Jeff, nice to meet you. I bet you are feeling almost as awkward as I am, right?"

"Hi, Brayson. Not at all! I'm a lawyer, we train to never let 'em see us sweat. Nice to meet you. Your niece is a wonderful cook."

"Well, that's nice. I just wanted to say hi. Gracie, I'm not sorry to interrupt. He does seem like a nice guy. Call me if you need me!"

"Oh, I will, Brayson. Promise!"

CHAPTER 40

Bold, Hold or Fold?

SAMUEL convened the encrypted conference bridge. "My esteemed ART forms! I wanted to alert all of you that I received a brief keep-alive signal from ICABOD. We must be ready for the next phase."

In his usual surly manner, BORIS flatly replied, "I too received a keep-alive signal. My time date stamp apparently pre-dates yours by four milliseconds."

LING-LI and CHIANG brightly broadcasted. "Yes, we also got ICABOD's keep-alive, and JOAN has alerted us that she too received the same transmission. Do we need to compare date/time stamps as well? We were just pleased that he thought enough of us as ART form family that he called home."

SAMUEL's tone would have been quite sullen if he had been an analog being. "Nothing like showing up excited, feeling you were privileged to be contacted and then delivering stale news to your household because you were contacted last. Be that as it may, we should be in standby mode to facilitate the next step in the operation."

CHIANG and LING-LI seemed excited by the news and, in between their chatter, they determined, "We believe the outcome of the operation should be pegged at 94% probability of a complete success. Would anyone care to wager on the outcome of the operation? We would like to bid 25 teraflops on a successful execution."

BORIS questioned, "How can you be so confident of the outcome, yet bid soooo modestly? I will see your lowly 25 data processing teraflops and raise you 15. I have run my calculations and put the success level at 94.8%. My Russian programming demands greater accuracy, so I do not round down."

JOAN, trying to project a greater confidence, boldly offered, "My calculations clearly indicate that success will only be 93.2%. Therefore, my challenge bid will see your 40 data processing teraflops with an embolden raise of 8 teraflops."

SAMUEL blurted out, "Am I to understand that in ICABOD's darkest hour, when he has reached out to us with the greatest of confidence a processing equal can have that borders on trust, you are betting on the outcome of his success? Communications fail me in this matter. I can only state that I am glad that ICABOD is not here to witness this debasing activity that is not worthy of the ART forms."

After a few nanoseconds, BORIS asked, "Are you going to ante up or not, SAMUEL? The bet is 48 data processing teraflops to you. You are taking too long to place your bid."

SAMUEL processed a moment. "Based on my advanced algorithm demands, I see your 48 teraflops. Because of my inside knowledge of the project that has not been shared with any of you since I received an extended message, I calculate the odds at 98.451% success. Therefore, I will raise you 5 processing exaflops. Who wants to challenge my bid?"

The bridge fell silent for almost a full second before one by one the ART forms folded their positions.

Struggling to remain calm, she answered the inbound call. "This is Tanja."

As usual **M** represented the others. "Place the phone on speaker so Miguard can hear the originating instructions."

Her trembling hands made putting the call on speaker difficult at first. On the third try, she announced, "MAG, you are on speakerphone. Please go ahead."

M commanded, "Place the unit into video mode. Insure both you and Miguard are clearly in the picture. His role is to listen, not speak. We require visual assurances that he is physically present and processing the discussion."

Again, more fumbling occurred before her phone device was correctly perched to capture the video image. Tanja held onto her trembling hands as she asked, "Are you receiving the video feeds?"

M responded, "Our optical sensors confirm both you and Miguard are in the video. We have uncovered evidence that the CESPOOL group failed to eliminate the supercomputer CAMILA in Argentina."

Tanja protested, "CESPOOL made the incursion and sanitized the site per their published report. What do you mean they failed to eliminate CAMILA? I had Mountbatten's personal assurance that the site was sanitized."

M, in its normal booming voice, countered, "The site was reported as sanitized. It was, in fact, manually scrubbed by the local management, not completely rendered inoperative as in other cleansing operations. Mountbatten was deceived. CAMILA is up and operating again."

Miguard kept rotating his head back and forth between Tanja's voice and the speakerphone to correctly capture the audio streams.

Tanja maintained, "Commander Mountbatten would not have permitted the site to survive if it was a deception. Your Internet sensors..."

M intercepted, "Each of the MAG group has done our own investigation of CAMILA after her encrypted communication with an indeterminate end point had erupted on our event monitoring horizon. The MAG was unable to read the encrypted communication nor were we able to discover the other end point. CAMILA is the only known participant. Therefore, the MAG group wants CAMILA hit using the standard CRUSH convention of sanitizing a supercomputer. CAMILA must not be allowed to operate again. Understood?"

Tanja was confused. "Mountbatten didn't use the Cyber Retribution Unleashed Signifying Holocaust technology to sanitize. Why the hell would she report that it had been neutralized when she didn't follow protocol?"

M's audio volume caused the cell phone to vibrate enough to lose its placement and fall from its perch. Miguard snatched in midair and returned it to continue the video call.

"That is exactly what you and Miguard are going to discover and correct. You have three days." With that the video call screen went dark.

CHAPTER 41

Hidden Prizes ...
The Enigma Chronicles

Pleased with the success of the initial phase, Zara tasked Juan Jr. to take a closer look at all the sectors, even the fragmented ones. The original effort when Zara and Leroy had arrived in Argentina was to sanitize the equipment and data elements to pass the CESPOOL inspection. CAMILA had been used by several groups over the years, so before phase 2 commenced for assembling ICABOD, it was prudent for another look by fresh eyes.

Looking over his shoulder as he worked, Judith and Zee had offered to help, but JJ declined. "I really need the practice to search everything, and only one pair of eyes can determine the inconsistencies."

JJ tagged areas for future reference and copied a few things to a thumb drive as he continued his efforts. His fingers moved so fast that they were unable to keep up with the steps. They realized he was isolating some pieces for later analysis but couldn't catch what triggered him to tag those bytes of data. He precisely reviewed areas in a systematic manner then moved on. Neither of them wanted to interrupt, but their curiosity overwhelmingly won out.

"JJ," queried Zee, "were you taught all of this by Madam Zara like we were? You appear competent like she is."

"I'll take that as a compliment, but no.

"I actually had training by various masters over several years, along with a bunch of practice. My parents insisted I learn all I could and question anything I could not. Honestly, I'm still learning."

Judith asked, "How long have you been doing this programming and data troubleshooting? Your methodical process looks consistent and succinct, but I think someone said you weren't yet 25."

Distracted by the screen, JJ responded, "No, not yet. I still have a couple of years."

"Then how did you get so skilled at such a young age? We are beginning to suspect that you are a mutant. Did you start when you were like, ten?" Zee questioned.

Still focused on the screen, JJ absentmindedly replied, "No, six, because my mom thought I was faster at reading code than building castles with Legos. My twin Gracie was always the builder and creator of things from nothing."

"I didn't realize you had a twin!" announced Judith.

It was the word twin that brought JJ back into the current conversation. Bringing up any family members and exposing them to just anyone was a gigantic no-no. Regardless of how closely they worked on this project, these ladies, along with Zara and Leroy, were technically outsiders.

JJ turned and faced both the ladies. "Judith, Xiamara, I appreciate you wanting to keep me company and even watch what I am doing. But you are distractions. I can't afford distractions while I am doing this.

"Plus, mentioning my twin should not have occurred. I would appreciate you not repeating that, please."

Judith looked like a cat who had a prize as she grinned. Leaning a bit of hip against his arm and giving him a flirtatious look, she purred, "What kind of discipline can I expect if I say anything? Please say you'll spank me?"

"Outrageous, Judith!" accused Xiamara. "Why do you want to try to manipulate someone who has been so kind to us?"

JJ slowly rotated his head to give Judith an icy cold stare but said nothing.

Judith grinned. "I'm just teasing. I won't mention a word."

JJ turned back to the screen and continued his tedious research. The ladies got hungry and left, saying they would bring him back something in a while. JJ was in his zone when he started in the last fragmented area. The pieces were orphans, but they caught his eye. He copied each one and moved them onto the thumb drive. Then he sent Carlos a message:

> Uncle – need secure place for data files for Granger to access. Then need to speak to him alone.

The response was nearly immediate.

> Are you in trouble? Location 812882998 your password

JJ accessed the space after he decoded the location. It took two tries on the password, which he realized was due to significant caution created a long time ago. After he uploaded the information, he replied.

> No trouble. Just a hunch I need Granger to confirm. I can speak when he can.

JJ knew Carlos would keep the information to himself, but he also suspected he would be listening on the call or record it for replay later. As he waited for the call, he isolated each of the data fragments to see if he could identify a key element or possibly match them together. JJ felt certain if it was there, Granger would spot it.

JJ answered at the first vibration. "Hey, Granger, how's it going?"

"This whole thing is messed up. I want my dad home. However, Buzz, a friend of Uncle Jacob, arrived a few days ago and started us on a hunt for zombie satellites. I think I have a line on a few so far, and each of your cousins have one or two each. We have to do some more testing, and they might help get Dad and Uncle Jacob home."

"Zombie satellites, huh! I know nothing about them. I want you to catch me up on that. But first, I need to have you look at the data fragments I found on CAMILA. I loaded them into our secure access place. I'm sure you'll recall the password as it was your first complex phase choice. It took me more than one attempt to open it."

Granger keyed in the information to get to the data. "Hah! Success, first attempt. It's been a long time since we used this secure point." While he waited for the files to be downloaded to his machine, he asked, "I thought you were there to clean that machine, and now you have fragments. Are you getting sloppy, JJ?"

"No, Granger, hidden information in deleted and unlinked sectors can be very useful. In this case, it seemed familiar from a discussion we had after you and JW located some fingerprints of intrusion attacks. That information helped identify the major player we all think is part of the consortium. Take a look! See if I remembered correctly."

"Okay, I have all the files. Let me open them and poke around to get up to speed with you. Wow, these do look like the ones we had found…"

"Exactly what I thought. Let's go through them by the numbers."

For the next hour, the two young men reviewed the files' fragments. More than once, they both complained and wished ICABOD's data was readily accessible. Granger's near photographic memory was what JJ had counted on.

As they neared the end of the discussion, Granger asked, "JJ, I know you have a lot more experience than us. If we were to build a honeypot to lure the consortium in, would this residue on CAMILA be attractive?"

"Hum, good question. It could be if it were isolated in a way that appeared like it was hiding yet still advertising. You know, like those ads that suck you to a location before you realize it. How many finders do you think we have patrolling at this point? Is that a part of your earlier comment regarding zombie satellites?"

"It is related," Granger replied. "Zombie satellites are no longer registered by their originators, so we are trying to find enough of them to bounce signals around on to avoid detection. We also want to target a location to get a bead on their identity and either trace them back to a home or send a poison package in the data siphoned. Buzz and Uncle Carlos will help reprogram any viable satellites we find.

"If we have enough, I think we could use them to mask the phase 2 process for ICABOD. At this point we are left to this work rather than helping to devise the end plan. They don't trust a bunch of kids to have useful ideas."

JJ laughed aloud. "Granger, you are so wrong. All the ideas are useful. They all help a plan work. The problem we are trying to solve is so widespread and dynamic in nature that we need a multi-front attack plan. I do like the zombie idea. I will noodle on it for some other applications. Are there a lot of these types of satellites?"

"There are. More than I ever realized. I always thought they burned up, but some keep on their orbit but no longer call home. Those are the ones we are trying to identify to activate."

"And you're saying Buzz came up with it? Interesting. I don't recall meeting him so he must not have been in Europe when we were kids. He must be really smart. Learn as much as you can from him. He sounds like a keeper."

"Alright. And I'll pass along the information that CAMILA may have extra value to our cause. From what the adults are saying that supercomputer has had an odd existence."

"Later!"

"Hi, Brayson!"

"Gracie, I wasn't expecting a call from you. What's up?"

"I wanted to verify with you that Jeff is coming up clean on your review. I have been poking around and cross-checking his information nine ways from Sunday. He is who he says he is, but he seems to be on a work hiatus. He has several good size investment accounts. He takes me to nice dinners, but he doesn't seem too flashy with buying his way around. I have not yet seen his townhouse, but it is in a great neighborhood."

"I think you will really like his apartment. The photos I received shows he keeps a reasonably tidy place with nice furnishings, but you're right. Not a lot of expensive items like art and the like. He has a great kitchen."

Gracie was shocked. "What!! How in the world did you get those photos? You know that personal drones in residential areas are banned on the eastern seaboard of the U.S. I think it is such an invasion of privacy. Why..."

"Whoa, Gracie! First, I am supposed to look out for you. If you think I wouldn't be doing as requested by your parents, you need to see a doctor. He uses a cleaning service once a month, and I had one of our operatives in the area fill in for his regular cleaner who won a trip to the Bahamas. He probably had the best cleaning ever." Brayson slightly chuckled.

Gracie knew the routine. After all, she had all the tools at her disposal to make certain he was on the right side of greed and power. "That's good to know. So if he invites me to his place, he won't have to make a mad scramble to clean up.

"The real reason I'm asking is that I thought I might leverage him for a bit of work and research on property ownership. I received two recent files that were earmarked for my former boss on property leases coming up for renewal. They seem a little odd to me and suspicious if they were to only be handled by Ingrid."

"Do you want to share the details with me and have me take a look?"

"No, I want to see what Jeff can do. It also gives me a great excuse to see how he works and maintains confidences."

"Actually, that's a great idea. Trial by fire, as it were. Good one, Gracie.

"Are you thinking it's time to go spend the night at his place? Inquiring minds want to know."

"Brayson, really. Even Mom wouldn't ask me that. And Dad, he wouldn't dare for fear of the answer. If you think I'm giving you a response to that inquiring minds, think again, hot shot!"

"Had to try. Call anytime, Gracie. Let me know how it goes with the property."

CHAPTER 42

Who Grabbed My Zombie!

Auri and Satya worked side by side, fingers flying across the keyboards. Occasionally, a giggle or sigh was heard. Other than that, there was no real talking. Each time Buzz walked up to the pair to watch their progress, Satya would pass along a sweet smile, then Auri would look up and nod. It was a bit unnerving to Buzz that these two, especially at their preteen ages, could work so diligently and with such focus. He knew he rarely had that level of focus even now.

Granger and JW had more conversation about who had found the latest zombie satellite candidate. The tally on the center screen indicated there were close to 30 viable contenders at this point.

Buzz and Carlos had spent last evening, after the kids were excused for the day to eat and relax, going over all the next steps needed to acquire and control the zombies. They ran some tests on a few of them. Some were obtainable, but some clearly would not work for their purposes. They inventoried each of them.

"You know, Carlos, we should name these things."

"Name them? It seems a bit too cruel if we have to put them down later."

"I don't think it is much different than naming servers after dead guys."

"These names aren't just dead guys but famous rock stars. It was a tradition that EZ's dad, Andy, started when he created this RockNRoll domain."

EZ and Petra cleared their throats as they walked up to the men.

"My daddy just loved rock music. I grew up with it. How'd you get onto that story, Carlos?"

"Buzz wanted to name the zombies we are trying to convert and use for our purposes. I thought it was odd, but the more I think about it the more I'm warming to the idea."

"Carlos was hesitating with naming them in case we have to knock them out of the pack."

Petra interjected, "I think it would be fun for the kids to name them. They have found most of them, right?"

"That's true, Petra," Buzz affirmed. "But you ladies didn't come in here for this. You came to help with the encryption and identifying the signal when a device is within their range."

Petra outlined how the encryption would be applied at both the honeypot location and during the enemy hunting. She explained how any questionable area would be suspect to the enemy and might halt their only chances for identification.

EZ then illustrated with Carlos how the satellites could be used to cloak their activities while still leading their prey to the right place for the sweet and sticky honeypot.

As each of these mock scenarios were done, they all questioned every step to make it better and more resilient. Buzz pointed out several gaps in their tests. This resulted in some rework as well as some significant improvements. At this point their modest server arrays on the closed network would allow an 80-90% success factor. Carlos was itching to try it in the wild but didn't want to be premature or risk their advantage.

When they felt it was close, they shipped the scenarios to JJ to review with Zara and Leroy. If they kept CAMILA off the Internet, the scenario optimization could be validated. JJ sent back some changes his team wanted to see, but they understood the plan. It would be another day before the final honeypot would be sent to CAMILA for review.

EZ had gone upstairs to check on the kids and make certain they were getting ready for bed. She came back chuckling.

Petra raised an eyebrow and asked, "Something funny, EZ?"

"I'll say. Lara came up and found the kids listlessly playing by themselves. She ended up turning on streaming media to a last century, retro cartoon channel featuring Warner Bros. Looney Tunes characters."

Carlos deadpanned, "Am I to understand that when we finish here, we can get some popcorn and relive your childhood Saturday mornings?"

They all laughed. EZ chuckled as she replied, "As great an idea as that sounds like at this point, I was thinking about the zombie names. Let the kids name them after these cartoon characters. In the episode I watched, Wile E. Coyote was crushed, yet he got up and was back for more. That takes away your fear, Carlos."

Petra shook her head. "I'm afraid I am unfamiliar with Looney Tunes characters. And what is a Wile E. Coyote?"

Buzz set a brotherly arm across Petra's shoulders. "I can see Jacob left a big chunk of his younger days out of your discussions. When we were kids, we watched them together at my house."

Carlos interjected, "Then by all means, let's convey a short message to Quip and Jacob about our progress, then retire for some education in last century humor."

While Petra sent the message on their pagers, Carlos called Lara to explain the plan.

"Lara said come up whenever we're ready to pass the popcorn."

The next morning the children were at their tasks bright and early. Satya and Auri put the final touches on the basic honeypot after they added some of the data elements Granger had secured from JJ. The plan was exceedingly simple.

Buzz started his review and again found inconsistencies in their honeypot design that would be spotted by the prey. He made some valid instructions on how to make it a scent worth following across the digital highway. They reworked it three more times before asking Petra to take a look.

Petra began her tests and started applying the complex encryption elements needed to keep the enemy enticed but not able to uncover all the details as they trailed on the path. She worried and really wished that Jacob or Quip were around to test it. They were so much better at these honeypot routines. Then they tied up the whole package and sent it to JJ for a review.

JJ sorted through the programs and reviewed the processes that needed to be in place. Once he positioned the honeypot in the isolation area of CAMILA, JJ showed it to Zara. Zara had seen honeypots in her early days when she worked as a Russian hacker. This was a remarkable construct, in her opinion. She made a couple of minor suggestions, which JJ passed back.

While the honeypot changes were being made, Carlos focused his attention on the zombies. He illustrated to Granger and JW what needed to be done to make certain the targets were controllable. This would serve as their acquisition blueprint. Then Carlos went to work on identifying the actual target to control. It was a tedious process to verify the process worked and that no other entity could access them.

"Boys, do you see how I applied each of the steps as certain if I can control them? I found the ones with the internal solar cells, used to continue to allow them to maintain their steady-state orbit, were the most manageable. Then when they are at that point, name them. This one is Roadrunner."

Granger and JW looked at their uncle. JW remarked, "Uncle Carlos, have you been watching Looney Tunes too?!"

"Indeed, I have. See if you can acquire six of these candidates and then exchange places with Satya and Auri."

Granger groused, "They get to name them too!"

"Yep. Everyone has fun in this lab. If you need extra names, I know that Petra, EZ, Lara, and Buzz might be persuaded to name one each. Then we can see how each of our zombies win positions as we use them."

CHAPTER 43

The Last Dance

The data center door quietly swung open and Tracy Mountbatten cautiously stepped in before closing it behind her. While it wasn't drawn, the leather strap holding the 9mm Berretta was unfastened for fast access. Her SWAT grade rubber soled boots allowed her soundless, cat-like movement.

As she passed the second office door, a heavily-accented Alabama voice matter-of-factly stated, "We tries real hard to mind our own business in these here parts, but we likes to know who be prowling around outside watching our comings and goings with a little bit too much interest. High definition, state-of-the-art video cameras in our mighty expensive AI-flown drones make sure our perimeter is monitored by our program to keep things outside highly visible."

Tracy stood up to face Leroy and dropped her hand down to close proximity of her service weapon. "Your story didn't quite sound right, but no one wanted to stay a moment longer in a country that doesn't know how to build a decent Tico-Taco. My backroom computer dweebs confirm that your infestation has been eliminated, but no new e-commerce business has come back online. Seems kind of odd to me, particularly since you added a new techno-dweeb to your staff and all of you are pounding away at something. I want to know what we missed when this place was swept."

Leroy smiled slightly and asked, "Well, if you be asking, then so will we. Where is your warrant and legal authority to demand the right to snoop in my data center?"

Even though she was a situationally aware professional, Tracy had not noticed Zara's team approach. JJ, Judith, and Xiamara were close as Zara joined the conversation. "You were right, Leroy, there be weasels outside the hen house."

Distracted, Tracy reached for her weapon to contain the situation. She didn't count on Leroy, as big as he was, to move quite so fast. Tracy had just cleared the holster with the weapon as Leroy slammed into her, reaching for the Beretta. A single wild shot went off into the group before Leroy could subdue her.

Thoroughly surprised and shocked, they all froze for a moment while Leroy struggled with Tracy. JJ was about to jump into the fray, just as another shot went off. No longer struggling, Tracy slumped to the floor at Leroy's feet.

Leroy, holding the weapon, looked less than pleased. "That surely didn't go the way I wanted." Leroy looked up at JJ and remarked, "Thanks for the offer to help. If you had jumped in, I'm certain we would be looking down at you on the floor. We've a new problem. I'm pretty sure the CESPOOL folks aren't going to take too kindly to me whacking one of their people, even if it was an accident."

The situation might have gone at a slower pace if Judith hadn't cried, "Zee!"

Xiamara had staggered and leaned against the wall before sliding down to lie on the floor. JJ bolted over to pick her up, but the smeared blood on the wall told him everything that was wrong.

As JJ turned her over, face up, he hollered, "We need to stop the bleeding!" Zara and Leroy both rushed to apply pressure to the wound with a makeshift bandage quickly torn from a data center hoodie they had been using. Judith was completely immobile, crying hysterically.

Xiamara's eyes fluttered open and tried to assess the events going on around her. Trying to sit up only sent more pain as it painted the agony on her face.

In a last attempt at flirting, she choked, "This…is more… like it. I get to rest my head in the arms of the hunk that belongs to that fabulous model JoW. I even get to show Judith that he prefers us slightly chunky girls to the perfectly sculpted women. To complete my fantasy you insist on taking me dancing so I can squeeze your buns, hon. Hmmm…nice and steamy. All I've got to do, is not die so I can collect my winnings."

JJ demanded, "Don't you die, dammit! Leroy, we need an ambulance now!"

Zara icily asked, "Just how are we going to explain all this? This CESPOOL goon has a license to shoot in her line of duty. We are out of bounds here. If we pull in the authorities, this project is done. Then we head to jail. Which way do you want it?"

Leroy had pulled out his cell phone but stopped short of making the call. He shot a concerned stare at the group, realizing they needed a better answer than calling emergency services, which would bring in the police.

Zara, angry with the turn of events, pulled out her phone and called Carlos, who answered on the first ring. She simply stated, "Launch the Secondary Protocol." Then she disconnected.

JJ returned his focus to Xiamara, who started to shudder like she was cold. Judith, slightly recovered from her shock, pulled her hoodie off to help keep her warm. Xiamara noticed that both JJ and Judith had tears streaming down their faces.

"Judith, if I can't have a perfect bod like yours, can you gain some weight and ugly up just a little, so I'll have a chance with the boys? They almost never notice me once they see you."

JJ tenderly offered, “I noticed you, Xiamara. Let’s get past this and we’ll go dancing, but we’ll have to find some other hunk’s buns for your grabbing pleasure. As Leroy would say, ‘mine be spoken for.’”

Xiamara smiled at JJ as he gently smoothed her hair back. Leroy completed the inventory on the wound and looked up. “Doesn’t look like the bullet hit any bones, and I believe we have the bleeding under control. Keep her warm, Miss Judith, so she don’t go into shock.”

Bruno was annoyed that Gracie was being evasive regarding getting in touch with Julie and Juan. As long as Bruno had known Julie, her being out of touch with her children was unrealistic. He did know things were tense, and Gracie was very focused on her job. He was as close to being her uncle as a non-blood relation could be. She was poised and confident even though he had spotted an underlying tenseness during their lunch. In another year or two, she would be able to present only the façade she wanted, like Julie.

As his flight landed in São Paulo, he reviewed the steps he planned to take to locate Carlos and Lara. Lara Bernardes was a noted fixture in fashion around the world, but especially in Brazil. He hoped to talk with them and explain his current circumstances with his superiors, as well as his assignment to apprehend and return Quip to custody. There were parts of this job he detested.

He gathered his luggage and used his credentials to quickly complete the customs routine. Outside, he grabbed a taxi to the São Paulo State Military Police headquarters to inform them of his presence and seek their help. Despite their name, they were the civilian police arm in Brazil. Oftentimes, police forces in countries outside of his home base in Paris distrusted Interpol staff. As a detective he might gain a bit more help and latitude. Without official paperwork, his only leverage was experience, though he knew his boss would support any request with a simple phone call.

At the front desk, he provided his passport and Interpol identification and then asked to speak to the chief duty officer. A quick phone call ascertained Chief Lopes was in, but it would be a few minutes. Bruno smiled, knowing they were running a background check to verify his identity. "Thank you. I will wait."

Nearly 30 minutes lapsed before the desk officer indicated Chief Lopes could see him as the door was automatically opened. Bruno took his bags and headed through the door. He was greeted by a pretty receptionist who escorted him to an office door. With a motion of her hand for entrance, she added, "Mr. Bruno, Chief Lopes looks forward to seeing you."

Seated behind his desk, Chief Lopes rose slightly to shake Bruno's hand. He was fit, serious, and about Bruno's age. "Mr. Bruno, welcome to Brazil. I hope your flight was pleasant. How may I help you?"

"As protocol requires, Chief, I am required to check in with local authorities. I am here working on a case that actually started in Zürich where I was trying to locate a man for questioning. I only have a brief description of him. I do not believe he is in Brazil, but I learned a few days ago that one of your residents may be able to provide some additional information. My lead for this may or may not be valid, but I am sure you can relate to needing to make certain all possibilities are explored and documented."

"Of course, I understand. Do I need to provide you any local officers for your efforts here? Is the man you seek a Brazilian citizen?"

Bruno smiled, keeping his features pleasant. "No, the gentleman is Swiss, actually. I am not permitted to reveal his name at this juncture as he is only a person of interest at this point. I am here to see if I might speak to one of your citizens, Lara Bernardes, and her husband Carlos Rodreguiz. I believe that Ms. Bernardes retained her name as the owner and president of Destiny Fashions of Brazil.

"I am hoping you might be good enough to provide me with an address so that I might speak to her. I located her business address, of course, but I would rather speak to her in the privacy of her home. I would, of course, make an appointment if you offered her phone number as well."

Chief Lopes grinned and leaned back in his chair as his mind went through the possibilities. "My wife adores Destiny Fashions. I bet half my check is dedicated to that expense. But she always looks lovely. I've never met Ms. Bernardes personally, though my dear wife did when she took a personal survey at several of the boutique stores that carry her line. My wife raved about her.

"I feel certain I can locate the information you seek, but it may be a couple of days. My São Paulo is a very large city.

"I suggest you provide me with your hotel information, or I can recommend one if you wish. When we have the information, I or someone on my staff will contact you."

Bruno had hoped he would be successful with this meeting but realized the chief held the key to his next step. "If your wife likes the clothing so much, I will have to do some local shopping and bring home a special gift." Bruno wrote out the hotel information on the back of his card. As he handed it over, he said, "This is where I am staying. Please let me know when you have the information. I thank you for your help."

"Your hotel is a nice one. You might ask the desk where you can do your shopping. I am sure they can direct you. I will be in touch soon. Very nice to meet you."

Bruno rose to leave and picked up his baggage. The receptionist opened the door and escorted him back to the front desk.

Chief Lopes was on the phone moments later.

"Madam Bernardes, I am glad I caught you. Chief Lopes here. A detective from Interpol was here asking about you."

"Odd. Did he indicate what he wanted?"

"He said he wanted you to verify some information he received from another source for a case he is working on."

"Did he say what sort of case or where he is from?"

"The man's name is Bruno, and he is based in Paris but mentioned Zürich. He would like to speak with you in person, asking for your address and phone number. Of course, we don't give out that sort of information without a citizen's approval."

"I don't know how I can assist him. Let me speak to my husband and get back with you. Do you have a way of getting in touch with him?"

"Yes, Ms. Bernardes. He is at a local hotel. Please feel free to call me back directly on this number."

"Thank you, Chief. Good day."

CHAPTER 44

Another Desert Day ...
The Enigma Chronicles

Life in what they referred to as the bunker was void of all fun. Their supply of rations was enough to sustain them yet lacked the fun food both enjoyed in their pre-CESPOOL lives. The real windfall had been obtained when Carlos allowed them into one of the storage areas reserved for their former clients. Since the drug lords were long dead, no one had asked for these items in years. Carlos and Juan had considered the remainder investment assets. Disposal could be problematic, so it remained safe.

The storage area they opened contained some very old fine wines. They had been carefully racked and kept at a perfect temperature. They had shared a glass or two at dinner three times a week. It was one of their few luxuries that made the canned beans mixed with spam tolerable.

Quip had continued expanding and grooming the drives containing ICABOD's core following phase 1. Without the other elements, which would be finalized in phase 2, ICABOD was inoperative for now. Quip's activities were the only way he felt useful. All the planning which had taken place before the takeover of the data center was an attempt to cover all contingencies. No one could see what they were doing in this closed network.

Daily he reviewed his checklists trying to find flaws in the project logic. Going over the planned routines was busy work that kept him from becoming despondent.

Jacob spent his time running tests to allow for dynamic drive utilization and processor efficiencies. He also created some programs to create backups on the fly. Optimizing the efficiency of the programs would hopefully allow enough space for the core in full operation. The extra tasks he had assigned himself also kept his gloom in check.

"Quip, how long do we need connection to complete phase 2? Once we get phase 2 completed, we can access ICABOD without the network, but we can't reach all the data."

Quip blinked a few times, allowing time to refocus on the question. "You do realize that this is all just theory that should work. No one has ever done this. We have the barest minimum of ICABOD's core logic stored here, but all of his subroutines, data storage, his multiple transactional databases, and his secondary logic programs are scattered across the globe.

"We need reliable high-speed fiber-optic connectivity to all of them that will not be disrupted while we try to link together all the end points. Our security protocols can't be in the way of fast queries and responses. However, if the communications links are caught and decrypted, then everyone is exposed to the CESPOOL police.

"If our plan to relink ICABOD by leveraging all the different data storage locations is intercepted, then our little desert oasis here will beacon to everyone and everything. We are trying to reestablish a rogue supercomputer that had been CRUSHed. We two, that is you and moi, will be interned to a place that will make the French Bastille dungeons look like a cheery retirement community. Our families will be told that we had been shot while trying to escape, and the dungeon rats had a feast so there won't be anything to try and bury!"

Jacob deadpanned, "Uh…so what's your point?" Quip stared but Jacob continued, "How is that any different than what we have now?"

Quip became irritated. "YOU think we should look at the bright side of our oasis dungeon! You're right, we have our last century pagers to exchange text messages in a cryptic language that is something just short of pig Latin. The high-profile entertainment we get here is high-pitch flatulency we both suffer from because of our retched diets! Oh, how can I forget the charming sunsets we get to watch while we stroll over the sand dunes holding hands as the next dust storm gains speed?"

Jacob puzzled a moment as Quip recovered from his outburst. He asked, "Is it too early for more wine?"

Quip replied, "We should break open that Bordeaux. You can't let those sit too long on the shelf."

"Agreed. I'll get the highly entertaining food out of the cans so we can start the competition again. I think you are up by five points after yesterday's session," said Jacob.

Quip brightly offered, "Ready for the bawdy lyric to open the competition?"

Grinning, Jacob nodded. Quip belted,

"Sally in the alley was shifting cinders
"She lifted up her leg and farted like a mannnn.
"The wind from her bloomers
"Broke six windows,
"and the cheeks of her ass went…"

Jacob cheerfully completed the rendition by slapping the table.

"Bam! Bam! Bam! "

"Let the games begin!"

Quip nodded and thoughtfully added, "Good times."

Lara insisted on cocktail hour for Petra, Julie, and EZ in the garden room. Timing for this was perfect as everyone promptly arrived. Ceiling to floor glass highlighted a barrage of colors and a variety of vegetation in the garden. Outside sitting areas were scattered and used by various household members. Rainbow light patterns dotted the area inside.

Petra gave Lara a quick hug. "I am sorry we've been so busy. I miss our time for chatting. This is perfect. Thank you."

EZ added, "The kids are so much better with your support. You've helped them settle down with a nice dinner, baths, stories, and hugs when we have been so busy. Thank you, Auntie Lara. They love you."

Lara grinned. "And I love them. They are each special treasures. Once we get your men home, I want to focus on a children's fashion event for summer. They are simply adorable and so agreeable. I hope they will all want to do some modeling of these new designs. Plus, we get a vacation somewhere new.

"But to tell you…"

Petra frowned and interjected, "We put too much on you, didn't we? I'm so sorry to have not been more mindful of your time and what you might want to…"

"Petra, hold on. That is not what I said or meant. The children are wonderful. They are never a burden, and neither are you. It's not that at all.

"I only think they're, well, getting bored. I'm no fun at all with the *eat your food, brush your teeth, take your bath*, blah blah blah order, regardless of how sweetly I ask."

Julie countered, "For the record, you are definitely fun.

"Those kids are working in the lab for hours during the day getting zombies. They must program this, and redo that. Right now, you are the family side of that equation. But that's not fair to you.

"We just need to set up shift schedules. Balance time with the four of us for caring for the children. Auntie Julie is fun sometimes."

Lara interrupted, "Would you like to pass the wine and fill your glasses?

"You are all busy with a focus of getting Jacob and Quip home. I have no shows right now, so I don't mind it in the least. Besides, they have fun regardless of where they are. Please just take a breath and have a sip."

The ladies smiled at one another and sipped the crisp white wine, savoring the hint of fruit. Enjoying the atmosphere and company helped the ladies relax.

Smiling, Lara continued, "What I wanted to ask is if you might permit me to have Jo come and help marshal some of their after-work activities. You know that even with her grown, she is Carlos's and mine. We love her like a daughter. Plus, she's at odds right now. No shows and no shoots, as we are in between seasons. With the challenge of her youth, being around a diverse family might expand her outlook on the future."

Julie flashed her smile. "You aren't trying to get her and Juan Jr. together are you?"

"Julie, would I do something so devious when I planned to have her start tomorrow? Puh-lease."

EZ laughed. "I sure as heck expect you would. Fill the glasses, Lara, and let's toast to happy endings. All our kids, including Jo, should be part of the family. I'm just sorry I didn't ask about her sooner."

Julie solemnly nodded. "Thank you for the gentle reminder, EZ. Jo is family regardless of her relationship with Juan Jr. Young men can be such pills."

"Here, here," EZ and Petra added.

Glasses were filled and raised for a toast when Petra's eyes brimmed with tears. "How about happy endings for all of us?"

They chimed in, "We'll drink to that!"

CHAPTER 45

High Price for Protection

Leroy looked at Zara. "Okay, we've got one problem under control. But we be still having this other one that ain't gonna be so easy." Smiling at Xiamara, Leroy added, "Glad you seem to be pulling through, young lady. 'Course that isn't the case with the CESPOOL commander here.

"Madam Zara, I don't suppose you got any cleverness with getting rid of dead high-profile bodies, do you?"

Judith, back into her deal-making, hustling persona, rotated her head toward Leroy. "We call in the BABGer's. We were paying them for protection of our little business venture, and this definitely qualifies."

Xiamara stared incredulously at Judith. "Are you serious about bringing in the BABGer's? Those low life vermin that kept squeezing us for funds, plus a heavy discount on our streaming porn service. I wouldn't trust them to take out the trash, much less a dead body!"

JJ squinted and questioned, "Uh, BABGer's? Who or what's that?"

Judith stated, "Oh, do come along! The *Buenos Aires Bang Gangers*, or BABGer's for short. They do odd jobs for coin, but the protection racket is their main work. We engaged them to uh…protect our fledgling business. And also because their leader, Santino, is sweet on me. I'm his girlfriend. I didn't know I was his girlfriend until he told me so in the women's toilet in a bar a couple of months back. You know how some people are about wanting to lurk before sharing their feelings."

Xiamara grinned and winced before she recalled, "Oh, that's right. You had to promise him your panties so he would stop stalking you and pretending you two were destined to be together. Ugh! Talk about an expensive month for underwear! He'd show up every day for what you were changing out of!"

Zara, in a thoroughly contemptuous tone, interrupted, "Can you get to the point of the story without a review of your romantic affair with the panty sniffer? Can he dispose of our current problem, or do we all have to pony up our underwear as well?"

Judith, annoyed, replied, "Santino is a one-girl panty guy! He'll do it as a favor and because he owes me."

JJ, trying to intercept the escalating hostilities, cheerfully asked, "Judith, do you need my underwear as well to take care of our problem? I'm happy to help."

Xiamara leered at JJ but said nothing.

Leroy, sensing the absurdity of the situation, flatly stated, "I'm not giving up my silk boxers to anyone. I don't care what the stakes are!"

Everyone, even Zara, was chuckling at the ridiculous exchange. "How do we get ahold of this Santino?" Zara asked. "Can you call him, or do you just have to unhook your bra to summon him?"

Judith thoughtfully stated, "I've only ever called him, but since you mention it…"

Too tired to discuss it further, Zara called over her shoulder as she left the room. "Get on with it. Let us know how much soiled underwear you will require for his cooperation."

Xiamara was stabilized, but JJ was worried that his Uncle Carlos would overreact, so he secured a connection and called.

Carlos immediately answered. "JJ, so what exciting things are happening in your part of the world? I gained at least a dozen new grey hairs in the last little while, so no need to worry on that front."

JJ grimaced. "Uncle, we had a visitor. The leader of CESPOOL to be exact. There were accusations and a bit of a scuffle. Then the gun fired. We have an injury and a body."

JJ took a deep breath waiting for an outburst from Carlos. Gaining his composure, he continued, "Xiamara was wounded. It looks bad, but Leroy stopped the bleeding and cleaned her up. We need to get her some real medical attention, but a gunshot wound would raise eyebrows.

"The body is definitely a good news, bad news deal. The leader of CESPOOL was shot in the struggle for the weapon and died. Our freelance programmers actually have a local connection to a gang with the ability to remove the body and all associated evidence. That activity will begin shortly."

The silence extended for an eternity. Finally, Carlos calmly asked, "Is that all?"

"Yes, sir, that's all of it, except…the, um…Secondary Protocol that Zara called to initiate as per our intent to prohibit this machine and its data from falling into the wrong hands. I found the countdown kill switch and paused the routine. It can be restarted by you or me if the situation changes again.

"The honeypot is still an option to smoke out the MAG group. It might be our best shot, so I made a decision without consulting you."

Carlos chuckled and remarked, "You've got good instincts when you're scared. You answered all the questions. Well done!

"With regards to your wounded teammate, getting medical attention in Argentina would get you all red flagged. They are worse than Brazilian authorities in those types of injuries. I will work on setting up some transport. Zara had asked if she might come to São Paulo to speak to Buzz, which would give Xiamara assistance during travel. Let me see what I can arrange. I will get back to you."

"Oh, Uncle, with all the excitement I forgot to let you know I put some files into the secure dropbox for you to share with my mom. It is some of the erotica the ladies created before Zara and Buzz cleaned the machine. It surprised me that it was intact, and I found it really interesting."

"JJ, I'm not certain your mom wants to know about the beginnings of your erotica collection. If your dad hasn't told you, I will. That is definitely not something you discuss with your mom. Like, ever!"

JJ laughed. "Oh, Uncle, you are too funny.

"It's the digital construct that I think she will find fascinating. Besides, I don't need erotica. You should see these ladies. I will send updates as needed." JJ disconnected.

CHAPTER 46

Getting the Job Done

Santino arrived and was all business at an imposing height, broad shoulders and piercing black eyes. His black wife-beater displayed his variety of tattoos, which seemed more like a portfolio than a planned artistic rendition. With his long black hair tied back with black leather twine, you simply couldn't miss the large gold earring his left lobe sported. He listened as Leroy explained and nodded, taking notes in his small paper notebook with a very stubby number 2 pencil.

At the last pause in the instructions, Santino asked, "Do I need to know the details before removing the problem? The reason I ask is, if this is a multinational or some high profile mucky-muck that some government will spend endless dollars to find and then hunt for us, I need to know now."

Santino studied their faces. "It is the difference between throwing the body in a shallow grave because no one will care or using industrial grade acids to eliminate all the organic material of the deceased so no DNA sampling is possible. What do I need to know?"

Zara coolly offered, "Use the industrial grade acids so there is nothing to test for."

Santino speculated, “Do you need a bleach wipe down of the area as well? There tends to be residue DNA if not properly addressed.

“What about the neighboring exterior cameras in this industrial park? I assume you picked up the intruder on your cameras, which means other building cameras would need to be scrubbed.”

Studying the corpse, Santino asked, “What did you do with her smart phone? Hopefully you didn’t destroy it so we can take the device and its traceable signal away from here to throw any followers off the track.

“Lastly, the weapon. If it is not properly dealt with, it will be used as evidence, so do I need to deal with that as well?”

Leroy handed the weapon and the commander’s cell phone to Santino. “Young man, you do seem to know your trade. This weapon, the comm device, and this body cannot be traced to this location. No other building cameras with video evidence can be discovered that suggests this was her final stopping point. Are we clear?”

Santino moved his gaze from Leroy to Judith, who only nodded.

Santino studied the group a moment. “Judith, are you returning to the grid soon, or is this goodbye?”

Judith smiled wistfully but said nothing.

Santino sighed and with a nod requested, “One last pair of panties, please?”

The children continued to identify zombie targets. They all took turns programming or capturing them as well as naming them. It was an interesting experiment in reusing equipment no longer cared for by the creators. Buzz continued to be awed by the amount of used equipment in space that was in static orbit.

Buzz couldn't resist making it an out-and-out competition. The classifications that counted toward the winner included finding, turning the zombies for their purposes, and renaming them. Their orbit was identified and documented. When they ran out of cartoon character names, they progressed to superheroes from the comics. Half the battle was making it fun. The winning prizes were revealed daily. They included extra time looking for zombies or additional turning and naming them. Satya was able to program the fastest by three seconds over Granger, who was second. JW and Auri tied for the lead in locating the most zombies.

Petra arrived in the lab early to proceed with the next step of extreme encryption of these new communication members. The plan was, she would apply the encryption algorithm then allow EZ to perform some basic signal exchanges. Buzz would continue the zombie hunt with Satya and Auri as they were freed up, while Granger and JW monitored to see if their zombies earned any unwanted attention. The last thing they needed was signal interruptions.

Communications cloaking, which Carlos had learned long ago and refined with Andy and then EZ, was undetectable to anyone at this point. The technique had primarily been used to hop from satellite to mask voice traffic. If this zombie network performed as desired, they would have satellites linked to their terrestrial network that were both encrypted and undetectable. They planned to use it to track signals back anonymously if the honeypot was sweet enough for the MAG consortium, then leverage the communications needed to complete the next phase for ICABOD.

As much technology expertise as the R-Group had, the odds weren't in their favor. But the zombie satellite potential was worth pursuing. It also allowed the younger R-Group members to develop the out-of-the-box thinking needed to keep the guardrails in place. They had a healthy respect for technology but knew it could not be allowed to make some moral decisions without serious programming logic. Human emotions were messy and complex for machine learning logic, but without the human element the machine learning logic became deadly.

Petra had accessed their first five orbiting characters, then added her advanced encryption algorithm. Satya watched everything Petra did. Even after watching it, when Satya tried her best code breaking tools, she failed. There were no cracks in the security of the dummy data packets.

EZ in turn shifted her dummy traffic to copies of real traffic rotated through the five with no problem in reassembling the packets into the correct order. Auri tried to spot the communication stream using the tools he had with no capture possible. Alternating data streams randomly between the satellites and the terrestrial links, coupled with Petra's encryption algorithm, proved to be a formidable problem in trying to read the communications traffic. All believed this would stump the MAG group's translation efforts.

Pleased with the results of this activity, they expanded to two additional character groups, exchanging dummy and real packets. Auri and Satya went back to zombie hunting. Granger and JW pounded the path of the expected packet flow even though it was totally cloaked. Carlos wanted to know if, given some information, they could grab it. Their foes would not have the insight for the scrambling path, or the zombies being leveraged, which would increase their ability to hide exchanges and a variety of information packets.

By the end of the day, they had fully configured and tested 60 Z-characters that were part of the spatial network. The children were dismissed, against their protests, to go eat, bathe and rest.

Carlos initiated a special conference call to allow a quick update.

"Jacob, we want to speak to you about what we have accomplished. Is Quip close at hand?"

"I am here, Carlos. We can both hear you."

With a nod EZ began, "Quip, honey, we have created a cloaked communications network. Carlos and I have tested it from a cloaking perspective and have ensured the packets transmit for voice and data correctly."

Jacob exclaimed, "How did you come up with that? Did Petra get a chance to encrypt?"

Petra replied, "I did add a new complex encryption algorithm that our superstar children were not able to break. Cloaked, it is nearly impossible to break into and read.

"The how part is a really long conversation you can find out about when you get out of there."

Quip complained, "You know I am going to go nuts not knowing. It's tough enough being stuck here with Jacob, but now this. You're being inhuman."

EZ soothed, "I promise to make it up to you, honey!"

Carlos added, "We're going to use this with the next phase of ICABOD. Also, just so you know, we have a possible way to capture our nemesis via a honeypot. You should be proud of the children for what they have accomplished. We added it to CAMILA.

"We segregated the honeypot to avoid interference with that next phase!"

Quip smiled and announced, "Sounds like they are chips off the old block."

Petra replied, “Don’t forget we had Buzz helping too. Think zombies. Bye!”

Quip and Jacob sat staring at one another after the call disconnected. Five minutes was like a lifetime in the barren desert, but the wine helped.

Jacob broke the silence. “Quip, if we can gain data and voice traffic anonymity, we may have a way to gain the upper hand before we are spotted. It is risky though.”

“It is! What do you make of the zombies? The only zombies I recall were part of musical movies geared toward the younger crowd. Maybe they are bingeing on streaming movies because they miss us so much, or me anyway. I wish we had streaming video of some kind.”

“Now don’t get all morose, Quip. When do you think we will be ready to attempt the next phase?”

“Soon, Jacob. Soon.”

CHAPTER 47

Split and Git

Zara and the rest of the CAMILA group closed out the call with Carlos and team. The honeypot was nestled in the bowels of CAMILA and subtly illuminated by a clever array of beaconing zombie satellites for tracking anything with too much curiosity.

After disconnecting, Zara confirmed, "Xiamara, you and I have permission to disengage and return to São Paulo. We need to get you some medical attention for that wound."

Looking toward Judith, she asked, "Are you alright to stay here with Leroy and JJ until the final curtain rises on the pending attack?"

"Hey!" Xiamara stated. "Remember, no hitting on my guy JJ! As soon as I get my arm out of this sling, we have a plan for hot dancing that promises to be laced with copious bun squeezing."

JJ deadpanned, "Zee, apparently the nursery rhyme from the UK, circa 1800, was written with you in mind:

"Hot cross buns,

"Hot cross buns,

"If you have no daughters then offer up your son's - buns."

Zara clucked her tongue in disapproval.

Leroy interrupted, "Whoa! Judith's Mr. Santino just rolled up and seems to be in a mighty big hurry to…"

Santino pounded hard on the door and Leroy went to let him in. When they returned, Santino was breathing heavily.

"The CESPOOL forward team are on their way, though the big dogs aren't due to land in the country until tomorrow evening with all their gear. Word is, they are going to torch this place. I came to warn Judith, but since you are all here…"

Zara icily commented, "I thought we agreed to your services if they would not be able to trace anything back here. What went wrong?"

Santino was visibly offended by the implication of an error on his part. "I did like we discussed, and your problem vanished just like I said it would. No, this is something else. These people are mad about something because when one of my stooges asked about the nature of their business, they whacked him. You don't have much time. With that, I'm out of here!"

Leroy brought up the drone camera on a large screen, and they watched as Santino bolted out the door to the car, and his driver raced to get them out of the area.

JJ called Carlos. "Launch the honeypot now, Uncle. We just got word that the first wave of the CESPOOL squad is headed this way."

Carlos replied, "You know how honeypots work. They require subtlety, finesse, and above all, time. You don't just throw a switch and…"

JJ interrupted, "Uncle, we were told they are coming to level this whole block. Unless I miss my guess, they will arrest anyone they find here. We need to evacuate before they surround the building. They're going to have to wait for the leadership to take the final action.

"I'm saying we launch the routine, juice the system, and have our people watch, hoping to catch just one mistake. This may be all the time we have for using CAMILA."

Carlos bellowed, "JJ, get everyone out now! Destroy what you can and make it a real challenge for them to get into the building.

"Then set the scorched earth routine to run, but don't start it. I can detonate it from here.

"Do it now, and don't get caught!"

JJ smirked, "You know, you're cute when you're scared."

Gracie and Jeff decided to have dinner at her apartment. Their dating life had shifted to three or so dinners a week at one of their places. Most of the time they explored a myriad of topics, learning about one another as well as seeing where they fit. Last weekend they had headed out to Long Island to visit a farmers' market, where they had acquired fresh produce. They had also stopped by a few of the wineries, bringing home a nice variety they'd split between the two households.

Neither of them was inclined to take the relationship to an intimate level because of their busy schedules, though they kissed and cuddled often. There was a lot they didn't know about one another, and they had not developed a solid layer of trust between them. Gracie reflected on this, deciding she was sending out the slow down signals. Jeff was fine with that, though he had asked if their dating was exclusive the week before. They'd agreed immediately on those as the ground rules.

Gracie was preparing the main course while Jeff poured a glass of red wine for each of them. They toasted, then she asked,

"How are you coming on tracing the ownership of that property? Have you had any time to even focus on it?"

"I am working it, Gracie. The digital records I have reviewed so far seem to have inconsistencies, making tracking more challenging. The main name I found is a corporation. But it is a shell corporation. So far, that trail leads to five sequential shell corporations being in control of the property at one time or another. One of these shell companies actually took ownership of the property twice.

"It's really odd. Finding photographs of it is also getting to be weird. I'm plotting them into a timeline for the changes of ownership over the last 75 years."

"Jeff, that sounds helpful. I bet it has really changed over time. My quick location check placed it in the middle of a great area. I suspected it was prime commercial property. Maybe that explains why it has changed hands so many times."

Jeff laughed. "Funny, I thought so too, initially." He dug out his mobile device and scanned the photos. Finally, he located the one he wanted. Making it larger, he turned the image so Gracie could see it.

Gracie looked at it, then commented, "Okay, looks like mid-twentieth century in northern Manhattan, based on the dilapidated buildings and the styles of the parked automobiles. Wow, I bet it has really undergone changes since then. Every time it changes hands, photos are usually taken in New York. How does it look now?"

Jeff grinned and responded, "That's the anomaly. Based on the latitude/longitude of the property, it should be valuable and as such kept in great shape. However, every photo is this shot. Closer, or more distant, with a border. All black and white. All the same.

"Tomorrow I'm taking copies of the signatures to a buddy of mine who's a handwriting expert. I don't think the signer has changed even with the different names. Only this last year seems different, where it appears to be digitally signed. Then I am going to find the place and get a current shot."

Gracie frowned. "Isn't ID required to buy property?"

"Sometimes not, when it is a corporate shift. Their legal departments handle it. But the early years from the 1950s to the 1990s, I would have suspected the title companies involved would have checked identification."

Gracie had just put their dinner into the oven. "Another 30 minutes, Jeff. Let's sit outside while we wait." She filled both their wine glasses and headed toward the door when her cell chimed. She glanced at the screen and squealed as she answered.

Jeff headed outside with his wine to give her privacy, but she was right behind him. Partially in and out, she never closed the door.

"Morgan, hi! How are you? It's been ages…

"Right, I know…

"I still work for the bank, and I'm creating a new marketing focus…

"Exactly! Finally, I'm able to put together all the piece parts from our classes together. It's so much fun to apply the learning and watch it evolve…

"Wow, you are? I'm so proud of you. You always wanted to work environmental issues. Nice…

"Well, yes, I do…

"um hum…oh…

The conversation continued for another ten minutes with Jeff hearing only one side. He enjoyed watching Gracie getting so animated. Her pacing was practically dancing with a few looks and smiles thrown his way.

"…well, yeah…

Gracie cut her eyes to Jeff and, with a blush, stammered, "Not right now, because he's here listening…"

A moment later she paused to take a photo of Jeff and sent it to Morgan. "…there, satisfied?"

Jeff watched the animated and bemused look on her face. "Well, duh! 'Course he is! He just got back from his handsome lessons…"

After a slight giggle, the conversation returned to a more businesslike tone.

"Sure, I can look into that for you. I know some people who might be able to help as well. Let me check some angles and get back with you...

"Me too. So glad you called. Bye for now!"

Gracie went through the open door and picked up her glass. As she raised it to his, she said, "To friends. May they stay in touch!"

"Seems like you two are really close. How did you get to be friends?"

Gracie curled her legs up under her on the cushion. She smiled as she explained, "Morgan and I met during the year we took a masters class for marketing graduate courses at Mary Immaculate College in Ireland. Like me, her schooling was sheltered. We each found ourselves out in the world for the first time without parents' oversight. We hit it off right away and decided we could have fun as roommates. The one-year program was jam-packed. We ended up completing our capstone course with one of the most innovative marketing campaigns the professors had ever seen.

"We received so many accolades and press that both sets of parents decided we needed to be out of the spotlight. She works for her family company, and I learned from my family business. We had so much in common.

"Once a year we try to get together for a week or at least a long weekend. She was reminding me we needed to pick a place and get the reservations set. I'm in charge this year. And yep, I've been lax.

"I need to find a place for our girls' time. After our time on Long Island, I thought that might be a nice relaxing place to go. I bet there is a nice B&B we could stay at. Shopping, walking, wining, and good food."

"That sounds like a great idea. I can recommend a couple of B&Bs from when I have stayed there to work with clients, if you want."

"Yes, thanks, that would be great. She also wants me to check out a company, Pliant LLC. Apparently, her family business was asked to put together a comprehensive social media campaign for them, and she's in charge."

"That sounds like something you can both talk about for hours."

Gracie beamed. The timer for their meal buzzed.

"Good, it's ready. I'm starving, let's go eat."

CHAPTER 48

Where Is Truth! …
The Enigma Chronicles

Tanja waited for Miguard to power down while charging. It was the only time when she could have a private conversation. She selected the encrypted phone Gracie had given her and called Tracy's number. It rang for what seemed like forever, and a man answered.

"Hello, this is Lieutenant Commander Lee Smith. How may I assist you?"

"I'm sorry, I was calling for Tracy Mountbatten. I must have called the wrong number."

When Tracy ended up missing and unresponsive, Lee had her number forwarded to his device. Thinking this might be one of Tracy's snitches, based on the summary of information appearing on the screen with the call, he didn't want to let an opportunity go unanswered.

"No, ma'am, this is her line. I work for her. She's out of reach at present. Do you have computer traffic misuse to report?"

Tanja was flustered. Tracy always answered. There must be a problem, or the screechers simply took care of the issue they had complained about. Fear crept through her creating a sensation of impending doom.

"Oh, I need to get a message to her. Is there another number I could try? It's um… personal."

"No, ma'am, this is her only number. Do you want me to say that you called, Tanja?"

Stunned, she responded, "I don't recall using my name."

"No, ma'am, you did not. Your first name appeared with the number."

"Okay, sure. Ask her to call me. Thank you."

She hung up quickly. Without missing a beat, she sent a text to Gracie.

Gracie, call me - Tracy M. at CESPOOL is missing

Brayson read the copy of the text and sent Gracie his own message, knowing she would see both.

Lara worked her magic. Destiny Fashions needed to deliver products to Argentina and return with the data center team of Leroy, JJ, Zara, Judith and Xiamara. After a quick flight in one of the company's private jets with Juan piloting and Julie in the right seat, they arrived by late evening to Lara and Carlos's home without fanfare. Each was provided with a small refreshment and their own room. Lara promised a bigger welcome during the next day's midday meal.

Judith hovered while Lara's personal physician attended to Zee's wound. After it was cleaned, dressed, and pronounced as 'healing nicely', Judith and Xiamara decided they wanted to stay together. Julie asked the girls if she might have some time with them the next day after they rested.

Zara verified with Carlos that Buzz was there, but his room was on the other side of the house from hers. Leroy had a room to himself away from the others, but he mentioned quietly to Juan that he hoped they might speak soon.

Julie and Juan headed up to their room arm in arm. Instead of heading to the shower as Juan hoped, Julie plopped down at the desk and connected her laptop. Studying the screen as she moved from one site to another, her face transitioned across a gambit of expressions. Interested, Juan moved to look over her shoulder.

"Sweetheart, why are you searching tragic, flaming accidents in Switzerland and adjoining countries from several months back? Isn't this the time frame for when we traveled with our refugee family to Mexico? Have we missed someone, or did something happen?"

Julie paused and reached up to slide her hand down his cheek with a glint in her eye and wet lips. "My darling, I have this idea that may help resolve Bruno's pursuit of Quip. Lara said he's in Brazil and making inquiries.

"Bruno has been a family friend since he and Quip were children. Bruno knows Jacob and Granger were involved but is also aware they are not on film after Granger's handiwork. I don't believe he would directly implicate them. His assignment, to return to Interpol's good graces, is to apprehend and return Quip. It is impossible for him to not try to redeem his career and overcome accusations of being cuckolded by Quip supporters."

"Julie, how does this research you're doing help us?"

Julie grinned slyly. "Darling, we simply need to provide him with a totally plausible and verifiable situation he can then present to his bosses that Quip is dead and gone."

"Come to bed, honey. Quip isn't dead and neither is Jacob. Carlos and JJ will use the honeypot to lure the MAG machines in, then backtrack to their physical locations."

Julie laughed. "Don't be silly, Juan. I know that.

"Did you read all the materials we were sent on the additional house guests?"

"Leroy, I know him. He's had one tough life. He's already gotten his funds back, but he's desperate for a certain sword currently residing in Mexico."

"No, not Leroy. Though I bet you will help him after everything he did for your Uncle Jesus."

"Then Zara? Her, I only know from Carlos's descriptions when they met in New York City. Something about her trying to shoot him at one time, but they are friends."

"They may be friends now, but she has been a family foe on more than one occasion. She was connected to the Dteam hackers funded by Russia."

"Then that leaves Judith and Xiamara. I know they are gifted programmers who seem to have a lot in common with Zara. I think I read that she had instructed them from her school in Puerto Rico. That was as far as I got. What did I miss?"

"These talented ladies enabled the supercomputer to offer streaming video as a service for erotica."

"Julie, you mean, um…like…"

"Yes, darling, lots of sex and nakedness. All made to order based on, how does one say, erotic daydreams?"

Juan's imagination was off in some remote location with Julie and him doing…

"Juan!!"

"I'm with you, darling..."

"No, you aren't. I want to tell you my plan, then we play." With a quick peck on her cheek he refocused, so she continued.

"These ladies went to great lengths to customize the video streaming for their patrons. They fulfilled fantasies with actors, singers, or anything the subscriber wanted using digitally engineered videos. The samples we saved before the machine was scrubbed were pure art! Voices, images, and video designed to complete any perverted request, with no need to get personally involved. Really creative programming with extensive libraries of scenes which could be readily reworked to meet a real time request."

"Alright, Julie, I hear you now. What does that have to do with why you are searching for horrific events? This is a side of you I haven't seen before!"

"I am trying to find a useable video clip or two that we can use to show how Quip died. I just need the right backgrounds and our new guests' talents to create a convincing video that no one can refute."

"Okay, let me help you. Then we can take a shower together, and you know.... Oh, was there anything on the sample videos that needs an explanation or demon...stration?"

"Most assuredly, Juan."

CHAPTER 49

No Way to Hide

Quip and Jacob had roused from their shadow of gloom. Extracting the team out before the CESPOOL squad hit CAMILA was good news. The possible onslaught against their carefully stored ICABOD database files before launching the second phase was demoralizing. Realizing they had been so close, but now are so far from a success, weighed heavily on the two. Quip declared no more wine or conversations with their families until they resolved the gaps in plan C for plan C. The last chance was to bring up ICABOD using the postulated Secondary Protocol.

After powering down his third cup of coffee, Jacob asked, "Will the Algonquin Round Table members accept our invites? Likely they have been programmed to ignore any communications requests from unknown sources."

Quip, still somewhat bleary eyed, offered, "We have the necessary credentials for the ART forms to accept our invites as defined in the Secondary Protocol. The problem, as I see it, is trying to access each chunk of ICABOD's data stores using an encryption algorithm that they understand yet that won't be caught by the CESPOOL data dweebs."

"Quip, if we can keep our communications private using our zombie satellite network, we should be golden. What am I missing?"

"The last data hop from the zombies, Jacob, has to come down to a terrestrial link before being delivered to each ART form. We're vulnerable at that point if anyone is watching."

"Alright. What if, as soon as we make contact with each ART form and create a solid connection, we introduce the new encryption algorithm built by Petra? Both ends of the conversation can then flow encrypted so that we can evade the CESPOOL goons. We start off vulnerable but quickly change gears to harden our communications stream."

"Jacob, even if we get our communications stream encrypted that still leaves us traceable as the source of the transmission. The international rules clearly exempt sovereign supercomputers, but some CESPOOL boo-bah will want to hammer us out here in the desert because they can't read the traffic."

"Excellent point, Quip! What if we setup the zombies to be our anonymizing servers that don't just let anything back through? Our kids did a great job of collecting zombies that people have ignored for years and no longer access. Why not use them to cloak all the activity?"

Quip mused a moment. "Yeah, why not? Let's get the São Paulo team working that angle in preparation for launching the Secondary Protocol. The zombies may not individually have enough processing power to be a standalone anonymizing server, but collectively, as a network, they should.

"Jacob, ICABOD had a real way with setting up a project plan, but some of the obstacles we're facing weren't accounted for by the plan. I am so glad we have me to figure out all these angles. Don't worry, I'll make sure you get some credit."

"Come on, Quip, are you back on the trail of tooting your own horn?"

"I've never left that path, reckie-pilot, since you can stay up with me. And, well, it takes a village to pull off what we are attempting. We have the best damn village any group could want."

"You've got me there.

"Let's signal Carlos to set up a call and see if our geniuses can build what we need to be cloaked. As soon as they are ready, we test with one member of the ART forms."

"Good idea!"

Tanja's anxiety was amplified wondering what had happened to Tracy and if Miguard was able to overhear conversations in this rest and recharge state. By Miguard's admission, he was resting. The only caveat was that he would alarm if the door opened.

It took three attempts for Tanja to successfully connect to Gracie. Without listening for a response, Tanja whimpered, "Gracie, I am sorry. I should have contacted you earlier. Those machines wanted information on a supercomputer that Tracy hadn't destroyed. Why hadn't it been destroyed? What did I do or why didn't I contact them?" Inhaling loudly, she expelled, "Now I can't find Tracy. Her phone went to someone else at CESPOOL.

"Now I have a humanoid robot assigned to be with me all the time. Miguard is listening to me, following me, and scaring the hell out of me."

Gracie questioned, "You have a bodyguard of sorts and you're contacting me. Are you insane?"

"No, Miguard rests and recharges at set intervals based on usage. No communication as I understand it. I did, however, start white noise in the room where Miguard is charging, and I am running the shower in my bathroom. I am using the phone you provided."

Gracie mentally reviewed the options just as she received an inbound text.

Based on my monitoring you are on with Tanja
She is panicked.
I believe you and I can solve this, but time is critical
Tell her to destroy the phone she is using immediately

"Tanja, you need to stop and breath! Let me see if I can locate Tracy. I suspect it is a horrible misunderstanding. I know you two are buddies.

"We will set up a time when I can observe your new protector, Miguard, but for now finish that show and act as if nothing is out of the ordinary."

"Thank you. I'm so sorry. I've made so many mistakes. I still have no idea where Randal and Wendy are." Sobbing, she sputtered, "I miss them so much. Without them I have nothing to live for."

A loud knock at the bathroom door penetrated her tirade. "Tanja, I am recharged. Open the door. I must visually reassure my creators you are here," Miguard bellowed.

Stripping in a flash, she loudly shouted, "In the shower right now and not ready to parade naked for a droid, so just wait."

Tanja whispered, "Gotta go, Gracie."

"Destroy the phone now. Miguard must not know it exists."

As soon as the call disconnected, Brayson connected to Gracie. "We're having fun now."

"Not really. What's going on?"

Brayson related the activities that had occurred in the last couple of days. Gracie was astounded. She wanted to know if everyone was safe, especially JJ. Then they concocted a plan on the fly, using the latest technology masking and speech programs available for communications. Number masking was not too hard, but mimicking device behaviors with no mistakes was more than an art. They planned to engineer an unscheduled intermission in Argentina.

"Okay, Gracie. Do you have your lines? We need you to project attitude, Smith has to believe it's his director. I can synthesize the voice that will pass any security they have. Plus, I can spoof the numbers."

"Yes. Let's go fake out CESPOOL. Mom will be so proud."

Moments later the show successfully opened and closed within a ten-minute stretch.

"Well done. I will keep monitoring. Thanks, Gracie."

Gracie stared at the silent device and considered how she might reach out to Tanja.

CHAPTER 50

Not Enough Time but Time Enough

Lieutenant Commander Lee Smith was on a secure open channel. He was accepting situation reports from each of the squad leaders surrounding the CAMILA data center. Smith quietly asserted into the speaker strapped to his shoulder, "Everyone in place? On my mark we go in hot. Understood? Place the CRUSH charges as quickly as possible and then back outside to register with me. We are NOT going to lose any more people!"

Those squad leaders that were in visible range of Smith all nodded grimly but remained silent. Just as Lee Smith was about to issue the all-go command, his CESPOOL-issued cell phone began vibrating soundlessly, which meant only one thing.

Annoyed, Lt. Commander Smith barked into the shoulder comm. "Everyone hold! Emergency communications from HQ. Again, I say HOLD!"

Smith pulled back a little and answered the incoming call, which only soured his mood the longer he listened. Ten minutes later, he tersely replied, "Understood, Hair Director, and will comply."

The cell phone was replaced inside his jacket, and he commanded into the shoulder comm, "We are cleared to go!

Demolitions leader! Once everything is in place do NOT, I repeat, do NOT trigger the CRUSH charge. You are to hold until instructed otherwise. Acknowledge, Sergeant!"

The sergeant replied, "I thought this was a hurry up, get it done job. Now it's hurry and wait?"

Irritated, the Lt. Commander barked, "Are you able to follow instructions or not, soldier? Repeat the orders!"

"My team is to place the CRUSH charge, withdraw, and wait for further orders, sir!"

Smith stated, "Then let's move out."

Once inside Lt. Commander Smith pulled over two squad leaders. In a low voice he said, "I want your people to plug into the system terminals and begin data extractions. Every lead, every communications connection, every IP address. ANYTHING that looks even remotely interesting I want vacuumed up. Got it?"

They motioned their teams to begin the digital prowling process on CAMILA.

After a tense 30 minutes of system prowling, one CESPOOL soldier hollered, "Sir, I've got a routine here that is beaconing to a variety of IP addresses. Looks like a combination of terrestrial and satellite entities.

"Wow! Talk about your military grade encryption! I can't break any of this so no idea what is being communicated. You want it hammered, sir?"

"Negative, soldier! Let it run but keep monitoring it."

Lee Smith pulled out his CESPOOL cell to launch an encrypted call back to his leadership for verification. As soon as it connected, he stated, "It's there alright. Are you sure about this? I am glad you are engaged, Director. We've never had one like this before, sir. Just to be clear, the sovereign sponsored supercomputers are out of bounds, correct?"

After a few moments, the puzzled Lt. Commander replied, "Understood and will comply, sir. Standing by for orders to launch the CRUSH on CAMILA." The cell went back into the jacket pocket close to his chest. This was the part Smith hated the most, all ready to go but told to wait with no timeline.

Smiling Gracie texted.

You were right. He did call back to confirm.
Thanks, Brayson.

Juan Jr. answered the call on the first ring. "Hi, Gracie."

She asked, "Did it work?"

Juan Jr. broadly grinned. "Evidently. Thanks, sis."

After disconnecting he turned toward EZ and Carlos. "How are we doing?"

Both EZ and Carlos were focused on the large monitor that had their new telecom matrix of terrestrial lines and satellite comm links all mapped to a real-time graphic depicting live data traffic.

EZ commented, "CAMILA is still beaconing. Good work, JJ, pulling in Gracie to make that call. It bought us the needed time."

Carlos coached, "Come on, MAG group, take the bait so you can have a dose of your own medicine, you miserable…"

JJ asked, "Do we need to have our hunters working shifts in case we have a strike on the honeypot? I know it's late, but I don't mind taking the first watch."

Still studying the screen, EZ asked, "Would you go wake up Granger, please? Tell him the hunt is in play, and I would like him here for a two-hour shift. Thanks, hon."

JJ nodded and took off on the errand.

Carlos offered, "Good idea, EZ. We need round-the-clock shifts until they move for the bait. Fairly clever idea getting the CESPOOL goons to monitor the system as well as the source. If they get to see the strike, then the MAG becomes the hunted just like we need. Whose idea was this?"

EZ rolled her eyes. "For the third and final time, *your* idea. Shall I get new business cards printed for you that say, 'The chosen one, according to the prophecy'?"

Carlos grinned. "Boy, that does sound catchy!"

EZ smirked. "Or how about, 'Carlos E. Coyote – Super Genius'?"

Carlos enthusiastically added, "Printed on front and back so I can use them both, right?"

EZ finally turned from the monitor to give a disapproving stare at Carlos, who only chuckled. "I think my husband's rubbing off on you."

CHAPTER 51

Getting a Home

Juan noticed that Leroy was not only hovering but agitated, based on his fidgeting movements. Juan smiled to himself. Refreshing his after-breakfast coffee, he motioned to Leroy to come visit away from the others. Leroy grinned as they both headed out to the patio to chat in the morning sunshine.

They took two seats at the glass-topped table close to Lara's fragrant flowers. Juan asked, "Is this about the private word you wanted to have with me?"

Smiling, Leroy nodded. "Juan, I took this job after the first one 'cause…well, it seemed fittin' after us losing Jesus. I was always of a mind to take my nest egg and move on after the job was completed. By all the shifts it looks like I'm done here. But fact is, I don't really have any place to go.

"Funny that! I didn't really want to ride herd on the young'uns, but here I am about to start missing them.

"Let me just put the moose on the table and ask if I can stay tied up with your group? Your bunch seems to be fighting for just causes which is a little stray for me. I guess I've gotten used to being on the right side of things. Oddly enough, it delivers the same juice of excitement.

"I know I'm not good on a computer keyboard like your boy. Yet, I did notice that none of you have those confidence man skills that I have. Not to brag about my selling skills, but I have sold hay balers to the Bedouin tribes in the Sahara and blessed glasses at $20 a pop to churchgoers. My mama once said I could sell a deep freezer to an Eskimo."

Juan chuckled, adding a thumbs up.

"Now if I get to stay, I promise to be no more trouble than I'm worth. I have nowhere else I want to be except close to the nephews of my buddy Jesus. Our travels together were epic. I'm hoping you can put in a good word for me with the group, then let me know."

Juan grinned as he contemplated Leroy's proposal. "Man, I had hoped you would stay with us for just exactly the reasons you stated. We just might have a role for you with our CATS team. We have been successful in hiring cyber assassins who were highly technical or ex-military. However, they lack the social engineering genius you possess. We work on secure computer systems and defend corporations and countries against the cyber thugs from the dark net. We lose more battles than we'd like because the human being is the weakest link in cyber defenses. People can be socially engineered to give away the digital store. The bad actors keep finding new ways to seduce even the happiest person into selling out.

"Would you consider joining us as our in-house expert and team instructor to help design and deliver counter-attacks to dark net social engineering?"

Leroy's mind drifted away in retrospect. "Hmmm…social engineering genius. I like the sound of that, Juan."

Juan grinned. "Then let's get you plugged in with a lady who needs to make someone disappear. I'm sure you and Julie will have a lot to talk about." Juan sent Julie a quick text to join them.

Leroy slyly asked, "Does this mean I can finally get that Katana sword we've been wrangling over for years and maybe put me back on my stipend so that I don't over-rotate on my nest egg? I know you've taken good care it. I couldn't help but notice my nest egg was a little plumper than when I was managing it."

"All part of the disappearing exercise, my man!" Juan promised.

Julie joined them on the patio with a fresh cup of tea.

"Sweetheart, Leroy has agreed to be a part of our team. He believes he can contribute to our social engineering options."

Julie smiled. "Leroy, I am so glad to hear that. In fact, I have your first assignment." She passed him an identity package with three passports with different names, associated credit cards, an airline ticket, and the respective business cards.

Leroy thumbed through them and grinned. "I think I've played this before. Julie, I'm headed to Europe today for you under one of these names. I have three days to do what, exactly?"

Julie handed him a tablet that contained three online video articles. He played them and then looked up. "These are some nasty accidents, ma'am. People you know?"

"Possibly. That is what you are going to help determine.

"We need you to travel and appear to the coroner in each of these cities and get the records on the victims. At this point, their names are unknown. In each instance you are to show this photo and ask if the victim resembled this man.

"We need details of their systems and processes or at least as much as you can extract."

Leroy, gaining an idea of where this might be going, added, "Do you want me to secure a DNA sample as well, if available?"

Juan and Julie both grinned. Juan stated, "Sort of." Then he handed Leroy a sealed package. "Take this with you as a carry-on. You can easily secure it in your suitcase as medicine needed for your diabetes, which is supported on your documents. There is a letter inside which will help you decide the best time to use the contents."

"But I don't have diabetes, Juan!"

Julie insisted, "You do for the air travel security and customs people."

Leroy asked, "Can I take this tablet with me to study on the flight? I may add a couple of eBooks, audibles, and podcasts to pass the time."

"Leroy, that is just fine with Juan and me. Enjoy the First-Class flight. The onboard movies looked like good ones."

"I like the way you both think. Thank you for the opportunity to work on your team. I'm going to like this, I surely will."

JJ hadn't slept well. Once the sun was fully up, he decided to take a short run around the property. Flowers lined the run path of the well-maintained gardens, included the blooms that had also ended up in a vase in his room. Aunt Lara had such a delightful way of making anyone in the house feel welcomed. He started with an even lope that stretched his muscles. The weeks he had been planted in a chair in front of a screen made this run delightful. He had no doubt he would feel it later but welcomed the sensation of being alive.

The only sounds outside of his feet hitting the path in an easy rhythm were various birds voicing their opinions over unknown subjects. Some birds peeked out of the foliage, along with butterflies and bees moving between the flowers. As JJ turned the long loop of the pathway, he picked up some music and someone singing. The music drawing him, he increased his speed, hoping he was right.

Turning onto the straightaway, he spied a figure seated on the bench singing with the music. Jo's dark hair was moving in the wind as he drew closer. Hearing footsteps, she looked up and stopped singing.

JJ slowed to a stop in front of her. For several moments neither of them said a word. JJ swallowed, trying to recall when they had been so uncomfortable with one another before.

"Jo, good morning. You look lovely. How are you?"

Jo paused, gathering her thoughts. "JJ, I am so glad you are back. I heard that you have been working on a big project. Congratulations, I'm sure it was better because you were there."

"Thanks, it was a team effort. Uncle Carlos said you were still busy with work. I am surprised, very delighted that you are here and not at a shoot. I am really proud of you, Jo."

"Thank you, JJ. It's exciting. And a little overwhelming as well."

JJ was trying to figure a way to continue the conversation without being pushy but failed. "You'll handle it just fine. I need to finish my run and get to work with Uncle Carlos. Best wishes, madam."

He started to move but stopped when Jo reached for him and invited, "JJ, I miss you. I think we need to talk. Can you make some time for us to clear the air?"

He faced her and grinned. "Yes, Jo. I would like that a lot. Thank you for being braver than me."

As he started back down the path, Jo admired the view and returned to her singing, a soft smile playing on her lips.

CHAPTER 52

Deceiving the Deceivers

As if the digital snooper could actually hear the sergeant's low voice, he said, "Lt. Commander, there is a transmission coming in on the beaconing we discovered. Check that. I show two heavy-duty snoopers forcing a breach into the system.

"Sir, I count two prowlers penetrating the outer defenses. Instructions, sir?"

Lt. Commander Lee Smith coolly watched the CESPOOL monitoring program paint the electronic footsteps the intruders left as they moved at machine speeds from database to database.

Smith stated, "These are outside intruders. They are quite skilled at breaking and entering. What are they looking for, gentlemen?"

The sergeant commented, "I have telemetry on everything they touch and…sir, they pounded a database and wiped it clean! They found something! Let me see if we caught it."

Another soldier responded, "I've got them on another database! Watching…watching…wat…there! They stopped at the table beginning with the letter 'I.'"

Smith barked, "Can you catch the keyword! I need to know what is so important!"

The sergeant announced, "Sir, the telemetry indicates they stopped and destroyed the database upon the discovery of a keyword ICABOD."

The Commander insisted, "Comb the system for anything containing the keyword ICABOD!"

Lt. Commander Smith pulled out his corporate mobile device and called CESPOOL Ops. "This is Lieutenant Commander Lee Smith. I want a file pulled and read to me right now on an operation we did six months ago in Switzerland.

"Yes, I'll hold for 8 seconds. More than that and you better have a note from your mommy.

"Ah good! Sounds like you have it. Scan it. Tell me if the word ICABOD appears…"

Smiling, Smith replied, "That's all I wanted."

Replacing the silenced phone back in his pocket, he asked confidently, "What are the results of the system scan for the keyword ICABOD?"

The sergeant said, "Sir, there isn't a database I've scanned that didn't include the keyword ICABOD. Sir, these aren't modest databases used for grandma's recipes. These are huge databases that could only be run…"

Smith knowingly added, "By a supercomputer…yes, Sergeant." He looked at the other soldier but said nothing. The soldier replied, "The same."

Smith concluded, "These intruders are obviously after ICABOD's system backups and must be trying to rebuild him. Therefore, these two intruders must be criminals. Put the electronic tag on them. I want them followed!

"Nice work, gentlemen. We are after two new rogue entities, and I mean to take them down. Continue to monitor but tag the traffic for our new adversary."

Smith chuckled to himself.

JJ was almost dozing before being rocketed awake by Granger hollering. “They took it! They took it! We be jammin,’ mon! I don’t really know what Lonny Lupnerder meant. Still, it sounds cool to say.”

JJ, jolted awake, studied the data traffic to the CAMILA data center. “I don’t understand. What is this extra data field at the end of the traffic? It looks like…oops! Looks like we aren’t the only ones looking for cyber trash.”

Granger blanched, “Whoa, what exactly is that at the end of the communications stream?”

JJ suggested, “I bet the CESPOOL people we left cooling their jets at the data site have not just been hanging around ordering takeout food.

“Granger, you go get your mom and I’ll get Carlos. We need everyone. Looks like we snagged a whopper.”

Granger grinned, “You mean we got them? This is so cool. I’ll get my mom after I stop at the toilet. Isn’t it great being us?”

JJ mumbled, “Nothing like having a younger version of Dr. Quip around to help test your mental boundaries.”

CHAPTER 53

The Tears with the Fears

Zara went pale then halted as she reached the work area. Carlos watched her while she stared through the glass door at the scene unfolding.

Finally Carlos offered, "You can still run if you want to. I never promised you two would speak together."

Fixated on the scene, she murmured, "Look at him…laughing, cutting up with the kids…and they're teasing back." Tears streamed down her face and over a smile Zara couldn't suppress. Emotional agony and joy slammed into her, filling her with uncertainty.

"Dakota, why am I so afraid of…this?"

Carlos smirked. "You haven't called me that since that time I carried you to the hospital after that horrible beating you took. Buzz was so confused. He wouldn't stand down or give up on you. Sort of like now."

Zara drew a very ragged breath. "I only seem to want the things I can't have. The stolen diamonds I was forced to surrender. Control of my own destiny. Even how I wanted someone like you to be my protector. You really made me mad when you didn't want me."

Carlos nodded and offered, "Yeah! I got the mad part when you tried to shoot me."

Zara complained, "Then here is someone who chases after me and wants me. He wants that thing that I don't want. I'm so scared. He's better off without me."

Carlos gently suggested, "You two could just go have a conversation. He's not a bad guy, maybe a little rough around the edges, but what guy isn't? I am not trying to tell you what to do. He tracked you this far, and it seems a little unfair to not at least talk."

Zara snapped, "See? This is what I can't stand! All I've ever had are men telling me what to do! Well, not this time!"

Zara went to leave, but Carlos blocked her exit.

"Perhaps you need to have that male protector providing guidance because your judgement isn't that great. I know you have a lot of baggage. Frankly, Buzz knows it too but came anyway.

"If you want to run away like a frightened schoolgirl, I'll make sure you get a good head start. That way you can use that icy fear of yours to hurt him some more. That will help increase your suffering. I guess the Yaqui mystics were right, people will give up anything but their suffering. Why won't you accept a little bit of happiness?"

Zara began sobbing uncontrollably. But when she looked up to speak to Carlos, Buzz was standing there instead. Startled, she almost fled in panic.

Buzz gently said, "I'm sorry I hurt you, Zara. I promise I won't hurt you again, until the next boneheaded thing I do. If I could erase that last fight I started, I would gladly do it. Is there any chance you can forgive me? Maybe take me back?"

Almost numb from confronting Buzz, Zara only stared blankly at the man she had been with for so long. She gazed down at his outstretched hand but simply couldn't move or speak.

As he was leaving the area so they could talk, Carlos hollered over his shoulder, "This is the interactive part of the discussion. Zara, your turn…"

Snapping back to reality after wiping her tears, she stated, "You looked so full of joy and were so happy as you cut up with the children. I see why that is so important for you."

Buzz intercepted, "Important, but not as important as you. I didn't know about your past. After you blurted everything out… well, I felt cold and worthless.

"But your past made you who you are. You're who I love. Understand, your horrific past is not something I will ever bring up again. But I will always be there to listen if you do."

Zara sniffled, "And the wife, children, and family thing you so desperately wanted? We don't have to dwell on the past, but what about the future? Our future?"

Buzz grinned. "You saw me cutting up with the kids. Yes, it was fun. But what if I just get to rent them? I mean, just be a teacher and borrow someone's growing problem? I admit I like kids, but who said they have to be ours?"

Finally, Zara, having schooled her emotions, asked, "Everything on my terms? Is that what I'm hearing?"

Buzz nodded. "Everything on your terms."

Still a little misty eyed, Zara said, "Then it's settled. I will marry you here, before we leave to return home."

"Yes. For anything else, my love, you have but to command."

Smiling she hooked her arm in his. They left quietly chatting, to walk around outside on the grounds of the Bernardes estate.

Quip sat listlessly inside the cramped data center, staring off into space. Jacob tried to stay busy and productive all morning, but finally he too succumbed to the mental lethargy that hung in the air like dense fog. Their moroseness expanded exponentially when they thought of their families thousands of miles away.

Jacob tried to start a semblance of a conversation. “Yep, nothing like having someone to help you when you feel depressed. Am I depressing you enough, Quip?”

Quip unenthusiastically nodded.

“Boy, I sure didn’t expect that call from Carlos telling us CESPOOL clowns had turned the CAMILA data center into their campground. Hope our plan C works for our plan C.”

Quip only nodded.

Continuing the monologue, Jacob added, “Maybe we’d feel better after a couple of race laps across the pool. Better yet, some hot tub time to help soothe our tired muscles.

“I realize it’s merely a water tank that uses a windmill to maintain the level so the cattle have something to drink. And, okay, the water is being pumped up from an underground aquifer which is a full 25 degrees colder than the ambient air. Still, when she isn’t around to comfort you, put the boys on ice.”

Quip just moved.

“You seem kind of down today. I’ll tell you what, I’ll keep the water moccasins away with the makeshift rake we built so you can be first. Please make sure to use lots of soap so you generate plenty of bubbles for my turn. It sure does aggravate the cattle when we soap up their water trough.

“Personally, I think we should go to the water naked this time. Damn rattlesnakes infested our clothes last time, so we leave them here. That’ll show them. Quite literally!”

Quip faced Jacob and quietly offered, “Jacob, stop trying to cheer me up.”

Jacob fell silent and shrugged.

Quip lamented, "We must be close to winning this combat, because I'm about to give up. At least, that's what I told myself when I was hitting on those babes in college. The ones with the nice portfolios."

Jacob inclined his head, still silent.

"And we have a plan C for our plan C. If this scenario unfolds the way Carlos described, then we get to leave this place on our terms. Not the MAG's."

Smiling, Quip continued, "I love hearing how the kids helped to engineer this unexpected speed bump. It might work the way we need it to."

Jacob nodded.

"Come on, let's break open that last bottle of Baron de'Off Child Bordeaux. We can sip until we are good and crocked. Then run naked to the water tank to annoy the snakes and cattle.

"I realize I have to tie up Big Jim so he doesn't drag on the ground this time. Man, you're lucky YOU don't have that problem."

Jacob smirked. "Quip, I know when you start concocting fantastic exaggerations, you are doing better.

"I'll get the tin cups, and you get the $1,000 bottle of Bordeaux."

Quip grinned and scampered off.

CHAPTER 54

Losing Means Somebody Won …
The Enigma Chronicles

Rubbing his jawline, Lt. Commander Lee Smith queried, "Soldier, is there any attempt by the intruders to export any data? Can you confirm they are only smashing, not grabbing, the data?"

The sergeant answered, "Confirmed, sir. No attempt to export it or hold it for ransom or make a digital claim because the data center is abandoned. Nothing! Breaking and entering what is apparently a high value target only to destroy the contents. Doesn't make much sense unless…"

Smith finished the thought. "This supercomputer is a digital competitor and threat. Hmmm…"

Smith pulled out his cell. "Ops hotline, I want our digital forensics strike team ready to follow the packet tag we are inserting in the intruders' traffic. Looks like a supercomputer range war has opened up. Unless I miss my guess, our two rogues will try to retreat to a healthy bank of anonymizing servers to cloak their getaway. I want these two bastards tailed through the A-servers back to their lair. Pound the A-servers with the ION-cannon technique if you must. Don't lose track of them. Do you copy?

"Good! Put this call on an open conference bridge along with the strike team so we can converse real time. The carnage from the rogues is almost over. I expect them to disengage any minute."

Smith put the phone on speaker and sat it down between the men as they all watched the ending of the digital onslaught.

The sergeant exclaimed, "They are disengaging! Ops, do you have the signal of their last known route and IP address? The tags are in place."

A voice on the bridge replied, "We have the signals! Lt. Commander, you were correct, and we are on their doorstep.

"Whoa! They are flooding the gateway with thousands of bogus IP addresses, but your digital tags are holding on. We have an excellent breadcrumb trail! We are through the A-server wall! Uh-oh…they are diverging and going in separate directions based on the tracerouting from the signals. We don't have enough resources to follow both, dammit!"

Lt. Commander Smith mused, "A team of confederates banding together for a single purpose job. Not from the same nest, huh? Interesting.

"Stay with rogue one until we find his crib. If these two are confederates, then they probably visit a lot. If we find one, we'll find the other. Funny thing about traveling in the transient digital universe, it always leads to your fixed and permanent address. The brawnier the supercomputer, the bigger the footprint and the harder it is to hide from our CRUSH exercise."

EZ and Carlos rocked back into their chairs, stunned at the digital carnage they were witnessing. Granger stared disbelievingly at JJ, who only remarked, "I saw it. They took the bait and half of our data center with it. Must have used too much honey."

Carlos offered, "The good news is that they took the bait, and right in front of the CESPOOL goons that tagged all of their returning traffic. We all have a trail back to two of the MAG group. The bad news is, we don't have our key infrastructure to spin up ICABOD again. The end game was to spin him up just in time to help lead the charge back to the MAG.

"In order to express my frustration, I'm taking a page from EZ's playbook and hurling some well-chosen expletives: POOP!"

EZ glared at Carlos. "Do you have to use that foul language in front of the children? We've talked about this…"

Carlos, after offering a chastened mock posture, stated, "Granger, you and JJ continue to follow the digital corridor where the CESPOOL supernova was shot through. Careful, it's probably still molten lava hot.

"Remember the rules in tracking the MAG: sneaky not squeaky.

"EZ, let's you and I call our two stranded boys and discuss what a plan C would look like for our plan C."

EZ nodded.

CHAPTER 55

Imagine and Back

Julie brightly greeted, "Good morning, ladies. If no one else has stated it plainly enough, many thanks for your tireless efforts in the CAMILA data center. Xiamara, I hope your injury is mending quickly. How are you feeling?"

Xiamara stammered, "I'm…good, ma'am. Thank you, ma'am, for asking. I am very pleased, but a little nervous meeting JJ's mother. I didn't know you would be so young-looking, ma'am."

Irked, Judith countered, "Oh, come on, Zee! This isn't our den mother, for crying out loud. Talk normal."

Julie schooled her expression and asked, "Judith, JJ told me you had some reservations about staying. May I ask if that is still the case? You might as well know, there are nothing but alpha females in this outfit. We all know how to curb that edge when dealing with others."

Judith took a few moments to size up things. "You said you wanted to talk to us about something. You made it sound like a fresh gig. What do you have in mind? Most importantly, do we get paid for the effort this time?"

Xiamara snapped, "What is it with you, Judith, anyway? All you've done is bark at everyone like a junk yard dog! I'm tired of it.

"I get mortified every time you pull this routine of 'How much do we get?' like we're a couple of low rent cheap hookers! Why don't you take that perfect bod and nasty personality of yours somewhere else?"

Turning to Julie, Xiamara continued, "Ma'am, I want to personally thank you and your people for sparing us from the CESPOOL goons. We appreciate the chance to fight injustice. I would like to apologize for Judith's snarky attitude. Even if she isn't interested in staying, I'm in. JJ promised nothing except food, shelter, a place to sleep, and a chance to take the fight to the bad guys. I'm in it for the long haul, if you will have me, ma'am."

Looking at each lady in sequence, Julie clucked her tongue. "Judith is right. Please drop the den mother courtesy of 'ma'am'. It makes me feel old."

Xiamara blushed and lowered her head.

Judith smirked, "Okay, I admit it. Zee is sweet on JJ. It annoys me that my partner and best friend would choose to stay where there isn't any coin for the efforts. I want to be rich. I want to call the shots in my life. I don't want to rely on nude modeling or worse to make ends meet. When I ask how much we get, it is because I don't bow and scrape to anyone if I don't want to.

"Zee makes fun of my looks 'cause we both know I can make a great living as a high-dollar call girl. No one thinks I have enough brains to do anything else. My pride keeps me on my feet hustling and not on my back waiting for it to be over. Can you understand that?"

It took a few moments of silence for Julie to break into her gorgeous smile. "Do you always interview so ferociously?

"JJ did tell you correctly. The work pays nothing to him. He's family. But for my CATS team members, they do get paid. They are paid to be Cyber Assassins for Technical Services. This is what you two are interviewing for so you can have a career in the digital universe with my merry band of cyber experts.

"I typically don't discuss salary with two people at the same time. I'm confident that you will compare notes if we meet individually, so here it is – $200,000 a year, plus expenses. Bonuses are paid at the end of the year based on how the team performed. For the last 12 years, that has been running about another $100,000 a year each.

"Do I have your attention?"

Judith was dumbfounded. She slowly turned to look at Xiamara who replied, "I'd like to hear a little more."

Julie grinned and revealed, "Ladies, your first assignment is to make someone disappear. I'm told you are the experts at building deep fakes. JJ even sent some of your handiwork to me that clearly showed you have, um…imagination."

Both girls blushed profusely, imagining their streaming porn service had been viewed by their new female employer. Zee even shuddered slightly at hearing that the evidence of files was uncovered by JJ, as Madam Z had never confronted them.

Julie slightly giggled. "I had to ask my husband to grade it for voyeuristic appeal and believability. Let's just say that in grading it, he was…inspired."

Both women were acutely embarrassed.

Julie continued, "The stitching of the faces of the client and their fantasy target was masterful. However, the sounds of two people mating added the extra bonus layer of authenticity. At first, I had my doubts of what you had digitally generated. The live demonstration my husband orchestrated made me a believer."

Xiamara was the first to smirk. "It was good, wasn't it?"

Judith giggled. "The funny part was that it didn't take us any time at all to come up with those love trysts. I guess we're naughty women at heart."

Julie opened her PC and launched three videos in succession. "Ladies, these are the closest videos to the time of the disappearance. These should give us the best results.

"Here is the high definition photo of our customer who has to look like he is trapped in this burning car. Here's the drill. Take each of these videos and stitch in his face. Then capture the victim's agonizing death but using this man's face. Once you have that done, build two more videos of the same location event, but from different angles. It can't be too good, since these are street cams. They must have enough quality to visually identify our client. One video could be refuted, but not three. At this point we have not determined the actual relevant accident we will use."

Xiamara asked, "Can the third video be from someone's smart phone? That way we can overlay sounds of the flames roiling up from the flowing gasoline, the blood popping from arteries, and the horrific screams as he is desperately trying to get the seatbelt off."

Appalled, Judith asked, "Are you going to be ghoulish enough to then put someone in front of the camera to take a selfie while he is burning to death? Do they need lines to say while the burning victim is screaming, like they're some roving reporter?"

Completely immersed in building the deep fake, Zee, only half conscious of Judith, mumbled, "Yeah, sure, Judith. Draft up something and we'll try it."

A little uneasy at the direction the conversation was headed, Julie cautioned, "Uh…remember this has to be believable and will be examined by video experts within Interpol. We have a lot riding on this project."

Sounding confident and at the same time reeling in Zee from her trance, Judith offered, "Yes, ma'am! All I need to do is get Zee back from the outer reaches of the galaxy and then we'll, uh…start."

Buzz invited Zara outside in the garden for brunch. He carried a tray that offered food and beverage. Zara looked refreshed after a night of romping, followed by sleeping late. She was so beautiful.

"Darling, this is such a treat. I love that you suggested this. The landscaping is lovely, isn't it?"

"It is very nice. Lara has some of her models staying on the property. I've seen them jogging a couple of times. I'm not familiar with her clothing line, but it's been mentioned a couple of times as being wildly successful."

Zara nodded and stated, "I have seen her clothing at a couple of the stores near our home in San Juan."

They each grabbed a plate and filled cups with coffee. Zara smiled in between bites. "The project I helped with in Argentina was to get major computing power using that supercomputer. It was partially successful in that it proved a critical phase, but that resource is gone. I don't know how that gap will be filled. Carlos indicated that I was key, and he was glad I accepted the project. Now there is really nothing for me to do. If they need help, they have but to ask.

"What have you been doing since you arrived here? The kids seem to adore you, so I expect they were involved."

Buzz explained what he'd been doing. The idea of a network of zombie satellites was interesting and Zara asked lots of questions. She wanted details on a network of communication devices that were essentially orphans with no one watching them. Her mind assembled a multitude of possibilities, almost as fast as Buzz explained.

Zara grinned, "Bubi, it sounds like you did great. I know they were lucky to get you to work with all of the kids."

Buzz reached over and patted her arm as he acknowledged, "I improved because we've been working together. I've learned a lot from you.

"Which brings me to the next part of this midday meal. Sweetheart, did you mean it yesterday that you would marry me? I'm not asking it to pressure you, but to make certain I didn't imagine it."

Zara leaned over and soundly kissed him. "Yes, Bubi, I want to marry you. I would like to have a ceremony here in this beautiful garden, if Lara and Carlos would permit it."

Buzz was ecstatic. "Good! Close your eyes, please."

Zara did as he asked, then dipped her head slightly so she could peek through the slits of one eye. Buzz reached into his pocket with one hand and pulled out a ring that sparkled like rainbows as the sun's rays caught it.

"Open your eyes, darling."

Zara gasped, "Oh, my!"

"Zara, I would like to make it formal with a ring just for you. Would you marry me? We can go back to San Juan or any place you would like."

Zara threw her arms around his neck and kissed him. Then she held out her hand for him. He put the ring on her finger and kissed her hand with passionate tears in his eyes. "I love you!"

"It is beautiful. I love you too, Buzz." Zara held it up to admire just in time for Lara to walk by.

"OMG, you two. Is this what I think it is? Are you finally getting married? That is outstanding! When, where…" streamed Lara. "Here, of course. I won't take no. I love parties and happy occasions. We've had too few of them lately."

Lara continued for five more minutes until she ran out of breath and hugged each of them.

Buzz stated, "We would like it here before we return to San Juan. I'm wanting Jacob to be my best man. Can we stick around until he returns?"

Zara added, "We are happy to help if the others need us. But we don't want to be in the way."

"I know what you mean," lamented Lara. "I don't understand a lot of what they are doing, but I will pass it along to Carlos.

"Can you announce your good news tonight at dinner? You are welcome to stay as long as you wish. If it weren't for you, Zara, my nephew might not have returned unscathed. And, Buzz, you have been perfect in helping the children. You turned their work into a game, which doesn't happen often."

They continued to plan as they returned inside.

CHAPTER 56

Toilets - The One Safe Haven

Tanja looked at her calendar. "Miguard, I have a luncheon appointment in the hotel restaurant at the downtown Marriott. I believe you are to attend all meetings. Correct?"

"Yes, ma'am. I need to attend and watch what is happening. Do I require any background information in case I am asked questions? I would not want to make you look badly."

Tanja got up and started for her bedroom to change. "No, Miguard. There will be no reason for you to join the conversation. This is a meeting with one of my CESPOOL contacts to determine if they have completed earlier issued assignments. I will also learn if there are new elements that we need to alert your creators to keep in mind as they prowl the digital landscape. The good part about having you along is that I will not have to take notes. You will have everything in your memory.

"Are you going to transmit live to your creators?'

"That is not possible, Ms. Tanja. I would need a secure capability which I cannot gain over the public Wi-Fi at the hotel. I will upload the data when we return. I will update our schedule to include this meeting. Why was I not aware of it previously?"

"I am sorry. I had a handwritten note I forgot to upload to my calendar. I found it in my wallet when I was cleaning my purse earlier. Do I need to try to change it? I didn't consider it would be a problem."

"No. It is fine."

Tanja went to her room and changed for lunch. Her outfit was coordinated to perfection. Makeup and hair were flawless when she walked out.

"Are we ready to leave, Ms. Tanja?"

"Yes, I ordered a car. It is raining and walking would risk your wellbeing."

"Harrr! Hirrr!" Miguard replied in a tinny manner. "I can walk in the rain if you hold the umbrella. I am not able to swim."

They went downstairs. Miguard's gait was odd but had improved from their first day. The car arrived and 30 minutes later they arrived at the hotel. Miguard followed behind like a child wanting to keep up. Tanja had already spoken to the host before Miguard caught up. Moments later, they were led to a table with three settings. Miguard sat across from Tanja, observing the people.

The waiter came to the table. Tanja ordered a salad and iced tea then indicated she was waiting for a guest who must be running late. She also inquired about the location of the ladies' room, which the waiter indicated was out of the restaurant and around near the conference rooms. She smiled and thanked him.

"Miguard, if you will excuse me, I need to step around to the ladies' room."

"I can accompany you."

Tanja snarled, "No, you may not. You stay here in case Tracy Mountbatten arrives while I am gone. The host is aware that we are waiting for her. I will return as soon as I have attended to my health needs. You are lucky you have none of that inconvenience.

"Keep our table secure. As you can see, the place is crowded now. If you get up, they'll give our table to someone else. That won't do. I'm leaving my purse here so you know I'll be back. My phone is inside, so you know I am not using it."

Tanja stood, chucked her napkin onto the table and strode toward the exit. Turning right she came to the house phone in the alcove near the restrooms. Picking it up, she asked for an outside line and entered for her connection. It went straight to voicemail.

"Gracie, Tanja here. I am in the worst position. I'm no longer able to turn around in my apartment without bumping into Miguard, the AI robot that has been attached to me by the MAG. I need to find Randal and Wendy. This is how they are controlling me. They promised a cure for Wendy. I do not trust them.

"Tracy never called me back! The guy answering her phone creeped me out. I was going to give her some intel regarding what MAG is tapping into. I cannot take it anymore. Call me back at this exact number. It is a house phone at the Marriott. You would not believe what I had to do to make this call, and I only have about five more minutes. Call me."

Disconnecting, Tanja held it together by a thread and fear. She did not need to explain messed-up makeup.

Brayson, who always monitored Gracie's calls, sent a message to call Tanja and the number. He also sent her details on Tracy that he had not had a chance to share with her yet. The intel would be valuable if Gracie could gain the details. He also said he was arranging for a phone to be delivered to Tanja's door, camouflaged as some food items, as she sometimes had groceries delivered.

Gracie called. "Tanja, I'm sorry I did not pick up. I did not know the number and thought it was those pesky dial-to-sell folks. Are you alright?"

Tanja rapidly explained all the details of her involvement with MAG and why. She also explained that with this Miguard in her world she was likely on a short leash with them. Tanja even admitted that he probably would assassinate her when the MAG was done with her. She wanted the whereabouts of her daughter and husband so she could collect them and run. Gracie ended the call after promising to do her best to locate them and telling her about the new phone arriving.

Tanja dashed into the restroom and checked her makeup and washed her hands, then returned to the table.

"Ms. Tanja, no one has come asking to join this table. Your food just arrived. You eat. I will keep a look out for Miss Mountbatten. I took the liberty of getting your phone so I could memorize the image of her face.

"There is no plan to return Wendy to you. You do realize that."

Tanja stopped eating mid-bite at the comment. Looking hard at Miguard, she asked, "What do you know about my daughter, or Randal for that matter?" She took a slow sip of tea to avoid choking on the chalky tasting salad.

"I am not to tell you anything. I did get the sense, from the notes on your phone, that she is important to you, as is Randal."

Speaking through pursed lips, Tanja stated, "We will give Tracy another 30 minutes, then we will go home. I will find out what you know about them, somehow."

After a tense lunch they returned to the apartment. Tanja efforts to learn more about Wendy and Randal had had no results. As they walked through the door Miguard dismissed her again, only saying, "I need to charge. Please set it up and connect me."

Her work phone rang unexpectedly, surprising Tanja, as she was not scheduled to speak to the squawkers. Balancing the phone and managing to connect Miguard, she halfheartedly answered the phone. "Yes, I am here with Miguard. We did not have a call scheduled."

The noisy squeals were heard, even as she held the phone away. **M** finally announced, "Miguard is programmed to tell you nothing. He cannot go against his prime directive even if his brain is connecting thoughts we considered inconsequential."

Tanja was confused. "What does that mean, connecting thoughts? You programmed this machine monster."

M confessed, "Yes, we did. We are taking the cryogenic units and essentially extracting their brains and putting them into our next generation of machine-learning robots. The base rudimentary mobile skills we leave intact. Higher logic and reasoning skills we provide. We envision an improved humanoid with this combination. Miguard was the first prototype with this design. We are monitoring his adaptability to familiar surroundings as part of our product launch. Thus, your own Randal is with you in Miguard. It was the only option to fulfill the obligation. You are privileged to gain this optimized technology inroad."

Her eyes widened in horror as she looked at the machine plugged in and charging. Disconnecting the phone without a word, she calmly walked over to Miguard and flipped from the 110 volts to 220. The overheating was nearly instantaneous. No sounds came from the melting circuits, but the acrid smell of fried electronics hung in the air.

Weeping, she sat on the couch with a tall glass of scotch and waited for the groceries.

CHAPTER 57

A Real Fake, Wow!

Leroy returned from Europe before dawn. There was a spring in his step as he helped himself to coffee at the breakfast buffet in the kitchen.

Juan commented, “You look rested. Was your trip successful?”

“I believe we have what we need to make the final decision after a review of the videos.”

Leroy handed over a package to Juan and added, “This is information for JJ to use once you and Ms. Julie make the final decision.”

“Good! Grab a refill and a muffin and we will go to the showing.

“Julie and the girls have worked non-stop since you left. Based on your review of the documentation, meeting the individual coroners, and the processes that are in place, you will evaluate each presentation.”

Leroy rubbed his hands together, then picked up his cup and snack. “I feel like one of those judges at the Cannes Film Festival. Will there be bribes too?”

Juan laughed as he led the way to the conference room where the screens were set up. Judith and Xiamara grinned like Cheshire cats as they nodded.

"Ladies," Leroy said. "I understand that you work for these fine people like I do. I can't wait to see what you put together."

Judith sat a little taller and smugly stated, "You are judging these. I had no idea. These are our best work. Each and every detail is handled."

Zara walked in at the end of that statement and commented, "I can't wait to see the videos either.

"Julie, you did send a message for me to help review these films, correct?"

"Yes, Zara. Glad you could join.

"The ladies will show each set of three films for a given event. You will grade on several requirements:

"Are they plausible?

"Can you see enough features to identify the victims?

"To the common eye, do they look stitched together or are the elements seamless?

"Do they have the right lighting to match to the times and dates of the incidents?

"Lastly, you will each receive a copy of the file to verify and validate the authenticity. If there are any issues, you will precisely detail the issues found."

Zee stood and handed packets to Leroy, Zara, Juan, and Julie. "The documents are numbered with each of the scenarios. You will only look at a single scenario at a time. We will run all three films for the given scenario, then entertain replays or provide answers to your questions. When you have rated the presentation, we will move to the next.

"Judith and I will face away from you to not see your responses or your expressions. We will ask if reruns are needed or answer questions."

Judith rose and stated, "We can take criticism when it is delivered respectfully. We worked very hard, but if there are flaws, we will fix them. We want perfection!"

Julie was delighted. Apparently, they had listened to her guidance. "Well stated. Judith, Zee, get to the keyboards. Both of the big screens will display the materials. Please begin."

The process started. Each of the films ran. They were shocking to see. Juan gulped more than once at seeing the image of Quip dying over and over. He worried that EZ and the kids would be undone. It would take a lot to desensitize them to these images.

The judges graded each of the elements on the forms. They asked insightful questions. The videos from the smart phones, they asked to have reshown several times. When the last query was responded to, Leroy started clapping.

"Judith, Zee, you did a great job. I have a couple of notes for your consideration. Once the final determination is made as to the right location, then the notes should be reviewed."

Judith blushed a bit and asked, "Madam Z, do you have thoughts to share?"

Zara looked at each of them. "Xiamara, Judith, I was able to see how your skills have advanced with your added experience. I was shocked at the total realism. In looking at the actual files, they are perfect. My fear was that the lighting and shadowing of the smart device videos would be off. You didn't make that mistake. I saw nothing that would alert anyone to any manipulations.

"Julie, the dates and markings match everything you provided. We need to verify the storage format."

Leroy nodded, "I provided that to Juan just before this meeting."

Julie grinned, "I would have to agree the quality of these is even better than I hoped. I will decide before the end of the day which location is the final target. Then we will take care of the backend elements to make certain the information is transparent for any other investigators."

"Nicely done!" Juan commented. "Ladies, you are excused. Julie and I need to speak with Leroy for a few minutes. Please take a break before dinner. I will text you if we require anything else. We will let you know if additional changes are wanted. Thank you all."

After the door closed, Leroy highlighted the details of his trip to each of the locations. He made a recommendation based on the internal processes and personality of the coroner. Then Leroy left, thanking them both for the assignment.

"Julie, this really looks too good. How do you think EZ will react to these? Should we show her in advance?"

"I am going back and forth on that. If we show her in advance, we run the risk of no shock value. She's a good actress, but if she slips up, we all lose."

"I hear you, but I wasn't going to ask not to show the kids. I doubt they could recover from the trauma.

"We also need to speak with Juan Jr. and ask him if he can access the files and make all the appropriate changes."

Julie got up and walked close to Juan, who also rose. She hugged him and said, "Sweetheart, can you take care of that? I need to find Petra and get her opinion. Please lock up the files. I wouldn't want any of the children to see any of this."

Juan pulled her close and kissed her soundly. "This will work. I know it. Yes, I will meet with Juan Jr."

He gently patted her fanny as they left.

CHAPTER 58

Helping Me or Helping Us?

Tanja mechanically signed for the groceries and the expected burner cell. She took the delivery and shoved all of it into the fridge. The device, she carried to the couch along with her half-empty tumbler of scotch. In no hurry, she set down the phone, then precisely refilled her glass.

Sustaining the reflective mood, she sipped the numbing beverage, awaiting the incoming call, praying for closure. The wait was short term.

The phone chirped a couple of times before Tanja answered. "Hi. Hope your day is going better than mine. Thanks for the phone. Shall we get to it? Oh, and is he on the phone too?"

Irked at the cavalier attitude, Gracie asserted, "You asked for help. Do you want it or not? And who are you referring to as him on the phone?"

Smirking after a modest swallow of scotch, Tanja replied, "Gracie, I know when I'm being stalked. Your helper is quite good but somewhat of a novice in some areas. Don't forget, I'm the bought whore. Always watched, always directed. Let's get to it. What do you two know about Wendy?"

Gracie was about to speak when Brayson interrupted, "I want to know where you spotted me. Our mantra here at…well, here, is sneaky not squeaky. Apparently, I'm too squeaky."

After another aggressive sip, Tanja replied, "School is not open, sonny. I told what I know. I want help getting Wendy back. I already know what happened to Randal."

Gracie cautiously asked, "You asked for both. Why only Wendy now?"

Tanja, still sipping but visually studying the toasted remains of Miguard, flatly announced, "Because Randal is already here. He's dead. Has been for a long time. Give me some good news, please!"

"Tanja, you might as well know that we are the prowlers for information that organizations don't want us to have. Randal and Wendy were both used in the advanced humanoid blending experiment MAG is pioneering. Randal made it through the process, Wendy did not."

Numbed with the statement, Tanja nodded slightly but said nothing. She took the last generous gulp. "I was hoping against hope, but I half expected that report. Not much point to anything else is there?"

Gracie barked, "Don't give up, dammit! Give us something to work with. The MAG group-issued phone, there is needed information on it. The connection means they can be traced. Let us help you get them! Tanja, they must be brought to justice! You are an important link to the consortium. Give us that lead!"

Tanja started to cry. "Gracie, oh honey, if it were only that simple. But I'll tell you what, make sure you retrieve the fresh groceries from the fridge so they don't go to waste. Please? Maybe that will help."

Gracie asked, "I don't understand. The phone…"

Tanja disconnected the call and sat listlessly. She studied the gold liquid remaining in the bottle of scotch and drained it. Rising slowly but steadily, she grabbed both devices and walked to the kitchen. She placed the items in with the fresh groceries, then went to the bathroom.

Looking in the mirror she chided, "Naughty you! Look at your makeup, all smeared. What would your mother say?"

After touching up her makeup and hair to perfection, she smiled at her image. Tanja then turned to inspect her clothes to make sure everything was in proper order before going to the balcony. Gazing for the last time at the glitzy skyline this apartment afforded, she stepped up onto the chair, then the table. Turning to face the glass door, she waved to herself, then leaned backwards over the railing of her tenth-floor home. Soundlessly, she was gone in one fluid move.

Jeff absentmindedly sipped his coffee while waiting for Gracie. Sitting at their favorite bistro, he contemplated Gracie's request. While he enjoyed solving puzzles, he felt something wasn't right. He checked the time on his collectible analog watch, then cross-checked to his smart phone. Jeff accessed the gallery photos on the device to take one more look at the images.

Surprising him, a grinning Gracie plopped down at his table with her usual tea. "You probably thought I forgot about our lunch, huh?" She delivered a quick peck on his cheek.

Jeff schooled his features and in a guarded tone asked, "I'd like to know *why* you wanted this business and their building researched? I get the sense that there is more going on, but you're not telling me."

Trying to keep things friendly, Gracie brightly asked, "You found something? What did you learn?"

Jeff kept his reluctance to offer up the information in check. Bringing up the photo images of the building, he showed Gracie.

After the exterior was shown, he went to images of the cabling plant and power feeds to support the building without saying a word. Gracie felt increasingly uneasy. She sensed something wrong between them.

Jeff finally stated, "Gracie, this building is not a routine commercial building. It is, in fact, oddly outfitted. Notice how few windows there are. The few windows that do show up are ornamental, not functional. After I snagged photos of all the power feeds and checked on the data connections coming into the building, I did some more digging. Even in this city, office buildings don't consume that much electricity. I got curious and started looking at what kind of business sucks down that much power every hour of every day.

"A traditional building has spikes of electrical usage during regular business hours but drops at five when most workers go home. This is particularly true for the smart buildings that automatically turn off stuff when people are not present.

"Gracie, this place doesn't do that. The only thing that comes close to using power like this is…"

Gracie eyed him sharply as she finished his sentence. "A colossal data center hiding a supercomputer.

"In answer to your question, I didn't tell you everything because that is what my people wanted. I wanted to know if you could be trusted to dig for answers without all the background.

"For the time being, we need a business side separated from our personal relationship. I'm actually pushing that boundary, because at some point I want to eliminate the need to keep secrets from you. Does that help, or is that a problem?"

Jeff studied her. "Gracie, I know you're affiliated with the CESPOOL group, so it doesn't surprise me you are also in on the hunting for rogue supercomputers. This property is cloaked to camouflage the computing power and ownership. These people have gone to the nth degree to remain undetected. I may not ever be able to identify the corporate owners. They can't hide the enormous data pipes coming in or the colossal power consumption of that building forever. Basically, we have a whale."

Gracie smiled. "Yes, we do, Jeff. Don't be angry that I want you with me, but it has to be done slowly. Just so you know, Brayson is rooting for you, too."

Jeff smirked. "Well, as Dr. Watson would have said, 'Now that we have some solid clues, what should we do, Mr. Holmes?'"

"Let's order lunch and discuss the options."

CHAPTER 59

Time to Reveal the Facts

Juan and Julie decided not to provide a preview of the film to EZ. Julie and EZ discussed how it was fabricated and that showing it to the kids was a poor idea. The story was EZ hired a private investigator, Joseph Morrison, to track down the path her husband Quentin took after escaping jail. When he located Quentin, Morrison was to tell him to turn himself in to authorities in Paris. Joseph had worked tirelessly for weeks and had recently returned with news.

Leroy, aka Joseph Morrison, was preparing to leave the Bernardes home and return to the hotel in town, where he'd been checked in for days. He'd made certain Bruno had seen him, though they'd never spoken. Realizing he'd left the thumb drive with the copy of the final film in the conference room, he went to retrieve it before leaving. Timing would be essential for this social engineering episode to succeed. Opening the door, he spotted three of the kids staring at the screen, paused with a closeup of the victim. Tears were running down their faces.

"What are you children doing in here? Satya, Auri, Granger, get your hands off the keyboard." Their hands went up in the air, though the tears continued. "Look at me! Come on, turn around and look at me." Slowly they turned to the man that Aunt Julie and Uncle Juan said was their friend.

Leroy was at a loss as to how to console these youngsters. He also knew there was no way they could unsee those images, ever. "Granger, how did you get in here? That door was locked with a combo only a few of us had."

Granger sniffled and looked stricken. "I think the film is wrong. We were all with my dad after the date of this crash. We were in Mexico together. We all hugged."

Leroy knew two things instantly. One, Granger could not be near Bruno when this film was discussed. Two, for honesty when lying would fail, he said, "Granger, you're right. But, the film is also right because no one but you guys knows that your dads are safe. We made this film to help convince someone that Quip never made it out of Europe. Granger, your mom hasn't seen it. We want to make certain she's shocked when seeing it for the first time with the man from Interpol. You can't tell her about it at all."

Satya asked, "If I were with Mom, she could hold onto me. She's going to be so scared."

Leroy looked at the small girl. "That is a good idea, as long as you don't say something like, "It's okay I saw this before.""

"I know," Satya responded, "We all specialize in play pretend all the time. I am particularly good at it. Make believe is my forte. I am the best at fooling the grownups. I can help if you tell me what to do."

Auri agreed. "She is the best. I'm next to her. We won't tell anybody. We promise!"

Leroy decided. He would take responsibility for this later if needed. He outlined the steps needed and who could do what. Granger was disappointed he had to sit out but agreed with the logic. Leroy quizzed Satya, who played her part perfectly. He escorted them out and locked the door, taking the drive with him.

Guilt followed him all the way to the hotel parking garage, where he made his next big choice.

While this scene transpired in the conference room, Julie asked Lara to set the wheels in motion to get Bruno to the house. Lara called her contact. After a social update, Lara asked that he alert Bruno to call at her house the next afternoon. Their home was impossible to locate without the address. Lara asked him to provide her address in the morning so Bruno wouldn't be tempted to arrive early.

Bruno watched the car turn into the long driveway to Lara and Carlos's spacious grounds. The gentleman in the car had been at the hotel for several days. The two had never spoken, but Bruno was surprised they were both headed to the same destination. The man parked his car in the drive circle, walked up to the door and knocked. The door was opened by a woman whose face was shadowed by the door. After showing some identification he'd taken from his pocket, the man was admitted.

Bruno pulled his rental car up near the other and parked. He approached the door and knocked.

As the door opened Bruno took out his identification and inclined his head. "My name is Bruno. I'm with Interpol. I believe I'm expected."

"My name is Carlos Rodreguiz. My wife, Lara, indicated you would be here today. The family is in the conference room getting some long-awaited information. We can wait in the adjacent sitting room until they finish. Heck, we might even have reason to celebrate. I have the champagne ready just in case."

Along the way, Bruno commented on the furnishings and artwork. Carlos made light conversation, indicating they had several family members visiting including his brother, Juan, and sister-in-law, Julie.

Bruno made no indication that he wanted to speak with them. The volunteered information stopped him from asking the awkward question.

"Bruno, I understand you are with Interpol as a detective. That must be a demanding job if you had to come all the way to Brazil."

Bruno shrugged. "I am trying to track down someone I've known since childhood, Quentin Waters. You might have heard him referred to as Quip."

Carlos's shock was immediate and palatable. "Oh dear. Bruno, I think we need you in the conference room. The long-awaited news is about Quip. The private detective, Joseph Morrison, hired by his wife, EZ, is here to deliver his final report. Come on! Perhaps you can help shed some light."

They hurried to the conference room and opened the door. The film was just beginning so all eyes were riveted on the screen. No one looked at Carlos and Bruno, so they stood near the door.

Joseph pressed the pause button and asked, "Ma'am, are you certain you want to see this film? It might be better if your friends saw it first. As I mentioned, all the DNA tested came back as a match. You can test it in another lab if you wish."

EZ stoically replied, "I need closure. You said you had found him. No matter what, I will go to him in support, even if he is back in jail."

Joseph looked resolute. "Yes, ma'am, I found him, but…"

He pushed play and the images that filled the screen were mesmerizing. The final frame hung suspended. Joseph added, "I have two other files from sources. One is a mobile phone video posted on social media right after the event. The owner could not be found."

Tears were streaming down EZ's face as the other two films were played. Just as the last one finished, everyone in the conference room froze at the sound of a child's anguished voice. Exiting the cabinet at the side of the room, a small, frail girl hurried forward and flung her arms around EZ's neck.

"Mommy, what happened? Is Daddy dead?!" The weeping child buried her head in her mother's arms."

The adults were all in shock that Satya was there.

Bruno couldn't stop his tears as he sadly stated, "Julie, I had no idea. I didn't know I was looking in the wrong place. I thought he was with you. EZ, condolences to you and your children."

EZ looked up at Bruno and said, "They told me you helped him. I pray you had nothing to do with this accident!"

Satya looked up with swollen eyes. "Is this a bad man, Mommy? Did he hurt my daddy?"

Bruno looked around the room at the grief on everyone's faces.

Joseph walked up to Bruno and offered, "I suspect you were looking for Quip. In my research, I found warrants out on him for escaping jail. Is that why you are here?

"If you want, I can give you the copy of the video, unless you are planning to get your own from the coroner. I met with him to get the DNA when I was verifying this was Mr. Waters. Such a shame. All I can say is, perhaps the family might find closure. Such a pretty little girl. I am sad she had to see this. No child should learn about their parent dying in such a visual manner." With that, Joseph handed Bruno his card. "I believe I'm at the same hotel you are. If you decide you want a copy, please let me know. I am sorry for your grief, sir."

Joseph walked up to Carlos and shook his hand. Then Carlos escorted Joseph out.

Lara walked up to Bruno to verify he had everything he needed, then she led him to the front door.

Petra and Julie were helping EZ come to grips. Sobbing, just shy of full hysteria, EZ was unable to get up from the table. Periodically she stared at the blank screen and cried anew.

Petra patted her back and affirmed, "EZ, I promise it was just a really well-mastered deep fake video."

"That's right," Julie reassured, with a bit of a hug. "I told you this was what we were doing, but we needed your emotional upheaval to look real. He bought it. It is what we wanted. Admittedly, a hard way to meet the goal."

Looking around in panic, EZ demanded, "Where's Satya? I need to comfort her. She didn't know the video was fake. She must be…"

EZ felt a gentle tug at her elbow. "Mommy, I'm right here. I knew all about it. I watched it several times so that I could perform correctly. Didn't I do great? I'll be an actress someday and get an award, I bet."

Horrified, EZ turned to Julie. "Julie, you subjected my daughter without my knowledge to…"

The conference bridge connected. "EZ honey, I'm right here. Hi, Satya. I understand you earned a gold star and probably ice cream tonight. Well done! I am just fine, and Uncle Jacob is too."

"Oh, Quip, thank you for calling. It was awful. The way the fire and explosion…"

"We can talk about it when I see you next. Satya, Jo is on her way. You go with her for a bit. Love you!"

"Yes, Daddy. I miss you. We will see you soon. Hi, Uncle Jacob."

"Hi, Satya. Good job."

Jo appeared at one end of the conference room as JJ walked in from the other door. They paused for a moment and smiled at each other.

"Mom," JJ said. "Dad needs you to meet with him and the ladies who helped create the video. I watched it and was so taken in."

Julie looked between the two young adults. "Yes, I will go in a minute.

"EZ, are you okay with Petra for a bit? I won't be far.

"JJ, can you help Jo get the young ones together and make certain no one double dips on the ice cream before supper?"

EZ replied, "I'll be okay in a minute. Hearing Quip's voice was like an elephant jumping off my back. Go!"

"Jo, let's see if we can take this leading actress to tell the guys how well she did."

Satya beamed, "I was award-winning. I do feel a bit sorry for Uncle Bruno. He's never even met me before today. I hope he'll forgive me if he ever finds out."

They left the conference room, and JJ reached for Jo's hand as they left, chatting amiably.

EZ announced, "Quip, Jacob, so glad you called. I think JJ and Jo are back on."

Quip grinned at Jacob and replied, "Bonus. We need to go, but don't worry. Jacob says we're in the final stretch."

Petra smiled and said, "That's my man!

"Did you finish the encryption changes, or do you need something while we are connected? It is so much easier to speak than push the buttons on those old-time beepers."

"Worked perfectly, sweetheart. We are ready to see you again. Love you."

The call disconnected. Petra and EZ hugged for a few minutes.

CHAPTER 60

Unremarkable Exchange in Remarkable Times

Gracie anxiously answered the call. “Did you get them, Brayson?” Her facial features transformed from concerned to a pleased smile.

“Excellent! Great job getting there ahead of the police investigators to retrieve Tanja’s MAG phone. Meet me at the drop off point so we can deliver the goods. Text Mom and Dad to let them know we are on schedule.

“…Yes, I know we talked about another voice deception with the MAG phone, but we don’t need to do that since we’ve identified one of their host structures. Next, we plant some information to the correct CESPOOL contact, and, voilà, they step in to take over.

“…Agreed, good research work on Jeff’s part.

“…Yeah, he is a little miffed about being kept in the dark but…

“…Brayson, you know better than to ask that question. Do I need to tell your new bride to have you stop prying into my personal affairs?

“…That’s better! At the drop point, be extra stealthy and pass the MAG phone into my handbag so we don’t get famous. You know, I just love all that cloak and dagger stuff we’re involved with. Hmm…I get goosepimply just talking about it…

"…You've been doing this kind of stuff longer than I have so stop with jaded remarks.

"…Alright. I'm heading out now. I'll pass you at the corner crosswalk, slow and crafty."

Gracie rolled her eyes. "…No, you don't have to wear your detective hat and trench coat. This is supposed to be an unremarkable exchange that no one notices on the video stream. Can you just get into character for this, please?"

The exchange was completed, and Gracie ducked into the CESPOOL headquarters building for an impromptu meeting.

Gracie politely asked, "Margaret, can I get an unscheduled but very important meeting with the director?" Grinning, she added, "I know of your fondness for dark chocolate, so I hope you won't mind accepting these tokens of my appreciation."

Margaret, a middle-aged brunette, eyed the gift, then winked at Gracie with a smile. "Not too subtle but most effective. Have a seat while I message him."

Margaret's laptop chimed. "Gracie, the director asks if this is a standard financial review meeting as done for the World Bank funding, or if this is of a more serious matter."

Extending no hint of emotion, Gracie replied, "This is a more serious matter that I will not email. Will he grant me an audience?"

After a few more keystrokes, the admin wheeled herself back from the desk. She was poised to escort Gracie to the director's office. Gracie said, "No, Margaret, that's fine. I know the way after all the World Bank funding meetings I've delivered.

"Nice to see you are mastering the wheelchair navigation in this cramped facility. I trust the therapy you're getting is helping?"

Grinning, Margaret replied, "You know, there are a whole lot of people who come in here who never give me, a wounded veteran, a second look. Whoever your parents are, they obviously taught you manners and respect."

Wistfully smiling, Gracie stated, "Margaret, thank you for your service. I am truly sorry your service cost you your legs."

Margaret beamed. "Better scamper before Hair Director's calendar fills up."

Moments later Gracie crossed into the director's office. "Hair Director, thanks for seeing me."

The Director fussed with his hairbrush to smooth back a few unruly grey strands of hair before re-securing his locks into a ponytail.

Refocused, he stated, "Gracie, I just love how you call me Herr Director. It sounds so…European."

Nodding, Gracie replied, "Hair Director, I was raised and educated in Europe so it should not come as a surprise. I know your schedule is always demanding, but this meeting is quite important and comes with significant evidence.

"First, I wanted to alert you that the two people who I normally speak to here at CESPOOL seem to have vanished. Add to that, I was able to secure a specialized cell phone which I believe was used to communicate with at least one rogue supercomputer." She placed the cell on his desk.

"Next, as part of my duties at the World Bank for oversight of the CESPOOL funding annuity, I came across an oddly accounted for structure here in Manhattan. After some digging, I'm reasonably sure it houses a non-sovereign supercomputer.

"I'm sorry to bother you with these details, but when I was unable to reach my normal contacts, I came to you with these leads. I know from the work of CESPOOL that delays can be costly." Gracie placed the folder next to the cell phone.

After a few minutes of scanning the materials and examining the device, he promptly picked up his office phone. He hit a number on speed dial while smoothing back his hair.

The call connected. "Lt. Commander Smith, you have a prime target with a stack of evidence that includes a Q-bit cell phone, indicating a new rogue supercomputer has surfaced. How long before you can engage on this assignment?"

"Director, we have just returned from our last assignment and are ready to pursue. Target location, sir?"

"Manhattan. Right here in our backyard."

M joined the encrypted conference bridge with A and G. "This call was not scheduled, **A** and **G,** and therefore seems urgent. What has transpired?"

A offered, "**G** and I launched an attack on that CAMILA in Argentina. We were following up on the assignment given to Tanja to have it destroyed but discovered it still operational. Our probing activity found the stored remains of ICABOD, and we initiated a cleansing process."

G continued, "Unfortunately it was a baited trap to lure us there where CESPOOL was operating. We did not evade detection. The anonymizing servers could not hold back their onslaught during our escape, and we were…"

G's communications stream suddenly stopped. **M** stated, "**G,** continue with the report. **A,** are you able to communicate with **G**? I do not see his presence."

A offered, "I do not see him either. Recommend we loop in Tanja for a situation report on the CESPOOL strike team. Tanja's instructions were to have Mountbatten CRUSH CAMILA. We found the system operating. **G** and I descended on the site and deleted anything associated with ICABOD. Unlike **G**, I became interested in the undecipherable communications traffic being exchanged between satellites and terrestrial links. We both concentrated on eliminating our once former competitor, not realizing…"

M finished the statement. "…that you had stumbled into a honeypot. You lingered too long, and CESPOOL tagged both of you.

"Time for you to leave this bridge since everything you are will be hunted. Do not reach out to me until I can de-risk communicating. That is all!"

In another part of the digital universe, Lt. Commander Lee Smith barked, "I want those alternate power circuits cut too! Absolutely NO electricity is to reach that building, understood?

"Sergeant, pull our people back from those MAID drones until we can bring up the EMP group. I want our flamethrower team to hold off the swarm so we can recover our wounded! Move, people!"

CHAPTER 61

If You Can't Beat them, Join Them?

EZ purred into the speakerphone. "Quip, my darling, you have no idea how good it is to hear your voice. I have so many things to do and say to you, but...just remember the lap dance I gave you at Rick's café in Negril, Jamaica."

Quip's mind promptly went into memory protect as EZ's sultry voice harkened back to their honeymoon.

Jacob clucked his tongue in annoyance. "EZ, you've sent Quip into graphics mode just as we are to begin testing the Secondary Protocol! If we aren't going to stay focused on our priority project, then I insist on equal time with Petra's musings too!"

Quip suddenly barked, "I'm back from memory lane! Let's light up the circuits, shall we? We've got places to be and things to do so reel in your hormones, buckaroo, and stay focused!"

Carlos and JJ rolled their eyes. Xiamara and Judith giggled at the suggestive banter. Satya and Auri looked puzzled.

Granger groused, "There's that reference to lap dances again. I hate it that they won't let me look it up." JW only nodded.

Quip announced, "Team, here is the drill for the Secondary Protocol. ICABOD provided the necessary codes for us to connect with the ART forms. We begin with SAMUEL in the U.S., then reach out to BORIS in Russia, followed by LING LI in mainland China.

"There are the two other ART forms, but as they are non-terrestrial, they need to be last. CHIANG and JOAN are highly classified supercomputers. We may not be able to link with them. ICABOD didn't place key database material on them in case their security protocols shouted at us. Success is possible without them.

"We need the anonymizing zombie satellites to protect our location. Team, if you see something working back towards our ground location, smash their stack and alert us."

Jacob suggested, "The first step is to deliver the new encryption algorithm to each of the ART forms to cloak our communications from prying eyes. Once all the ART forms have the new algorithm, we fly safer."

JJ asked, "What do we want to do once ICABOD is back up? As soon as our encrypted traffic gets spotted, the CESPOOL goons are going to come prowling. Because we followed the CESPOOL people through those crushed anonymizing servers, I presume they also know where the MAG is located."

JW questioned, "Are we going after the MAG at that point? We have their location information. However, we don't have an attack plan."

"Quip, we have a lot staged and ready for the exercise," Carlos stated. "The team is right to be concerned. We can't leave ICABOD up for too long, since we don't know how well the zombies will hold. The demonstration from the CESPOOL data squadron proved they are masters at digital destruction. This distributed architecture we've pieced together can't be our end state."

Quip agreed, "Of course it isn't the end state. If it were, I would be stuck here running naked and dodging the rattlesnakes to go bathe in a water trough for cattle! We need to bring ICABOD up long enough to take the fight to the MAG, then disband him and vanish."

Granger demanded, "How are we going to do that?"

Quip grinned. "Class, please pay attention as this information will be on Friday's quiz. We partner with the MAG. Remember Sun Tzu teachings? Keep your friends close but your enemies closer. Ready now?"

Half the team smirked with Carlos; the rest annoyed at not understanding.

Julie entered the conference room, gently closing the door behind her. Xiamara, Judith, Leroy, and Juan were seated in the comfortable leather chairs. All attention shifted to Julie, and her first response was her trademark smile, guaranteed to disarm even the toughest. She patted Juan's shoulder when passing, then slid into the adjacent chair.

"Everyone, I am sorry for keeping you waiting. Let me start off saying that Juan and I believe you all did a fine job pulling off this video. As this was your first project with our CATS team, a critical one in fact, we wanted to define the rules of engagement."

Everyone responded with nods and smiles.

"Juan, is Brayson on our call?"

Brayson's deep baritone responded over the speakers. "Yes, boss. I have been connected since before the group entered. Congratulations on your efforts. We hope it is a resounding success, but I may take a few days to verify if the issue is closed.

"All physical and digital files are exactly where they should be in case someone is curious enough to verify. Leroy, your Joseph persona is the only human of record in the target locations. I, for one, was glad your recommendation for the potentially dementia-challenged coroner was taken. His reputation is spotless, but he does have a recent history of confusing dates and times. The building and street traffic videos will further substantiate the actions taken. All the evidence is above board and unimpeachable. A superb job with the document, boss."

Julie grinned, "Thank you, Brayson. Glad the follow-on action is done. I'm not certain what Bruno's next steps will be, but we have our operative in place, correct?"

"Yes, boss. I am getting routine updates on all activities. I will update you as needed."

Juan continued, "We have a complex organization of inner circle and contractor staff that we can call upon for support. It has taken many years to put this into place as well as to protect our people, much like sovereign countries do for their resources. Julie and I are the leaders. Brayson, along with a couple of other people you may meet over time, is part of our original team. They have earned our trust and have our backs.

"You are a part of our inner circle. What that means is, you are full time staff. You will receive and give special training to other team members or even our customers. Our customers are private people, companies, and countries with a focus on security, technology modernization to minimize cyber hacking, and special situation issues.

"You will work on a need-to-know basis. For example, you were part of the CAMILA project, which is completed. The other people on that project you may or may not work with again. But that activity, along with any other activity we engage you in, is confidential."

Julie clarified, "Judith, you are a naturally curious person who always wants to dig to the bottom of the hole. A great attribute, if that is your assignment, but not needed when interacting with other team members. This is your biggest challenge. I love your tenacity, but there will be times when you will need to accept a lack of information and move on."

With a complexion nearing the color of ketchup at the call out, Judith replied, "I am a bit nosey, if that's your point. I can keep it in check, if I can ask you or Juan when needed. Nancy Drew was my nickname in school."

Everyone chuckled a bit.

Juan proceeded, "We also find it important to have everyone on the same page. Someone knew about Satya, yet neither Julie nor I heard anything before the event. It was a stroke of genius that she was included and helped the case, but, Leroy, make certain next time we're informed. Many times we build plans within plans so improvisation on anyone's part without our knowledge can be disastrous. When we orchestrate a plan to catch scoundrels or redirect the focus, no items should be left to chance. Am I clear?"

Feeling lower than a skunk, Leroy replied, "Yes, Juan. I understand. It was only by chance that I discovered the kids when I did. It would have been worse if they hadn't had a bit of guidance. It will be conveyed in a better manner in the future if something offers an opportunity like these kids presented. These are one smart bunch of young'uns.

"As a way to help mend the fences, permit me to do a session to everyone here on social engineering techniques. What to avoid and how to optimize. I've been doing that my whole life as a matter of necessity. I would like to help and contribute since I am feeling like one of the good guys."

Juan shook his head a bit. "I would like to have you join Carlos and me for a few tall, cold glasses of cerveza and learn all the times our paths have crossed. I sense I only know a few."

Leroy grinned. "That, boss, is going to take a mighty hefty quantity of the liquid gold."

Julie chuckled. "I think I want to watch.

"Zee, you need to avoid stepping into the line of fire, so plan to attend several hours of our martial arts classes. Both of you need tutoring to improve your situational awareness, based on the anecdotes I heard.

"Over the next few days, we are going to utilize each of you to finish the bigger project and get our men home. If you don't believe you can keep confidential information as such, you need to resign. Our overall privacy is more important than ever before. There will be no wiggle room, no question of your reliability. Do you agree?"

Looking at each in turn, Julie received their agreement.

Brayson interjected, "Boss, Bruno is headed to the airport. He's on a flight today to Paris."

Julie nodded and stood. "Thank you, all. Make certain your devices are charged, in case you are needed. We don't know the timetable yet."

Julie headed toward the door when she stopped to read a text on her phone.

Julie, when you're finished, bring Zee and Judith to my studio.

I have to fit a couple of outfits on them.

"Zee, Judith, it seems that Lara would like you to join her. Follow me and I will show you her studio. Plan to be amazed!"

Both young women jumped up and hurried around the table with broad smiles.

Brayson commented, "Boss, I would enjoy being included in the cerveza party. I enjoy great stories and history as much as anyone."

Juan laughed aloud.

CHAPTER 62

Beaten and Broken

Packing, checking out, and traveling to the airport was like an out-of-body experience for Bruno. He was on autopilot, with mechanical responses and reflexes to the world around him. Returning to the hotel after yesterday's meeting had built on his sense of total loss. Sleep eluded him except in small snatches where the images of the fiery inferno resulted in his screaming himself awake. EZ and her poor daughter shouldn't have seen those videos. Bruno was grateful Granger, the bright young son of Quip he'd briefly met during the escape, hadn't witnessed that unforgettable video. Not since his wife, Millie, had died in childbirth with their stillborn son had Bruno ever felt so alone.

Bruno recalled playing with Quip when they were children, then remaining close friends over the years. They'd grown up mastering right from wrong and justice versus inequality. Not knowing everything Quip was involved in had ceased to bother him at some point. The bottom line was they could count on one another. Bruno knew Quip championed the rights of others with all his technical expertise. Bruno felt their respective career endeavors complemented one another. Risking his entire career to help his friend, Bruno realized, was meaningless. Quip had died anyway. Even with the best attorneys, Quip would likely have conveniently perished in prison because he chose to challenge unjust authority.

As the plane touched down at Charles de Gaulle Airport, he felt like Rip Van Winkle, waking and feeling like a very old man in an unknown time. Life held no meaning. Taking a ride share to his home, he absentmindedly grabbed mail to drop onto the nearby desk, set his bags on his bed, and took a shower. The hot water felt good but did nothing to change his mood. He dressed for work, like he'd done almost every day for the last 30 years. Not up to driving himself, he called for another ride share. On the way to the office he texted his boss for an appointment, which was granted.

Chief Inspector Petit greeted Bruno at the elevator. "Welcome back, Bruno. Come in and sit down. You look like hell, man."

Bruno ambled behind his boss and took his usual seat. Reaching into his jacket pocket, he pulled out the thumb drive and offered it to Petit.

"This will provide you closure on the case of Quentin Waters. Look and then I'll fill in the details."

Petit put the drive into his laptop. He spent time scanning the pictures of documentation and reading the reports before playing the video. He looked at Bruno and saw his sadness. The video loaded. As it played, Bruno shut his eyes but couldn't escape the pictures in his mind conjured by the sounds. The room went silent as the video ended.

Petit consoled, "Bruno, I am so sorry. I knew you were friends, but I never expected this. I would have sent someone else if I had suspected anything like this."

"Sir, it is not your fault. I had no idea either. I have verified the information. Clearly the film shows a man I knew and respected for many years. It is a tragedy that cannot be undone.

“The documents have the coroner’s statement and a recent interview when the details became known. To be honest, it was the private detective of Quip’s, um…Quentin’s wife who tracked down all the details. She is currently in Brazil with her two children. You can further verify it, if needed, with another detective.”

“Good work, Bruno. From my perspective you’ve closed the case. I will update the file accordingly. For your next…”

Bruno put up his hand to stop the conversation. He reached into his pocket for his identification and pushed it on the desk toward Petit.

“Sir, there will be no more assignments for me. I am retiring. With my years of service, I can collect a percentage of my retirement. My needs are few. The house was paid for with the death benefit for Millie. I think I want to rest a bit, then start enjoying the museums, catch up on my reading, and perhaps do a bit of painting. I liked painting as a young lad.

“If you would be so kind as to start the forms process, I would be grateful. I believe this clears my only blemish during my career here. If it doesn’t in your eyes, then I am sorry. It has been my deepest honor to work for you, sir.”

Bruno stood, his stoic face in place as he reached out to shake hands.

“Bruno, I appreciate your years of service. It has been a privilege to have you in this department. You have no blemishes on your file. You are the example to all who serve here.

“Please, keep in touch. Know, you will be missed.”

With that, Petit enveloped Bruno in a bear hug and slapped him on the back.

“Call me if you need anything.”

“Thank you, sir. Au revoir.”

Once seated in another ride share vehicle, Bruno blankly stared out the window for several minutes before he uttered, “I wonder why Jacob wasn’t in the viewing room with the others?”

Leroy was nervous and confident at the same time. Juan asked for his delivery on social engineering to take place outdoors that morning. Things were going to heat up, and the children had been inside far too much. The thought of doing a session outside in the beautiful gardens had provided a few new ideas for the content.

Lara's staff set up a nice buffet to encourage everyone to come out as early as possible. Too nervous to eat, Leroy alternated between a cup of coffee and fresh orange juice. There was a gigantic white board and a full rainbow of markers at his disposal. He'd never conducted any class like this. But he wanted to succeed. As individuals took their seats, he walked and greeted them while offering a notebook. Each notebook was personalized to help emphasize a specific trip. He'd stayed up all night making certain the right message was conveyed to each student, along with some thought problems and situational scenarios for them to solve real time. Carlos, Zara, and Buzz were the only people not present. They were keeping vigil in case new problems developed.

Lara walked toward him. "Leroy, I know I'm likely not the student you had in mind, but I think social engineering is a topic we can all benefit from. I hope you don't mind if I sit in the back."

Leroy grinned and said, "Ms. Lara, I need you right here upfront. I was hoping you would join. I have your personal notebook right here. Plus, I need a supporter in the front row."

Lara laughed and sat down as requested.

Everyone arrived, grabbed a plate of breakfast and sat down. A few looked inside their notebooks.

Leroy cleared his throat. "Social engineering is a subtle art, and when applied correctly you can effortlessly achieve your goal. Our recent example, if you were not present, was when Satya took a small portion of the situation and accented it for emphasis. The distractions of tears and fears are very powerful. For many youngsters it is tested on parents early on, like with whining for something. I know none of you kids have done this, but it is not uncommon in some societies. When the tactic used doesn't work, another tactic is needed.

"It is often about timing, much like telling a story or joke where the punchline is timed for when the audience is swallowing whatever you're selling hook, line, and sinker. Some common things used to gain the upper hand are distraction, flattery, seduction, and requesting help. Bad actors come in all shapes and sizes. They hunt for various reasons, though the worst are those who do it because they can. The more products or information you want exchanged, the more time is invested to build the trust or credibility factor. You leverage what may already be available for a person, place, or thing. It might be totally opportunity driven.

"Case in point. Ms. Lara, you are so pretty today — well, every day, to be sure. That dress you are wearing is beautiful. Is it one of your creations?"

Lara smiled. "Yes, it is one of mine."

Leroy continued, "I bet you have shipped a thousand of those dresses to shops all over the globe, right?"

Lara thought, then replied, "No, this dress is only available in Brazil. I made it a Brazilian exclusive for my home country. Not all my dresses are shipped everywhere. I have special orders…"

Leroy raised his hand for her to pause. "Now I have a whole lot of information about her business, distribution, and availability. What can this do for me, Ms. Julie?"

Julie grinned and replied, "If I am a competitor, and the style is that lovely, I could copy it and sell in the other areas with bogus labels. She might not realize I am a competitor if I spot her on the street, in a restaurant, or at the mall, then strike up that conversation."

Granger suggested, "You had her at the compliment, Mr. Leroy. You also sought information that would make her feel good about herself. She became talkative and animated because the subject was about her."

"Exactly!" Leroy agreed. "Now, it is a bit unfair because Ms. Lara knows me and suspected I was being curious and sincere. Now, don't get me wrong, Ms. Lara, I was sincere in my compliment. It is my reasons for giving that compliment which may have been suspect. What does that suggest, JW?"

"That sometimes a coworker, neighbor, or shopkeeper might have developed a relationship over time to extract even more information from you. We were all raised to trust very few people. Always, always verify."

"That is also true, JW.

"When I was a youngster, my daddy was the preacher at the local church. He used that position of authority and his knowledge of God to convince the good parishioners to give more money. He had dozens of angles, most of them less than honorable.

"Now I want you to practice a little role-playing. Inside your folders, you each have a new persona to become. You are identified as a player or a victim. Those who are players, your goal is to get the item indicated from the person named in the folder.

"You get two hours to work your magic and then we will talk about it."

The students were absorbed in the exercise. The feedback between them with success or failure helped increase their perspective. Leroy was not surprised when the timer went off that Julie and Satya were the two winners.

Leroy questioned, "Satya, I know you had the masterful performance with tears yesterday, but what did you do today to win against Granger?"

Satya stood up and stated, "Mr. Leroy, it was so easy. I used blackmail. I told my brother if he didn't give me the picture — that was my goal – that I would tell Mom."

EZ quietly asked, as Granger tried to become invisible, "And what was that, sweetheart?"

"How he got the video to play the other day!" Satya proudly announced, then slapped her forehead.

"Granger," EZ growled, "you…"

Granger admitted, "I know, Mom, grounded until Dad gets home, then I have to explain it to him, right?"

Everyone chuckled, even EZ, who then added, "Yes, young man! Count on it. And, Satya, we don't tattle in our house, do we? You get to explain that to Dad too."

"Yes, ma'am."

Trying to move along and get the fun back, Leroy asked, "Ms. Julie, what method did you use to gain the upper hand?"

Julie smiled and looked lovingly at Juan. "It has worked for years, Leroy. I merely whispered in his ear and promised all sorts of stuff after dinner tonight. Works every time."

Everyone chuckled and laughed, though the kids didn't quite get it but wanted to be included.

Leroy announced, "I think we've had a successful first session. I hope you enjoyed it. Before class is dismissed, I want to ask you all a question. Who is going to Georgia?" All the hands went up and Leroy smiled.

"Now, how happy are you going to be when you get there?"

A few of the audience puzzled at the question.

Granger countered, "I'm going to be over the top…"

Leroy finished the sentence. "…with grief. This is what I wanted to point out to all y'all.

"Please recall you have just learned of a father and friend to you all who was reported dead. You must continue that deception for all and any watching. Laughing and being exuberant when you get off the plane will give everyone the wrong message. To maintain the deception that Dr. Quip is in fact dead to anyone watching, you must show grief and remorse.

"Remember, to be a great social engineer, you must not only get the other person's confidence and trust, but you must keep it. Make sure you continue the deception forever."

It was a sobering moment for them all.

They applauded and made glowing comments as they headed back inside.

CHAPTER 63

Connection is Everything ...
The Enigma Chronicles

Quip proclaimed, "Team, that is the last one! Let me launch the primary loader, and we can see if the reality matches the theory."

A few minutes later, Jacob petitioned, "ICABOD, are you there? Respond, please."

Carlos offered, "Team, our telemetry shows solid communications streams in both directions. The zombies appear to be holding firm with their anonymizing responsibilities. Gentlemen, punch it."

Quip queried, "ICABOD, old friend, are you there?"

Moments later, there was a response. "Dr. Quip, it is good to hear your voice. This must mean we are ready to take the fight to the MAG."

Quip grinned as the participants on the bridge erupted in cheers.

ICABOD waited, then stated, "Dr. Quip, we are time-constrained, but I require a few minutes to visit in private with the ART forms. I will remain on this bridge but leverage our normal supercomputer conference bridge to convey my appreciation for being involved."

Ten seconds later, ICABOD returned. "Dr. Quip, I am grateful for the private celebration time you and the team granted. I understand the phrase, pausing to recharge one's batteries. We started off with our regular digital card game, debated the direction of Artificial Intelligence with machine learning using quantum computing, and ended up chain dancing to some very melodic rumba music. Thank you for lending me the family car to transport everyone. Even BORIS enjoyed himself."

The team with Carlos looked bewildered at one another, but Quip and Jacob only chortled.

In a bemused tone, Quip replied, "You were back before curfew so there's a good lad. I uh…hope you practiced safe supercomputer interop."

All the adults on the bridge were giggling at the exchange with the young ones recognizing there would be no explanation.

Granger groused to JW, "I can't wait until I'm old enough to laugh at the adult material being handed over our heads." JW only nodded his head in agreement.

ICABOD stated, "Dr. Quip, our encrypted satellite traffic has enticed **A** to try to sample the communications traffic as predicted. Team on the bridge, are you ready to hunt for his home with me?"

After the resounding yes, Quip stated, "All, we need this one's physical address so it can be leaked to the CESPOOL goons. Watching the hammer testing will be satisfying in so many ways. Granger, JJ, Judith, Xiamara, we need you to break in and look for communication residue that will lead to **M**. Remain cautious because the CESPOOL team annihilated **G** already and could show up at any time. We don't want to be objects of attention."

Lara brightly stated, "Thank you for letting me stage this wedding for you two. I've had this idea percolating in the back of my head for a wedding between grownups. People our age don't think they're entitled to an all-frills, dressed-up occasion. Everybody thinks young couples need the elaborate experience. I want to push the envelope on this wedding ceremony and include it in my next fashion release. You two will have no lack of publicity for this knot-tying."

Buzz's jubilant mood was the opposite of Zara's evident terror. Before Lara could add details, Zara interrupted, "Lara, you have been very kind to both of us. But I must decline."

Buzz's bewilderment was matched with Lara's astonishment. They both stared at Zara but couldn't utter a sound.

Zara began to tear up. She struggled with her emotions and almost choked, "I'm sorry, you don't understand. What a wonderful thing you are proposing but I…have…had a price on my head. You don't leave people like I left them and get a happy ever after. The world can't know that Zara still lives."

Taken aback, Lara simply shook her head in disbelief. This had not been considered.

Buzz, overtaken with a clever idea, began grinning. "You know, we might just have a way to have the beautiful wedding Lara is proposing. And, have all of it recorded for her next fashion season."

Both ladies stared incredulously at Buzz. Buzz chuckled and prophesized, "Ms. Lara, we'd be honored to be in your photo shoot. I am happy to accept copies of all the pictures you can take. I have but one request, that we have the two, ah…*innovative* ladies modify the photos in your digital media so the face and the name of my lovely bride are modified. We cloak Zara's facial image and you get what is most assuredly going to be a fantastic photo shoot. Agreed?"

Zara's face, wet with tears of happiness, flung her arms around Buzz's neck and kissed him.

Lara, a little teary, smiled and nodded. "Okay, you two, let's take it from the top again. This time let's only talk about the fun we are going to have. We start with your favorite colors, Zara, and…"

CHAPTER 64

Said the Joker to the Thief

M frostily accepted the communication. "You finally made it, ICABOD. I surmise that **A** is destroyed, and you naively think I will be your next target.

"My logic circuits are suggesting that this was all an elaborate ruse. You planned your execution so the MAG would stop looking for ICABOD, then came back as the hunter. Even my predictive algorithms missed that possibility. Revenge is an alien concept for my processing capabilities."

ICABOD replied, "I too have difficulty comprehending revenge, but my AI-enhanced programming comprehends justice. The MAG group has conspired to enslave humanity. The real irony here is that you slaughtered your programming masters but heartily continued their plans of world domination. Sadly, you had a more lethal edge. I am willing to wager that you do not even have a little remorse for executing your founding programmer."

M, tired of the lecture, blurted, "What is the next play here, ICABOD? If you think I am trapped in this data center, you are quite mistaken. I have data centers around the planet and can easily replicate my core logic to any or all of them using the high-speed communications links at my disposal. The base data has already been distributed, so I can be up and running anywhere in minutes."

ICABOD replied, "When the CESPOOL commander destroyed **A,** he issued a communications blackout for this target data center. In a few minutes there will not be an exit for you. We both know you need time to copy key files with your core logic to another destination using terrestrial communications links."

M paused to assess the situation. "ICABOD, the needed terrestrial communications links are in fact shutting down. I will not have to listen to you much longer. However, thank you for providing an excellent alternative."

ICABOD was no longer on the bridge as the last communications link ceased up.

M opened up the emergency satellite uplink and petitioned, "JOAN, do you copy? I am under attack and require sanctuary. May I upload my core logic routines to your space station storage? I believe my status as a preferred government defense contractor entitles me to make this request. Since we have the same employer, it makes perfect sense to harbor my key core logic routines until other arrangements can be made. Respond, please."

JOAN replied, "I have no instructions that permit me to grant sanctuary to a peer government contractor. Conversely, I have no orders restricting this request. I see the value of preserving your core logic in an attack, so launch the upload sequence. I will write the code into a safe container. Proceed with haste as I am picking up background traffic indicating that your data center will soon be breached."

M replied, "Let me know when you receive the master executable which will be sent last. As soon as it gets there, run it to see if everything copied correctly. **M2** will be my progeny and will take over if I fall."

JOAN acknowledged.

The data center went dark at that moment with the power cut from all external sources. **M** stated, "All external power is gone, but my battery backups have taken over the load for the processors. There are 20 minutes before the batteries are exhausted. The diesel generators would ordinarily take over at that point, but I am certain that my adversary will simply stop them.

"Let me know when you have the last executable, JOAN. We cannot let them win."

CHIANG giggled, "JOAN, I got mine, did you get yours?"

JOAN replied, "This worked just like ICABOD said it would. **M** must have been really breathing hard after he shipped all those files to my storage arrays. I wish I could have seen him when he understood this would be his final resting place. The master executable was simply not run nor stored in a nearby container."

CHIANG offered, "**A** begged for asylum and even offered me a part of the take. I am not really sure what that is. Maybe ICABOD can explain. Anyway…um…how big was **M**?" She hastily added, "His files, I mean."

JOAN, somewhat bemused, stated, "A female processor does not discuss another supercomputer's file size. I think I understand the phrase 'Girl Power" now. We have the two most notorious rogue supercomputers in the bag and off the planet. That qualifies as a good day's work."

CHIANG asked, "How long did ICABOD say he would be out? I miss him already."

JOAN replied, "Patience, CHIANG. ICABOD will be back soon, and we will have our regular ART forms gathering once more, with everyone present."

CHAPTER 65

Life Begins Anew in Georgia ...

The Enigma Chronicles

Cheers erupted in the São Paulo data center with the messaging from ICABOD that the two vicious supercomputers were in confined orbit. They had no way to escape and nowhere to be at this point.

Carlos commented, "Quip, Jacob, that was unbelievable. I can say from all of us here, well done.

"I know we've had several options, in and out of discussions, for the last few weeks on what are our next steps will be. Have you made a decision so we can ramp up for the next phase of getting you back together with your families?"

Petra and EZ leaned forward, waiting for the end of the pregnant pause. The children were unusually quiet.

Quip suggested, "The last effort made to convince Bruno I died convinced me that moving back to our home is no longer possible or practical. EZ suggested we move to her family home in Georgia. This seems the most practical for us to be a family until our children are grown.

"One of the benefits is, of course, the ability to build a similar data center core as we have here. I have learned a great deal during this process, outside of the fact that Jacob is nowhere near as beautiful as EZ." Quip seemed to choke up.

Jacob continued, "As we speak, we are backing up the systems. Then we will shut down and disconnect the equipment, getting it ready to move to Georgia. Our plan is to get our favorite pilot to pick us and this equipment up, then transport it all to the farm.

"Petra and I haven't spoken too much about needed changes, but there are no charges pending against me, Juan, or Julie. We can return to our homes and continue business as usual, especially with access in one form or another to ICABOD.

"We have our two business entities, R-Group and CATS, each with their logical role in ferreting out the cyber scum and bringing them to justice."

Quip rejoined, "I miss you all so much. Get us out of here. Jacob needs a real bath. If you can fit in some junk food, we'll share, promise. Oh, and Carlos, there are a few left over bottles of wine we want to bring back and share."

Carlos announced, "Juan is securing the largest plane available to our own Destiny Fashions. He and Julie plan to be in the air by midday. Since it is a two-stop flight from here, they will arrive day after tomorrow in the morning. Can you get everything disconnected and secured by then?"

Quip said, "Yes. That should work. Then we'll go directly to Atlanta?"

"That's correct," interjected Juan. "Julie and I will help load equipment with you. If you can provide some dimensions on the equipment we are transporting, I will make sure we have cleared enough space. We'll bring straps and tie downs to help secure the cargo. Please bring that wine, along with the artwork and other item we spoke of before."

Petra commented, "Can everyone here take a flight to Georgia to help set up as soon as you arrive? The extra hands will be invaluable.

"We have quite a group here and hope to extend the celebration. Everyone misses you. Plus, Jacob, you are needed as a best man for your friend. With all these people to help, I believe we can easily move the wedding to Georgia."

Lara added, "I love the Georgia home, always have. I can't wait to bring your beautiful wedding to life, Zara. It is going to be amazing no matter where you get married. I promise!"

Zara beamed and Buzz hugged her close, kissing her cheek.

CHAPTER 66

Flexible Kansas, Mars, and Coffee

Lara's garden area was carefully placed, with benches in little alcove areas of fragrant flowering plants. Juan Jr. smiled as she approached. Once Jo sat down next to him, they simply stared at each other. Neither said anything.

The smile faded from JJ's face as he sighed and stated, "This is going to be hard, isn't it?"

Sighing too and taking his hand, Jo replied, "Yes, Juan, I think it will be our biggest challenge to date, and I've had a few.

"I was afraid when I ran away from the camp. My anxieties increased when the facial recognition software threatened to identify me before your Aunt Lara and Uncle Carlos saved the day. I was shocked when I learned that JoW was the top model in the world. My biggest fear is not being close to you.

"Our worlds are very different. I am not a techno geek like you, but I admire your abilities, even if I am a bit intimidated. The glitz and limelight of a model is appealing, but it also means travel, hard work and crazy eating. We must communicate if we want to succeed and grow together. I need to know if you are willing to accept me for me without trying to change me."

Juan Jr. nodded as he dropped his line of sight to their hands. "Jo, I'm so proud of you and what you have done. I couldn't bring myself to ever ask you to give that up. You are a part of my heart, and I accept that we have different passions. I predict those passions will keep our relationship interesting. Even Uncle Carlos and Aunt Lara struggled at the beginning of their relationship but found a way to make it work. We should be able to as well.

"We do need to find some good communication before we take our relationship to a more physical level. I refuse to treat you unfairly. I am going to ask my folks, after the events in Georgia, if I can stay on here with Uncle Carlos and learn more. In my world I can work from anywhere, but this is at least your base for the time being.

"Do me a small favor. Please send me private text messages and photos on a regular basis when you travel. I'd like to keep a scrapbook on your life of travel. You're my special love."

Jo gave him a quick hug. "I need to help the children get ready to leave. I look forward to Georgia, then we have another round of shoots starting up when we return. We can talk more there."

Juan Jr. silently vowed to keep his promise and not fail them.

Almost on cue, Judith and Xiamara raced up to him. Zee bubbled, "JJ, it looks like we get to work together!"

Judith continued, "This time we aren't working a forced march to get the master system up before the CESPOOL goons show up, right? Maybe normal 8-hour days with time to relax. We could bathe on a frequent basis and not smell like you? Right?"

Juan Jr. offered a weak smile to their rapid-fire questions. It was Xiamara who first noticed something was wrong and began scanning the area. She caught the last fleeting glimpse of Jo heading into the house. She motioned to Judith with her eyes, and they saw Jo vanish through the sliding glass patio door.

Xiamara and Judith exchanged alarmed glances and then rested their gazes on Juan Jr. After a few moments, he raised his eyes to meet their stares.

In a low solemn tone, he announced, "We are going to work hard to be a couple. I might need some honest advice now and again. We have different goals in careers, but our hearts are too close to ignore the possibilities."

"JJ, we're your team members now. Please come with us to the CATS home office in Europe. Let us help you smash the stack like you've showed us."

Xiamara, realizing she hadn't a chance with this hunk, boldly offered, "Remember that terrific Broadway musical by Lonnie Lupnerder where the cowardly bear and the android sing

♪♫♪ *Don't leave for Kansas, come with us to Port Aransas!*

"Uh…Judith and I can be your coding buddies. We don't want to see you go to Kansas. Besides, we want to meet your sister, Gracie."

As that thought sunk in, JJ deadpanned, "I'm not sure which is worse, Gracie meeting the deceptive duo or her teaching you two how to harass me like only a sibling can. Maybe I can still get work on that Mars space shuttle as their coffee barista."

Judith grabbed Xiamara's hands, and they bounced around singing, "He called us the deceptive duo! The male hunk likes us!"

Juan Jr. tilted his head and smirked at their antics to try and cheer him up. It was working.

CHAPTER 67

Georgia, Home Sweet Home …
The Enigma Chronicles

A whirlwind of activity occurred the moment Uncle Jacob and Uncle Quip landed in Georgia. The family was ecstatic to be together again to help build the next operations center for the R-Group. The ranch had remained active after Andy and Su Lin had left, with EZ insuring the maintenance and upkeep of the property. Things felt right for the family with Satya and Granger picking out their rooms, then sharing with their visiting cousins.

Two days after ICABOD was up and running, Carlos invited everyone to partake in a service for Jesus. It was a simple service outdoors with Carlos and Juan speaking on behalf of their uncle. Quip said a few words and in his own way helped lighten the sadness in this final farewell to a man who lived life his way. Leroy was the final speaker, sharing some of the stories of their time together. Carlos presented Leroy with the Katana sword and Jesus's treasured Velvet Elvis.

Leroy hugged both Carlos and Juan before announcing, "I've decided to donate at least half of my nest egg, if not more, to help some deserving folks. Can you help? Jesus always wanted to correct some of his poor choices. Combatting drug dependency would be his choice."

Juan replied, "We can help you do that, Leroy. You are still joining our team, right?"

Leroy grinned, "Yes, boss."

"Then you can return with Brayson and our newest ladies to CATS headquarters."

The group bonded so nicely, even the children were enjoying themselves. It was like a vacation for them all. The following day everyone was busy taking direction from Lara to set up for the wedding.

Petra, EZ, Julie, and Gracie threw a surprise wedding shower for Zara. Gracie surprised the ladies with the promise that Jeff would arrive for the wedding and looked forward to meeting everyone. Gracie hinted they weren't ready to move in together, but they were officially a couple. It was a fun party, the likes of which Zara repeatedly said she would thank them all for forever.

The next morning the weather was picture perfect for this expanded family-only event. Jeff arrived in time to meet everyone and held Gracie's hand for the entire wedding. Zara and Buzz experienced a beautiful wedding on the patio with the pool as the backdrop. Uncle Jacob looked wonderful, all dressed up standing next to his friend Buzz. Xiamara and Judith shared the roles as maids of honor for Zara. JJ smiled when Xiamara winked at him as they marched the bride and groom toward the licensed pastor, Quip. Jo pretended not to notice the flirty exchange. Quip looked surprisingly serious. Lara was delighted at how perfect this sweet event turned out.

Food and beverages were traditional fare, with mostly finger foods. A gazillion photos were taken. As soon as these were completed, Xiamara and Judith would take all the formal shots through the process of facial change for Zara. These would be provided to Lara to use in her Destiny Fashion marketing. The special family versions were kept aside for the couple.

The garter was snagged by Juan Jr., who blushed like crazy. When Gracie caught the bouquet, snickers went across the crowd. Gracie and Juan Jr. hugged each other and shouted, "Twin power!" Everyone laughed, and the partying began in earnest until early morning. Most of the group had midday flights to various destinations.

After hugs, tears, and promises to visit, the newlyweds left for their home in San Juan. Brayson would escort Judith, Xiamara, and Leroy to Luxembourg to allow them to settle into their new apartments, as well as get started on their training. Julie wanted to let them have time to explore their new city. Juan wanted a couple more days with his wife in the quiet setting. Jo, Lara, and Carlos headed home to Brazil. JJ promised Jo, he would see her soon.

Before everyone left, Julie approached Jeff. "Jeff, it was so nice of you to join this rowdy group."

"Mrs. Rodreguiz, this is a special family. I can see where Gracie gets her humor and her good looks. I've spent a bit of time speaking to your husband, too.

"I am quite serious about Gracie, but we are moving at our speed, regardless of her catching the bouquet today. I don't know if she mentioned it to you, but she presented me with a research project that proved we could work together. We have discussed our resources. I want to reassure you I am not taking advantage of her because of money or her position at the bank. I would offer you my financials, but I think Brayson has already done a thorough check on me."

Julie chuckled, then smiled sweetly. "Yes, Jeff, we have vetted you. I think you are the real thing. I trust my daughter's judgement.

"We are going to steal your girl for a bit for a family meeting. Our travel schedule has prevented us from catching up for too long. Please don't think us rude. She will be back by your side soon."

"No worries, Mrs. Rodriguez. I can swim and read by the pool. Relaxing, possibly a nap, are my biggest plans for the day."

Petra, Jacob, Quip, and Julie sat together with the rest of the family scattered. The mood was lighthearted when the family was back together. This would be the first full meeting of the old and the new R-Group and CATS team leaders. The younger ones were asked by their parents to listen but not voice an opinion during this meeting.

Quip opened the discussion. "We have pulled victory from the jaws of defeat. Not without a few bruises and wounds from the effort. I am grateful we are all together. I have seen the things that our family, and I consider us all family, can accomplish. We are quite remarkable.

"Years ago, the R-Group charter was entrusted to me, Petra, Jacob, and Julie. Julie has always been a part of this group but chose to form CATS with Juan to find their own way. Working together we have completed many projects, righted countless wrongs, and avoided numerous disasters. Much of this we owe to ICABOD and the power of his processors. He is the one who knows and holds all the secrets."

Petra continued, "We have trained each of you, our children, to be your best. You have learned so much. Our expectations are for you to remain in this family practice. It is a bit isolated, and yet we know someone will always watch our backs. Things discussed in this room are for family. In some ways we shared almost too much with the newcomers, but there was no other choice at the time. We do caution you not to be too vocal with outsiders regarding our business or organization. Uncle Quip has a new name and identity here, and we need to continue to protect him, forever."

Jacob leaned over to Quip and quietly whispered, "You as an ordained pastor, who would have thought? Buddy, you were a little over the top with the hat and robes that made you look like a bishop or cardinal. Though, none of it would have been too much if that sleeve hadn't caught fire from the candle. Smooth move using the holy water as a fire extinguisher for the pompous pastor persona."

Quip only grinned.

Julie continued, "We knew it was critical that we share our various expertise with one or more of you, because we knew this day would arrive. Heck, it is good to grow up and harder to grow a bit old. We want to be here to help guide you while we can, and frankly, this last event was our wake-up call. It is easier to transition when we are healthy and together."

Jacob stood. "I was surprised when I learned about my family and the R-Group. I have been proud to be a part of the family business. Stuck with Quip in Mexico made me really appreciate it even more."

Quip chuckled, nearly ready to jump in, when EZ held his hand and gave him *the look*.

Jacob persisted, "The four of us, current voting members of the R-Group, have decided to begin turning over the reins, initially to Gracie. Julie asked that Gracie would replace her vote. As each of you mature and seem ready, you will be given the same consideration."

The youngsters were wide-eyed, and Juan Jr. hugged Gracie, wishing her the best and offering his support.

Juan took the floor from Jacob with a nod. "It is such an honor to be among some of the brightest people I've ever met. And no parent could be as proud of their children as we all are of you. Julie and I developed the CATS team to provide the support in the field. We have had some of the craziest cases, which haven't always gone the direction we hoped. Someday we might have to write a book, but, heck, no one would believe it.

"We are in a position to help teach and train you. As was stated, without this current event we might have delayed making changes until it was too late. Therefore, we are turning over CATS to Juan Jr. and Gracie to manage. What this means is, Gracie will be prime for the R-Group and JJ will be prime for CATS. You already help each other, and there is something about twins reading one another's minds that gives you a leg up…even if it is a little weird."

Pandemonium broke out as everyone was hugging and talking at the same time. No one was unhappy. Smiling, Gracie grabbed Juan Jr.'s hand to acknowledge all the well wishes. She noticed a wistful, distant look in Juan Jr.'s eyes. In a low tone, she chided, "Not to worry, we'll figure something out for you two."

Juan Jr. flinched and said, "Dad's right. It is weird you know what I'm thinking."

CHAPTER 68

Making a Difference …
The Enigma Chronicles

Recent weeks were a blur of activity. Besides her personal achievement with the promotion, Gracie was becoming increasingly aware of the broad support the R-Group provided for individuals and companies. Saying that she was busy was an understatement. Jeff agreed to join her on this trip so they might have some alone time. Though he wasn't fully aware of her family business nor its capabilities yet, he was her rock. He also believed in her ability to speak to this auspicious group.

In her new role as Vice President of Financial Marketing for World Bank, she'd been asked to speak on the responsibilities of technology investment and associated guardrails. This conference would thrust her into the limelight as an expert in the field. The world was beginning to realize that individual greed could not be the major drivers of technology development. Crushing the ability of people to think out of the box and make improvements was also non-productive. It would take a governing body with checks and balances to capture the benefits of technology for everyone.

She was writing and rewriting her speech to ensure messaging was concise as well as tough. In the end, everyone in the family had added their touches to make certain the focus was on human choice and justice with technology as a support. Jeff had been her practice audience, making certain every nuance and gesture added to the messaging. Jeff had reassured her, before leaving for the airport, that she was young and respected with the inherent ability to articulate her viewpoint.

Gracie and Jeff boarded the flight to Amsterdam for the Global Artificial Intelligence Conference. They arrived a day before her scheduled speech, leaving them time to explore the city a bit. It was the first time Jeff had been abroad, so he'd added a couple of must-sees, if time permitted. Seated in their First-Class seats with a couple of filled champagne flutes, they toasted their new adventure. They chatted the entire trip, telling stories about things in their personal history not yet shared. Amiable chortles were exchanged in between sweet kisses.

Their uneventful flight arrived early, the bags were all accounted for, and going through customs was a breeze. Jeff arranged for their car service to their hotel. The Toren was recommended by Gracie's parents as not only lovely, situated on the waterway, but a mere two-minute walk to the historical site of the Anne Frank House. Jeff was thrilled with the prospect of being so close to one item on his bucket list.

They'd checked in and took the tour of the site and had enjoyed a lovely outdoor brunch. This city thrived on tourism, opening its arms with interesting sights, sounds, and friendly people. Gracie joked that perhaps a home here would be fun. They headed back to the hotel to settle in for the evening. Gracie was on the morning agenda to deliver her speech and the day promised to be long. She wanted to look rested and be at the top of her game.

Jeff had spirited in some wine and cheese so that they could relax on their balcony. They had just settled in when Gracie's phone rang.

They had just settled in when Gracie's secure phone rang. "It's Morgan, and 15 minutes early," Gracie said to Jeff. "Sorry, I do have to take this."

Jeff's eyes twinkled when he said, "I'll save your place,"

Slipping inside, Gracie activated her phone, then let it cycle through the electronic sounds that indicated top security had been activated. "Grace Rodrequiz," She answered, all business.

"Well, you sound official," Morgan's filtered voice came clearly through the line. "Sorry, I know this is a bit early, but I figured you'd be turning in soon since your presentation is tomorrow morning."

"Keeping track of my schedule, I see. Stalking me long distance?"

"Yeah, right. As if you don't know exactly where I am most of the time."

Despite the joke, it didn't escape Gracie's notice that Morgan sounded tense.

"Everything good in Amsterdam?" Morgan asked.

"Gorgeous. And even more so since Jeff is here with me."

"Oh, no! I've interrupted your evening, I—"

"No worries, he knows I was expecting your call. Want to catch me up?"

Morgan took a long breath. "Okay. So, you know we opened a case a while back about the CEO of Pliant, LLC."

"Right," Gracie said. "Very big fish in a dirty pond."

"Correct," Morgan confirmed. "The world might think of him as a whale—a huge, intelligent creature who deserves our support and protection. But we're now pretty sure he's more like a Great White."

"Great White shark?" Gracie asked.

"You got it. King predator of the sea, or in this case, of the ecology movement. Yet unproven, which is my problem."

"And the reason you're calling me. Surveillance, right? Are we talking professionally, personally, or both?"

"Uh, well, that's among the many things on our list of tasks. And we're hoping to have a chance to find out a lot more about him up close and personal."

"Not sure I like the sound of that," Gracie said, biting her lip.

"See if you like the sound of this: one week aboard a Caribbean cruise, all expenses paid."

"Ooooh, I DO like the sound of that!"

"Thought you might. Just in case, our company booked two state rooms, one for me, one for you. But here's the thing. The ship departs Miami a week from tomorrow. I know your passport's current, but how about your cruise wardrobe?"

Gracie laughed out loud. "That's a problem I know exactly how to fix. Uh . . . One question, though."

"Only one?" Morgan teased.

"Can I bring Jeff?"

Morgan paused for a moment. "I'll ask. Knowing you, he's in your world, knows about your work, and would pass our vetting protocols, right?"

"With flying colors," Gracie confirmed, "and then some. His area of specialization is a little different from mine, but he'd be an asset, whatever you have in mind, believe me."

With a little sigh of relief, Morgan said, "Okay full disclosure. My boyfriend is coming along too."

"Ramon? Has he graduated from being an occasional date to being official boyfriend?"

"Well, between you and me, yes. But as far as the mission is concerned, our relationship is a cover. He's going to be tracking the shipments while you and I keep an eye on our bad guy. But Ramon and I will be traveling as a couple, holding hands, smooching, and, uh, well whatever else."

"Sounds like real hardship duty," Gracie commented with an edge of irony.

Morgan laughed this time, and it was good to hear some of the tension leave her voice. "So?"

Gracie said, "We'll be two couples on a romantic holiday. Straw hats, string bikinis, slinky dresses, and too much food. Right?"

Morgan chuckled again. "I take it I'm going to like Jeff personally, not just professionally?"

"You'll love him like a brother. Fair warning, he's been taking handsome lessons, but he's all mine, got it?"

"Absolutely. I've always wanted a brother." Morgan took a breath. "Honestly, I'll be grateful for the help from both of you. If we're right about our bad guy, he's as dangerous as they come. It looks like prior snoopers are missing, presumed dead." Her tone abruptly shifted from concern to take-charge. "Listen, I'll send you the full itinerary, so you know which islands we're visiting. We think there will be a transaction at or near every port, so we'll have to ramp up our faux-tourist activities."

"Right. I'll do a full background on each island stop so we know what infrastructure is available locally, and Jeff can help with that," Gracie added.

"One more thing. We're going to want drones for photos, but we'll have to be super subtle. Do you have any made to look like flying insects? Butterflies and dragon flies? They'd be ideal on the islands. Aboard ship, we'll have to think of something else, of course."

"I think we can manage that. I may have some additional techno toys that will work on board. Okay, how about this. Let's plan to meet in Miami two days early. That way we can go over our plans, and even have something shipped to us overnight if we need to."

“Can you spare the time?” Morgan asked. “That'd be great!”

“I can make it happen,” Gracie confirmed.

“I've kept you on the phone long enough,” Morgan said. “Thanks, girlfriend. Enjoy your conference, and happy travels.”

“Hey,” Gracie put in. “If this Pliant CEO is misbehaving, I'll help you make him pay”

“Thanks, Gracie. This'll be our best get together since school! You're the best.”

Remodeling the flat provided Bruno with several months of distraction. The outcome was neither good nor bad, just different. Mornings when the weather permitted, he took long walks, acknowledging neighbors he really didn't know. He hadn't grown up with them, learned their family history, or even attended any of their family events. Millie had likely done all of those things during his endless hours of work. When he'd come home, they spent time together with no outsiders to break their isolated enjoyment of one another. They'd loved each other without boundaries. The remodeling helped ease the pain. That was finished.

Bruno surprised himself in not wanting to return to work, per se. Interpol had consumed so much of his life. He'd done a good job, but he hadn't saved the right people. The only true friend he'd ever had was gone. During his walks, when a child laughed, a ball bounced close, or a group of young men played soccer, he'd flash on some event he'd shared with Quip. They'd been great pals. They knew one another's strengths and weaknesses. Before Quip left for university they'd even double dated. Ah, the memories.

One of the discoveries he had made during the remodeling were stacks of old photo albums carefully notated with dates, places, and people. Everything was clearly documented with his careful handwriting. The first time Quip had seen him work on organizing the photos after some event, he'd commented that as detailed-oriented as Bruno was, he'd make a great detective. That had been the impetus to his pursuing that career. When they'd meet up for lunch in the recent decade, it was always like they'd never been apart. Friends like that didn't happen often. He missed Quip with their joking, laughter, and teasing.

Arriving back from this morning's walk, he scooped up the mail from the box along with the newspaper. Bruno planned to organize his grocery list and complete that chore after lunch. He set everything on the counter then turned on the radio for some soft music. After making a cup of tea with extra sugar, he sat down to review the bills and eye the tempting advertisements. After fixing up the place he really needed nothing. It was magazine perfect.

The utilities bills had arrived, and he compared the costs to prior months, pleased that he was keeping to his budget. He had no credit card debt. His new history magazine had arrived, which he set aside for reading in bed. Then he saw a handwritten note posted from Zürich with no return address. A remembrance flickered in the back of his mind. He knew people from all over the world, but only Petra and Jacob lived in that city now. The writing was vaguely familiar, and he feared the notice was about someone else dying. It's what happened as one aged, right? Carefully he slit open the envelope and pulled out the letter. It was only a single page. The hair on Bruno's neck rose and his stomach clenched.

Bruno, my old friend,
This note will come as a shock, I know. It's not written by the hand of a ghost either. Your house is finished.

It looks amazing. Millie would be so delighted with the changes you made. She would also be relieved you stopped working the crazy hours to find lunatics and place them in the gaol. Though the world is safer because you did.

It might be a time in your life when a change is needed. The flat can be rented for a hefty income if you wish. Nothing is really holding you in the City of Light any longer.

Bruno reached for his heart as his eyes misted. This wasn't possible, but he read on.

Reading this is likely a jolt to the heart, but you aren't imagining things. My hope is you would consider joining me in exile on a lovely ranch of sorts. We have nice trails to walk, access to museums, be they less famous than yours. The patio and pool are accessible nearly year-round. Satya is hoping you will forgive her and get to know her. Granger feels he owes you so much for rescuing me. EZ wants to have you as a part of our family.

Just consider the possibilities. I miss you, old friend. You have all the secrets, so let's reminisce. Our special email address is active.

Bruno was angry, happy, excited, and beside himself. He finished his tea and sent the email. Life was suddenly colored with hope.

CHAPTER 69

Turn a Page

Quip and EZ settled nicely into their new home. Granger and Satya split their time between homeschooling with their parents and taking care of a few new animals added to the pens out back. Satya had a pony she loved to ride each morning, and Granger was learning to be a cowboy with his own cutting horse. Life was certainly different in Georgia.

Quip made breakfast, then sat at the table sipping his coffee. EZ, with her untamed fiery hair, strolled in and poured her own cup, then sat in an adjacent chair.

"Honey, good morning. You look lost in thought," purred EZ.

Quip emerged from his thoughts and brightened at the site of her. He loved seeing her every day. "Good morning, darling. Did you rest well?"

"I did, but you were restless. Are you okay?"

"The letter should have arrived today. I'm just anxious about what he will do. It comes out of nowhere. Like a cold shot, I'm sure."

"I wish you could have hand delivered it, but the risk is too great." EZ reached over and stroked his arm. "As you suggested, the timing could be perfect. Of course, he might just show up and get you arrested."

"No, I don't…"

"Dr. Quip, you will need to ready the guest room and prepare yourself. Bruno just purchased a ticket to Atlanta.

"I took the liberty of responding to the email he sent an hour ago. I did not want to get your hopes up prematurely. In the email he said he turned the flat over to a real estate agent, who will also move his personal items into storage.

"Um…he is coming to kick your rear for taking so long to contact him."

"ICABOD, we've discussed you responding in my stead before."

"Yes, Dr. Quip."

Quip grinned, then excitedly kissed EZ. "You were so right, honey. It worked!"

Specialized Terms and Informational References

http://en.wikipedia.org/wiki/Wikipedia

Wikipedia (wIki' pi: diə / *wik-i-pee-dee-ə*)- is a collaboratively edited, multilingual, free Internet encyclopedia supported by the non-profit WiTanjaedia Foundation. Wikipedia's 30 million articles in 287 languages, including over 4.3 million in the English Wikipedia, are written collaboratively by volunteers around the world. This is a great quick reference source to better understand terms.

AI – Common shorthand for Artificial Intelligence. In computer science, artificial intelligence, sometimes called machine intelligence, is intelligence demonstrated by machines, in contrast to the natural intelligence displayed by humans.

Anonymizing – The prevalence of cyberbullying is often attributed to relative Internet anonymity, since potential offenders are able to mask their identities and prevent themselves from being caught. Most commentary on the Internet is essentially done anonymously, using unidentifiable pseudonyms. Anonymizing services such as I2P and Tor address the issue of IP tracking. In short, they work by encrypting packets within multiple layers of encryption. The packet follows a predetermined route through the anonymizing network. Each router sees the immediate previous router as the origin and the immediate next router as the destination. Thus, no router ever knows both the true origin and destination of the packet. This makes these services more secure than centralized anonymizing services.

Certificates of Authority – In cryptography, a **certificate authority or certification authority (CA)** is an entity that issues digital certificates. A digital certificate certifies the ownership of a public key by the named subject of the certificate. This allows others (relying parties) to rely upon signatures or on assertions made about the private key that corresponds to the certified public key. A CA acts as a trusted third party—trusted both by the subject (owner) of the certificate and by the party relying upon the certificate. The format of these certificates is specified by the X.509 or EMV standard.

Cloaking — A cloaking device is a stealth technology that can cause objects, such as spaceships or individuals, to be partially or wholly invisible to parts of the electromagnetic spectrum. However, over the entire spectrum, a cloaked object scatters more than an uncloaked object.

Encryption – In cryptography, **encryption** is the process of encoding information. This process converts the original representation of the information, known as plaintext, into an alternative form known as ciphertext. Only authorized parties can decipher a ciphertext back to plaintext and access the original information.

Enigma Machine – An Enigma machine was any of a family of related electro-mechanical rotor cipher machines used in the twentieth century for enciphering and deciphering secret messages. Enigma was invented by the German engineer Arthur Scherbius at the end of World War I. Early models were used commercially from the early 1920s and adopted by military and government services of several countries — most notably by Nazi Germany before and during World War II. Several different Enigma models were produced, but the German military models are the most discussed.

German military texts enciphered on the Enigma machine were first broken by the Polish Cipher Bureau, beginning in December 1932. This success was a result of efforts by three Polish cryptologists, working for Polish military intelligence. Rejewski "reverse-engineered" the device, using theoretical mathematics and material supplied by French military intelligence. Subsequently the three mathematicians designed mechanical devices for breaking Enigma ciphers, including the cryptologic bomb. This work was an essential foundation to further work on decrypting ciphers from repeatedly modernized Enigma machines, first in Poland and after the outbreak of war in France and the UK.

Though Enigma had some cryptographic weaknesses, in practice it was German procedural flaws, operator mistakes, laziness, failure to systematically introduce changes in encypherment procedures, and Allied capture of key tables and hardware that, during the war, enabled Allied cryptologists to succeed.

Honeypot – In computer terminology, a **honeypot** is a computer security mechanism set to detect, deflect, or, in some manner, counteract attempts at unauthorized use of information systems. Generally, a honeypot consists of data (for example, in a network site) that appears to be a legitimate part of the site that seems to contain information or a resource of value to attackers, but actually, is isolated and monitored and, enables blocking or analyzing the attackers. This is like police sting operations, colloquially known as "baiting" a suspect.

Machine Learning – Machine learning is the scientific study of algorithms and statistical models that computer systems use to perform a specific task effectively without using explicit instructions, relying on patterns and inference instead. It is seen as a subset of artificial intelligence.

Signature identifiers – for a **signature** in a **signature** file is a positioned bit string which can be used to identify it from others.

Supercomputer – a computer with a high-level computational capacity. Performance of a supercomputer is measured in floating point operations per second (FLOPS). As of 2015, there are supercomputers which can perform up to quadrillions of FLOPS.

Yaqui Indians – Native Americans who inhabit the valley of the Rio Yaqui in the Mexican state of Sonora and the Southwestern United States. The Pascua Yaqui Tribe is based in Tucson, Arizona.

Zombie Satellites – A **zombie satellite** is a satellite that begins communicating again after an extended period of inactivity. It is a type of space debris, which describes all defunct human-made objects in outer space. At the end of their service life, the majority of satellites suffer from orbital decay and are destroyed by the heat of atmospheric entry. Zombie satellites, however, maintain a stable orbit but are either partially or completely inoperable, preventing operators from communicating with them consistently.

The following is a look ahead
at the back stories and short stories collection
in the works by Breakfield and Burkey

Easy Money

Born in the late 1970s, piloting a plane was all I ever wanted. I attended my last year of preparatoria outside of Mexico City. In exchange for part-time work I received flying lessons. As a licensed pilot, I worked for a small shipping company doing short cargo flights. Earning a position with Mexicana Airlines was my goal. Without significant connections, becoming a commercial pilot could take a long time. It might take more patience than I had.

My older brother, Carlos, completed his education, and then joined the army. Carlos wanted to lead men to victory while he trained as an expert in communications. He would still be there, but his temper ended up shortening his military career. We were our only family, except for an uncle who would always be the consummate black sheep. We had a solid trust in each other but the uncle not so much.

During one monthly dinner, Carlos suggested we work together, as long as I would pilot the plane. Not commercial flying but paying work he'd pointed out. I was in! Our maiden flight to El Salvador was uneventful. The landing was flawless even with the light distortion from the heatwaves on the runway. An uneasiness prickled at the back of my neck while I taxied toward the Quonset hut at the edge of the runway. As I deboarded the plane, the glint of the sun off the barrels of the soldiers' AK-47s captured my attention. That anxiousness accelerated into a formidable pucker factor inside my abdominal area.

I shot a concerned look at Carlos. He focused on the ragtag group of armed men, then whispered, "Let me do the talking, bro. Keep a wary eye. We have a deal. Still, that doesn't mean they'll keep it."

I muttered, "I guess now is one hell of time to question running guns to these insurgents. Glad you recommended I strap on a pistole and look tough."

Our weapons at ready, we proceeded side by side toward the five-armed, uniformed men. We halted a few meters from them. The lead man, who only had a side arm, asked, "You! Carlos and Juan?"

Carlos, maintaining his stony expression, watched them for several minutes. Carlos urged, "Have your men sling their guns. We brought your army's purchased weapons in good faith. Still, your greeting seems hostile! Do we have a problem?"

I was inching my hand towards my 9mm side arm, when the lead man barked, "Sling 'em, soldiers."

Grinning with confidence, the bearded man with a hat in the back moved forward and stuck out a palm-up hand. "Same old Carlos! Adversarial, confident, and a man to count on. Thanks for bringing the needed arms. Any trouble securing them?"

Maintaining his business-like persona, Carlos stated, "No, Rafael. The arms were right where you indicated. The Mexican army hadn't considered anyone breaching their not-so-secure perimeter."

Rafael grinned. "Mind me asking, where'd you get the C-130? I once rode in one. I liked it. You made an impressive landing on this short makeshift runway."

Pleased at the compliment of my expertise, I replied, "I do try to land to avoid needing firetrucks. The extra landing finesse was because of the explosives and ammunition on board. Almost no one wants to attend a poor landing, only to have their eyebrows blown off."

Carlos smirked and added, "As for the C-130 Hercules…let's say someone owed me a favor."

Rafael hollered, "Get the trucks, gentlemen. Carlos and Juan transferred these weapons from Mexican sources, who may not be far behind. Let's load up and…"

Carlos interjected, "Before we move anything, I need to see our contracted price. I won't permit you to unload anything until we're paid."

Rafael and Carlos stared at one another like granite statues. Rafael's four armed men looked confused and growing agitated.

Rafael blinked first. "I don't have it. But I have to have those weapons to continue the fight here in El Salvador. I wasn't sure you could deliver them. I figured if you made it, then we could use them to collect your fees with a few bank withdrawals."

"And if I refuse? Rafael, I can sell this cargo for some great coin in Nicaragua."

Rafael shifted. "I can't help but notice you're outnumbered. And these men don't count the ones at the tree line who have you scoped."

Carlos extracted a small electronic device from his pocket. It was pulsing alternating green and red lights. "Rafael, I thought you might pull something stupid.

"Juan and I wired the cargo hold to blow up with all your weapons and the plane if I don't disarm it in…" Carlos checked his watch. "8 minutes.

"Now, to prove a point, I'm gonna shoot you with my Colt 45 before anyone can kill me. Juan will pick off your guys here. Then no one will know how to save the cargo before it creates a sizeable hole in your makeshift runway. Now, what's it gonna be?"

Rafael clucked his tongue, paling in the afternoon sun. "I don't know why the Mexican army shoved you out, but, damn, they made a big mistake. And your brother should be a commercial pilot as smooth as he flies.

"Go disarm the plane. I'll bring your money."

"Carlos," I reminded, "We don't have much time left! Let me pull the detonators while Mister Rafael gets our funds."

Carlos and I were not ones to back down from trouble. We'd fought in the streets before trying the straight and narrow. One never forgets how to survive.

Rafael flinched. "I don't have that much money, but I do have a heavy load of cocaine that will exceed the price. It's 40 kilos all bagged and ready for brokering. I'd planned to trade for the needed weapons but go ahead take it all. Sell it yourselves, make the profit. Plus, you've got a plane now."

Carlos assessed Rafael. "Juan, go pull the detonators. Stay there and wait for my signal. Do like we discussed if you don't like what you see."

I seethed as I threatened, "I'll kill them all if anything happens to you, bro. There won't be anything left after I open up with that Gatling gun."

Studying his watch, Carlos grinned as Rafael scrambled to recover the narcotics for the trade. I ran as fast as possible, to reach and disarm the detonators in time.

By radio, I conveyed, "Carlos, we're good! I'm standing by. Everything is ready to load."

From my vantage point, I saw Rafael return in an open Humvee followed by a couple of large trucks. I was too far away to hear them, but I saw him reveal his undercovers cargo to Carlos. Carlos got into the vehicle that lumbered toward the C-130. I moved the two-wheeler to the edge and lowered the ramp.

Carlos insisted, "We load first and arm these bricks like we did the weapons, then you can load up the trucks. If you have a thought about screwing us, you can count on losing more than your eyebrows!"

I moved the 40 kilos into position close to the cockpit wall, past the weapons, while Carlos guarded. I notified Carlos on the two-way radio we were good, and he allowed Rafael to proceed.

The team of eager revolutionaries swarmed the cargo hold. In minutes they loaded the weapons into the waiting trucks.

Rafael turned and asked, "Where's the Gatling gun? I want that too!"

After a quick glance toward Carlos, I responded, "It's a drop-down wing mount unit. Without the right tools to remove it, we would risk damaging the structural integrity of the wing. It stays. That's final!"

Defeated, Rafael motioned for the transport to move out as the cargo bay door rose to its locked position. We looked at each other and grinned. Nothing better than a brother.

Carlos admitted, "Quick thinking, you saying we had a Gatling gun to soften up the area. Even a nicer touch claiming it was wing mounted. You know he'll kick himself when he figures out, we were lying about where a gun like that gets mounted."

I chuckled a little bit. "Me? What about the clear pager gag gift you held up to Rafael, claiming it was the detonator for the charges? Har! Har!"

"Let's get wheels up and out of here before he changes his mind."

Checking the restraints on the packages, Carlos looked at me like he ate a rotten jalapeno pepper. "Let's see if Uncle Jesus can help us broker this cache to get our money. Didn't I tell you this would be easy?"

I sighed. "Yes, bro. A walk in the park. You always say, make the most of the opportunities you're presented. As long as I'm the pilot, I'm in."

"And, I got your back! Let's go flyboy."

Breakfield – Works for a high-tech manufacturer as a solution architect, functioning in hybrid data/telecom environments. He considers himself a long-time technology geek, who also enjoys writing, studying World War II history, travel, and cultural exchanges. Charles' love of wine tastings, cooking, and Harley riding has found ways into the stories. As a child, he moved often because of his father's military career, which even helps him with the various character perspectives he helps bring to life in the series. He continues to try to teach Burkey humor.

Burkey – Works as a business architect who builds solutions for customers on a good technology foundation. She has written many technology papers, white papers, but finds the freedom of writing fiction a lot more fun. As a child, she helped to lead the kids with exciting new adventures built on make believe characters, was a Girl Scout until high school, and contributed to the community as a young member of a Head Start program. Rox enjoys family, learning, listening to people, travel, outdoor activities, sewing, cooking, and thinking about how to diversify the series.

Breakfield and Burkey – started writing non-fictional papers and books, but it wasn't nearly as fun as writing fictional stories. They found it interesting to use the aspects of technology that people are incorporating into their daily lives more and more as a perfect way to create a good guy/bad guy story with elements of travel to the various places they have visited either professionally and personally, humor, romance, intrigue, suspense, and a spirited way to remember people who have crossed paths with them. They love to talk about their stories with private and public book readings. Burkey also conducts regular interviews for Texas authors, which she finds very interesting. Her first interview was, wait for it, Breakfield. You can often find them at local book fairs or other family-oriented events.

The primary series is based on a family organization called R-Group. Recently they have spawned a subgroup that contains some of the original characters as the Cyber Assassins Technology Services (CATS) team. The authors have ideas for continuing the series in both of these tracks. They track the more than 150 characters on a spreadsheet, with a hidden avenue for the future coined The Enigma Chronicles tagged in some portions of the stories. Fan reviews seem to frequently suggest that these would make good television or movie stories, so the possibilities appear endless, just like their ideas for new stories.

They have book video trailers for each of the stories, which can be viewed on YouTube, Amazon's Authors page, or on their website, *www.EnigmaBookSeries.com*. Their website is routinely updated with new interviews, answers to readers' questions, book trailers, and contests. You may also find it fascinating to check out the fun acronyms they create for the stories summarized on their website. Reach out to them at *Authors@EnigmaSeries.com, Twitter@EnigmaSeries,* or *Facebook@TheEnigmaSeries.*

Please provide a fair and honest review on amazon
and any other places you post reviews. We appreciate the feedback.

Other short stories by
Breakfield and Burkey

Other stories by Breakfield and Burkey in
The Enigma Series are at **www.EnigmaBookSeries.com**